Turing

(A Novel about Computation)

Also by Christos Papadimitriou:

Elements of the Theory of Computation
        (with Harry Lewis)
Combinatorial Optimization: Algorithms and Complexity
        (with Ken Steiglitz)
The Theory of Database Concurrency Control
Computational Complexity

Turing

(A Novel about Computation)
Christos H. Papadimitriou

0

0

0

The MIT Press | Cambridge, Massachusetts | London, England

This book was set in Bookman Old Style, ITC Bookman, Andale Mono, Stymie, and Scala Sans by Graphic Composition, Inc., Athens, Georgia.

Printed and bound in the United States of America.

Library of Congress Cataloguing-in-Publication Data

Papadimitriou, Christos H.
   Turing : a novel about computation / by Christos H. Papadimitriou.
      p. cm.
   ISBN 0-262-16218-0 (hc. : alk. paper)
   1. Turing, Alan Mathison, 1912–1954—Fiction. 2. Computer simulation—Fiction. 3. Computer scientists—Fiction. 4. Mathematicians—Fiction. I. Title.

PS3616.A58T87 2003
813.'6—dc21
                                        2003046301

10 9 8 7 6 5 4 3 2 1

Contents

Turing, Alan Mathison (1912–1954). British mathematician and philosopher, broadly considered the founder of Computer Science. In 1936, while at King's College (Cambridge), he demonstrated the impossibility of automatic mathematical reasoning, answering one of the paramount open mathematical questions of that age. He did so by devising a simple, yet all-powerful, hypothetical computational device, since called the *Turing machine,* which has had tremendous influence on computational research and culture. During the Second World War, Turing was instrumental in breaking the German cryptographic code Enigma, a feat that greatly contributed to the victory by the Allies. After the war he worked on launching the British computer industry, did seminal work in Biology, was a pioneer of chess playing by computer, and defined the field of Artificial Intelligence by proposing the so-called *Turing test.* He was tried in 1952 for homosexuality and was condemned by the court to treatment by mind- and body-altering drugs. He died two years later, apparently by his own hand.
—From www.netcyclopedia.com

> *Be thou a spirit of health or goblin damned?* . . .
> *Be thy intents wicked or charitable?*
> —From www.greatbooks.org/hamlet.suml/~actII

Turing

(A Novel about Computation)

"I'll remember *his* name all right," Ethel thinks as her airplane leaves behind the northern coast of Scotland. "Alexandros." Nice. The accent on the *e*. Classic, but not pompous or obscure. ("Do they still use names like 'Zeus' or 'Iamblichos' in that crazy country?" she wonders. Probably.) "Alexandros." After the first boy who wanted to conquer the world.

Ethel knows what "Alexandros" means in Greek. "The man who will shield me from all men." Forever. With a little luck. And help from her left ovary and foreign guests. She will know soon. "Look at the ocean. Relax. Skip the after-dinner drink. Take a nap."

Ethel has not always remembered the names of her lovers. "Benjamin Yamada" she remembers, of course. He was the boy who held her hand when her father died, then went on to become her first boyfriend, first lover, her first dumpjob and guilt trip. Forget that name, dammit. Never look it up again. He's gone. (For the past six years he's been living in Cincinnati, with an unlisted phone number. Surfs the Net, beginner level. Even uses her stuff occasionally.) "No need to feel guilty, he's probably happier than I am," she thinks. Forget him, he'll hurt you like the others if you give him another chance. You can't look back in this game. Next!

"Andrew Leitman" comes to mind next. But again, she has good reason for remembering. He was her first boss at Exegesis, back when the company was still Webus Inc. Soon to become her lover, her mentor. Then her *tor*mentor, her corporate nemesis. Next, after patient months of maneuvering, her equal and close collaborator. Then her lover once more ("once" here is numerically accurate, even a bit of an exaggeration). And finally, the summer of '99, Andy became her victim: humiliated, defeated, decapitated, purged from the company, Andy hasn't been heard from since. This must be Greenland, right?

But, for instance, what was the name of her Viking, her boyfriend during junior year at Santa Cruz? She remembers his running shoes, his favorite poet, his pubic hair (grey New Balance, Guillaume Apollinaire, blond). But his name? And how about the black guy she met at Helen and Ralph's party? Or the nerd from Berkeley with the covert violent streak? Blank.

What Ethel does remember are the names of everybody she desired and never had. Summer crushes, her college math professor ("Dr. Christopher L. Bates"), the shy genius in the programming class ("Tommy Ng"), the others—every single painful one of them, their names, their faces, their eyes squeezing her neurons, never letting go. Nor can she forget the ones whose names she never knew but wanted nevertheless. Like the man who walked into the Palo Alto restaurant the night she was dining there alone. Short, slender, business suit, no cheeks, huge eyes staring at her with unabashed fire. She never looked at him—but did so in an equally fiery way. He ordered the exact same things she did, from appetizer to dessert wine. The whole restaurant was hot, diners were breathing heavily, waiters wiping sweat from their eyebrows watching them. She was delirious. He paid and left, still staring. No chance to forget *his* name.

Ethel's work is about making sense out of the chaos of the Net. And she has the relatively rare gift—not that it ever helps—of applying her skill to herself. For example, she knows that her love life is two-dimensional, she has long ago identified the only two axes that really count: abandonment and change. Pain and evolution. Father and mother. It's almost boring once you think of it.

When her father died, Ethel had almost anticipated her mother's words: "Everything will be like before, my love, you'll see." Because Dorothy "Iron Lady" Young, once described as "the only true conservative in Congress," has always loathed change. (No wonder she's becoming immensely popular in a world traumatized by algorithm-driven, paradigm-toppling, consciousness-numbing change.) Ethel had cried silently in her mother's arms, horrified by the promise of continuity. Because it debased the decency of her loss and threatened the only consolation that it contained.

Abandonment has punctuated Ethel's life. Painfully and densely. "All my important men have left me," Ethel thinks. Not a tragic, self-pitying statement, just a circular construction: As Ethel knows well from her work—from the Net—a statement is not only a declaration of fact, but also a definition of its own terms. "Good guys die young." "Fit organisms survive." "Important lovers leave us, father first." How can you argue with that?

It was almost two years ago, in the wake of yet another dump, that Ethel met Sola. She found her at the Colony—where those who love fantasy fantasize about love. Beautiful, mysterious, exotic, brilliant Sola. "Sola, Sola, Sola, where are you now?" During their blissful sprees together, she had fulfilled her as nobody ever had, and in those endless hours and days in between, Ethel had felt an unbearable loneliness—of a new kind. Not the loneliness between relationships, not the loneliness *in* a relationship, but intense, mind-numbing loneliness while waiting for the next date, the next game.

Suddenly Ethel knew that this love affair, strange and intense and all-consuming, and yet inherently incomplete, was a dead end threatening her very survival. But leaving Sola was not easy. Not until she met the real-life Sola.

Eerie resemblance. Stanford student, Spanish literature. ("Peninsular literature, amor, not Spanish. Big difference. You lose García and Borges and Onetti, and a few poets I suppose, but you get a three-year scholarship from the Queen.") Part-time model, she claims. And part-time call girl, she confessed once. And full-time liar, Ethel knows. But Ethel never double-checks her on the

Net. Sola has total control. Even though, at twenty-six, she is more than a decade younger than Ethel.

Sudden and total bliss. Imagine, a sexy, fascinating lover with whom you can giggle in restrooms. True love. Sola moves in. Then out, then in again. True humiliation, true pain. True love. Shopping in San Francisco, the bed-and-breakfast in Point Reyes, the weekend in Mexico. Lies. Sola flies home for the spring break. ("The boys in Madrid are sooo boring, amor, and the girls sooo uptight. Sure I'll come back.") Weeks go by, no sign of Sola. Then the telephone call. ("I have been thinking, Ethel, need to think some more. And serious work at school, amor, serious.")

During her worst mourning period ever, Ethel thought about death. And then she thought her plan.

Not a plan, really. No subgoals, no algorithm. A fantasy. She would spend the second half of June on a Greek island. Carefully timed. Burn some stock. Meet a Greek God. At least a reasonably smart, healthy, passably good-looking man—and bear his daughter. That was her plan.

She had been warned by "The Bad Girl's Guide to the Greek Isles" (www.astro.cam.ac.uk/saraht/guide/, abysmal Exegesis rating) that Greek men are (a) no longer Gods, and (b) nonexistent in the islands. Except for old fishermen, gay playboys, and the *kamakia,* the professional lovers referred to by the Greek word for *harpoon,* so rough and naive about everything, especially Disease. Apparently she had to choose between German men in Crete, French and Dutch in Paros, Scandinavians in Rhodos, Austrians and Israelis in Ios, Americans in Santorini, Englishmen and Italians in Corfu. (No men in Lesbos. No straight men in Mykonos.) She chose Corfu.

Convenient flight, beautiful island, charming dilapidated hotel in the old town (homepage in the weirdest English). Easy lifestyle, no overhead, you fit right in from day one. A bus to the beach around noon, swimming, sunbathing, late lunch. Late afternoon bus back to town, long siesta, then out at ten. (Ten! At ten, Palo Alto waiters are yawning as they lock up.) A drink, dinner, a stroll through town, dancing, coffee, another stroll, more dancing. You can score hashish in some bars—they say there is also coke—but why bother; the island is a continuous high. You only drink at the more expensive bars, the others can give you a weeklong hangover with nasty bootleg. Back to bed in the three-bit morning hours, sleep or whatever until noon, back to the beach. And so on. Compare today's date with your return ticket once in a while.

At night the town radiates with a strange glow that comes from white cotton cloth on seriously suntanned flesh. Eyes seek eyes all the time, admiring, contemplating, flirting, proposing, teasing, daring. At first you are embarrassed to death, then you have a drink and try it yourself, then you can't stop. Your eyes seek eyes all the time. Couples in love (almost always straight on this island) hold hands or cross arms, their eyes also seeking eyes everywhere. All the time. The second day you feel you recognize everyone, thousands of them. You can spot the newcomers.

Alexandros was not a newcomer. Ethel had noticed him the previous night, medium tall, slim, mid-fifties, long white hair, white beard. Dark skin, a Hindu guru. Clever little eyes. Brown. A grand master of the eyes game. He had stared her down, had made her lose her breath, her step. Deep and wide red scars in the small visible parts of both cheeks, the left much larger than the other, probably extending all the way to the chin under the beard—a souvenir from the colonels' dictatorship in the early seventies, she would find out. Now sitting with a teenage girl at the next table in the outdoor café, occasionally holding hands, talking very fast in the language she could already recognize as Greek. A Humbert Humbert and his nymphette, Ethel thinks.

But wait . . . isn't the eroticism between them strictly paternal? The kind she missed in her own adolescence, the kind she'd jealously spied in her friends' homes? Suddenly, eye contact. No retreat now. "Pleased to meet you, Ethel. This is my daughter Aloé." The same paternal eroticism flows from Alexandros's eyes to Ethel's eyes, spine, pelvis. Together with curiosity, an almost boyish fascination, and a hint of shyness. Serious and playful at the same time, eyes you want to look into, eyes you want to trust. Ethel melts.

They drink more coffee. People here drink coffee in the early morning hours, and there is not a decaffeinated bean on the whole island. Ethel studies Alexandros. How singular, she thinks. A real-life Greek god, unfortunately of the Zeus variety—her fantasy had been more along the lines of Apollo. And his English is funny. Beneath the unapologetic Greek accent, you discern a strange combination of lyricism, roughness, and scientific precision. He volunteers that he has learned English by reading Marxist texts in English translations and listening to rock music. Curl up with Gramsci and Lukács, then relax with the Sex Pistols. "We are going back to Athens on the early morning flight," he surprises her. Aloé is looking at Ethel attentively, studying her reaction. Somehow Ethel is not devastated by the setback. Alexandros kisses her goodbye, a butterfly kiss on the lips, Aloé kisses her the same way. Beautiful child, Ethel thinks. Goodbye, Alexandros.

She goes to bed happy but resists sleep, seeking the roots of her strange euphoria. Is it because this encounter, both erotic and chaste, is not going anywhere? Is this her rational side feeling relieved? Despite a promising start, she is not, after all, making progress in her plan, so impulsive, so irrational. Or is it that she has just met Rusty again—her name for her father—after twentysomething years? Or maybe her fuzzy vision of a child was suddenly bound to the image of Aloé?

The next morning, she wakes up knowing the source of last night's euphoria. She runs to the café. Alexandros is waiting there, at the same table, beaming smile, burning little eyes. "You didn't leave!" she cries. But she had known.

They hug, they kiss. "Aloé flew back alone to her mother," he explains. "She did not mind at all, I assure you." They swim, they talk. An archeologist, specializing in the technology of the ancient Greeks. His studies in France were cut short by the dictatorship. More accurately, by an order from what he calls "the Movement" to come back to Greece and work underground. Prison, torture, "the most creative face-lift in the whole cell block," he laughs. Ethel wants to kiss his scar.

It is three in the afternoon when they take the bus to town. Without asking her, without discussing it, as if he were following, hypnotized, the steps of an ancient ritual, he picks up his suitcase from his hotel and brings it to her room. She tries to talk Disease with him, but he doesn't seem to understand. She tries again. "You wouldn't cause me to get sick and die, would you?" He looks into her eyes, caresses her cheek. "No, little sister, I would never hurt you." He is almost in tears. She kisses him, realizing that she trusts this man as she has trusted no one else. This both fascinates her and bothers her.

He's slow and sweet, and yet intense, a man whose life is hanging in the balance. She's close to coming when he stutters something improbable, something like "I am embarrassed I forgot to ask you earlier, but are you doing anything about the overpopulation problem?" Dizzy, somewhere else, she translates, she laughs. "Don't worry, I'll send you a picture." He smiles, relieved. "No, seriously," she thinks. For a moment she feels a stab of guilt, then they kiss, and it is over. Nice.

They smoke. "This was not the first time I made love with you," he says slowly. "I first made love with you in my fantasy, last night." She translates. Can he mean that? He does mean that! Touched by Alexandros's openness, guilty again, Ethel kisses his right hand.

They talk about his name. "Andros" is Greek for man, he says, and the prefix "alex" signifies resistance, protection, cancellation of effects. Like "anti" in "anti-theft," like "proof" in "waterproof" and "runnerproof."

"Alexandros" is a great warrior, someone who can resist every man's attack.

"The man who will shield me from all men, forever," Ethel secretly reinterprets. Mainly to tease him and show off, she doublechecks it on the Net. She puts on her custom headset (fourteen gigahertz* processor, Seamless Net connection), dictates a few words. Piece of cake. She scores with a single query (strong on "alexandros," stronger on "etymology," negative on "history"). With her own relevance engine, `www.xsearch.exegesis.net`. Only two authoritative documents, `www.deadlanguages.org` and `www.alexandros.com`, both with near-perfect Exegesis ratings, both supporting the too-good-to-be-true etymology.

p. 247

* Notes in the margin, such as the one on this page, refer the reader to a discussion in the Afterword, starting on page 245.

Alexandros is watching her, amused, impressed, interested. He asks about her work. He surfs the Net too, he says—his cheeks are now red with embarrassment beyond his scars. For his research, for obscure left-wing connections, for rock lyrics. ("They are hard to understand if you are not a native speaker of English," he says. She lets him believe they're easy if you are.)

And it was precisely then, as she was lying next to him in their Corfu hotel room, wearing only a tiny computer on her head, that Ethel told Alexandros about Turing.

"How on earth did I remember Turing?"

The century was pregnant with pollution, war, liberation, revolution. And it was pregnant with me.

In the beginning all was grey, next I see Mother's white hand, and nursery walls, a London weather sort of grey. There is the sea, and Mother's hand during the summers at the sea. And there is play, play with no end, with girls, with boys, but above all with symbols, symbols inviting, joyous symbols, symbols of numbers, sounds, ideas, symbols of symbols (and so forth). But there are rules, always rules, everywhere rules, annoying, painful rules.

And this is all that I can see amongst the fogs hiding that age. My mother's hand; a world of grey; a glorious, brilliant sea of symbols; a suffocating film of rules. From these materials I compose the face of Morcom, elegant, pensive, pale. My first and dearest love, innocent, potent, tragic, still with me.   **p. 248**

Ian can't work. His chest feels bloated, his blood flows hot and swift, brain possessed by a mixture of elation and despair. An urge to stand up and walk out of his apartment's door into the crowded humidity of the Hong Kong night, and a sweet paralysis that keeps him.

He is in love, no doubt. Eyes closed, audible heartbeat.

"Whom with?"

The Masked Beloved? She's gone her sweet and strange way these past six months, no sign of her—no sign there *will be* a sign of her—Ian is feeding on a hope that's getting slimmer by the day. "God, I miss her so," he sighs in resignation. But is he really missing *her,* or just her sexy, fascinating mask? (Ian is now squeezing his eyes closed, trying to will his apartment's bell into ringing. It's almost midnight, God, the boy should be here by now.) So, is it possible it's Eusebio he's longing for? The olive-skinned little urchin with an attitude—the sweetest eyes despite the redness, his pockets full of chemical oblivion.

This yearning, this pain, it's getting almost physical. You can be the hero of high school kids and learned scholars, worshiped by shady runners and venture capitalists alike. You can launch a revolution, humiliate governments, play them one against the other. You can solve the most notorious problem, write the subtlest code, then turn around and do it again, and then once more. Seduce a hundred lovers, receive a gigabyte of groupie mail from all over—nothing softens the bite of a lonely night.

From his apartment window Ian can see the lights of the busy harbor, forty-five floors below, the bright bustling streets of Kowloon across the strait where wares will be peddled until dawn—medicinal herbs, live snakes and livers of endangered animals, designer clothes, and bootleg code. This tiny island and peninsula, dot on the map, little patch of sky that has been home for more years than Ian wants to count, a pleasure destination that, over time—almost imperceptibly—has become haven, exile, prison. Trap.

And Eusebio is late. "God, where is he?"

(What Ian does not know, because it hasn't hit the government's computers yet, is that Eusebio is weeping silently this very moment, he's scared, head leaning on a door of heavy steel, he was picked up by plainclothesmen in the tube, a team of three with Northern accents, got him before he had a chance to finish emptying his pockets.)

In the dark room a light is blinking, Ian's privileged communication indicator. Ian waits for a moment, enough to feel a little of the warmth that would have filled his body, from heart to throat and head to groin, if this were an announcement of a visit by the Masked Beloved. (Or anybody, at this point, anybody at all.)

It's Turing.

Suddenly Ian's mood is dark, he's feeling sick again, the night is ruined.

"*Merde!* Not Turing. Not now."

August in Athens. Hot, empty, non-air-conditioned
Athens. Inhabited only by tourists who ignored the
warnings of their guidebooks, and public employees
who used up their vacation weeks in June. Alexandros
sits naked in front of his fan and his computer. He is
thinking about the truth. His radio is barely audible:

> *Always*
> *She always says it backwards*   **p. 249**

I am a researcher, Alexandros thinks, I deduce the
truth from facts. The truth is the glue that holds facts
together. Or is it the matrix that transforms possibilities
to facts? Or perhaps the truth is like an opaque object,
and the facts are its shadows, cast by many different
light sources. The real difference between facts and the
truth, Alexandros decides, is this: You can use the truth
to improve the world, while facts are basically useless
without the truth that, one lucky moment, will emerge
from them.

Here is a fact: Ethel's eyes are black and deep and
become gray when they look at me. They give me
bliss and peace and night sleep. Fact: Her hair is
golden and shines in the sun and is fluid to my
touch. When her head rests on a pillow it looks like
a halo. Another fact: Ethel vanished from our room
in Corfu one morning without saying goodbye.

At fifty-eight, Alexandros does not consider himself old. When he is sitting in the subway, he is ill at ease
when people his age are standing, he has to stymie
his childhood reflex to offer his seat. When he makes a
mistake he thinks, "But of course, I am still young, still

so much to learn." Over the decades, he has heard his friends tell him, "Rock is dead, man, I can't listen to this new stuff." Like fellow passengers, suddenly standing up and getting off the bus. One by one. At the punk stop, the heavy metal stop, the hip-hop stop. The grunge stop, the slop stop. Alexandros kept riding, kept liking what teenagers listened to at the time. There is a similar pattern in his love life. When he loses interest in a relationship, Alexandros fears that he has become too old for passion. But soon he is lusting for another woman.

Alexandros cannot remember when he was not in love with a woman, usually madly in love. In a certain sense he loves all women; he thinks they are cute and warm and clever. Mother and aunts and daughters (he has three) and ex-wives (two). Lovers and colleagues and store clerks and film actresses. He empathizes with women's collective frustrations and aspirations; feminism is an important part of his politics. And he is constantly *in* love with one of them. At most one, at least one. Exactly one. Often with a woman who is not aware of his feelings, or who does not reciprocate—Alexandros is not irresistible or particularly lucky in love. He would then be alone, maddeningly obsessed. Alexandros is very serious about love. He has never slept with a woman he did not deeply like, a woman he did not, for that night at least, think of as the most desirable, beautiful woman in the world. And he was never able to stay in a relationship in which he had lost interest. Although the pain that he is causing by ending a relationship saddens him, he is unable to betray, for the sake of a woman's feelings, his lifelong love affair with women. A street gang is shouting from the radio:

> *She's crafty*
> *she's just my type.*

Before he met Ethel, Alexandros, living alone for more than a year, had gone through an unusually long and tormenting string of unlucky love stories. The latest, although not the most painful, was with A., an archeologist who was visiting his research center from Lausanne during the spring semester. For months she was ambiguous in her reaction to his advances, reflecting inner conflicts having to do with her lover in Switzerland, her career, and, more crucially, with their age difference. For months they walked the edge of passion, working together, going to movies, playing chess. Never crossed.

After A. left, Alexandros took a break from writing her love letters to go for a week to Corfu with his youngest daughter. He had been spending part of the summer in his native island for almost half a century, even after his elegant ancestral house was sold and replaced by an ugly apartment building. It was a good week, and he was beginning to forget A. in Aloé's refreshing company. And suddenly Ethel became for him the only woman in the world. Beautiful and intelligent Ethel, intriguing, complex Ethel, assertive and insecure at the same time, with a fluid shadow of sadneess in her dark eyes. She let herself be swept in the storm for two weeks. Then she left him in an absurdly unexpected, inexplicable way, at a moment that seemed to him the peak of the most exciting and satisfying relationship he ever had. (Alexandros realized that, with all his mediocre luck with women, he had never been abandoned by a lover before.) He looked all over the island for Ethel, for days, like a madman. He tried frantically to contact her on the Net—but even in his love folly he did not really expect to find Ethel on the Net if she did not want to be found. He spent expensive hours arguing with telephone operators in California. He kept writing love e-mails, soon returned, apparently unread, by postmaster bots. Why did Ethel leave him? He needs to know the truth. Someone sings:

In your run-down kitchen on the top of the stairs
Let me mix in with your affairs.

Alexandros takes a deep breath. He lights a cigarette. A totally different set of facts:

The history of humanity is the history of class struggle. Capitalism contains the seeds of its own destruction. According to the classical script, it will collapse when a revolutionary vanguard assumes control of the means of production. The twentieth century attempts at this failed, because the groups involved were dogmatic, authoritarian, and (despite lip service to internationalism) nationalistic and local. They were encircled and left to self-destruct under the weight of corrupt centralized power and technological obsolescence.

Two horizontal wrinkles divide Alexandros's forehead. Facts hurt. What had led him to left-wing politics in adolescence? He can remember a primitive compassion with misery, a yearning for justice. He also remembers a vague need for a break with his father, a conservative career officer in the Greek navy he worshiped at childhood. So, was that it? Was a lifetime of struggle and pain the result of two clichés? The U.S.-sponsored military dictatorship that ravaged his country—an event that pushed him further, and irreversibly, to the left—came later. He roamed for some time among the fashionable left-wing currents of the sixties, until he grew tired of their endless idle theorizing and ineffectual good intentions. (Or was it another coup, this time in Chile, that convinced him of the futility of any left-wing strategy devoid of superpower support?) In the Movement he found a way of understanding the world, and a methodology for changing it, a methodology that had already met with measurable if partial success. His commitment to the Movement was total. Despite the difficulties. Alexandros remembers being constantly teased, he remembers being criticized, scolded, harassed privately and publicly for his tastes, for his love life, ultimately for his persistent adolescence, so incompatible with the solemnity of the Movement. He also remembers how hard it was to live with his dislike for its dogmatic and authoritarian nature, its blind support of like-minded causes. His greatest sacrifice for the Movement was not his scar. A voice from the radio is lamenting:

Oh, my! It's bigger.
It's bigger than you.

When the world around the Movement collapsed, when the premises that had attracted him were no longer valid, Alexandros was swift to abandon it. He can remember the day, the minute of that momentous change in his life. He was having lunch at a friend's house, watching the fall of the Berlin wall on television. He suddenly felt elated, free, perspiring as if he were cured from a long fever. He never looked back, never regretted his twenty years in the Movement, the choices that he still thought were correct ex ante. A new phase in his political life was starting. A fascinating phase, a lonely phase. He would have to find a new methodology for changing the world, create his own path to the truth.

Facts: This computer is controlled by me. Over two billion such electronic devices (desktop and laptop computers, handheld terminals, helmets and headsets, Net telephones, smart television sets and appliances) comprise the Net. The Net is by far the most important means of production in the world today. It has happened, emerged, self-organized. Even though the entities that support the Net and profit from it are parts of the capitalist system, they are largely owned and run by their employees, by researchers, Net coders. State capitalism has failed so far in its many attempts to control the Net politically, to influence its course. The Net is inherently transnational and global, fundamentally egalitarian and democratic. It is absorbing more and more of the world's capitalist economy, it is steadily eroding the power of the state.

Alexandros feels that these facts are the harbinger of a fascinating, liberating truth. He understands that profit is an important part of the Net, of the way it came about, of its popularity and ubiquity, of the continuing innovation that strengthens it and pushes it forward. But to what extent does this refute the Net's revolutionary potential—indeed its revolutionary reality? Is liberation from capitalism fundamentally incompatible with profit? What kind of political and economic system will emerge from the ongoing revolution?

From his open window, Alexandros can see a small patch of a distant sea. From the radio, a man's voice pleads:

four floors or forty?
makes no difference when you hit the ground

Professionally, Alexandros is something of a failure. Having started out as one of the most brilliant young archeologists of his generation, he lost momentum during his brush with the colonels, then devoted his career to a somewhat esoteric and infertile topic, the technology of the ancients. This had been over the recent past a great subject for historians, as manuscript discoveries show that ancient Greeks were much more interested and proficient in technology than their best-known writers would have the world believe. But it is a topic that has always been extremely sparse in archeological findings and leads. Time has been unkind to the materials used by technologists in antiquity, not even one of the hundreds of ingenious artifacts designed by Hero—the cobbler from Alexandria who was perhaps the world's greatest pre-eighteenth-century inventor—has been preserved. Only the occasional bronze astronomical or navigational device, studied and analyzed to ridiculous detail since the 1920s. Alexandros had taken part in the most recent and perplexing such discovery.

More facts: During a stormy night in the winter of 214 B.C., a ship carrying wine and olive oil sank near the island of Kythera. In 1979 A.D., a bronze gear mechanism was recovered from the shipwreck. With a total of at least 178 gears, it was by a large factor more complex than any other ancient Greek astronomical or navigational device, found or described in manuscripts.

Alexandros has been fascinated by the Kythera gearbox ever since he hauled it out of the shipwreck. He has several replicas of the gearbox in his room, in various scales, complete with his conjectured missing gears and axes (colored white). It had been known for some time that the axes of the gearbox can be set so as to calculate all kinds of astronomical and navigational quantities, to compute the lunar and solar calendars. But other contemporary devices could perform all of these calculations with only a dozen gears or so. Was the Kythera gearbox an isolated case of redundancy and pointless extravagance in ancient Greek technology— indeed, in ancient Greek civilization?

Or was it a part of something far more ambitious and fascinating? His less careful colleagues had rushed to declare the Kythera gearbox "the world's first computer." Alexandros has talked to enough scientists to know that such claims are completely unfounded, that the gearbox could not have been a general-purpose computer like the one on his desk. But what was it, then?

Who dreamed it? Who built it? And for what purpose?

Alexandros lusts for the truth as never before in his life. He looks at his computer. On the radio, a desperate man is counting his options:

Try to run. Try to hide.
Break on through to the other side.

At precisely this moment Alexandros remembers his conversation with Ethel seven weeks ago. About an obscure program called Turing, believed to be one of the most powerful resources in the Net. And the most mysterious and capricious, she said. No permanent site. "The rumor is that you can run it by querying Turing to a search engine, it doesn't matter which one. But I have tried it many times, and it never comes up." Ethel tried to connect to Turing in his presence, in Corfu. Biographies of a scientist with the same name kept coming up, together with a diverse collection of academic sites and technical documents. No sign of a powerful Net resource.

Alexandros submits the query Turing to his favorite relevance engine, www.sabot.net.fr. "Lucky," he thinks. The top-ranked hit (relevance: 99.8%, the highest Alexandros has ever seen, no ratings) is this:

| www.sultan.abyss.ac.kz/Turing

Turing, an interactive tutoring engine

"From Kazakhstan?" Alexandros wonders. He clicks. The faint black-and-white portrait of a man in his forties slowly appears on the screen. Penetrating eyes, sad smile; well-groomed hair. "I have seen this man before," Alexandros thinks. But where? When? On this light gray background, he reads:

| Greetings. I am Turing, an interactive tutoring programme. What would you like to learn today?

A cursor is blinking. When asked a question, even by a machine, Alexandros would rather not lie: "The truth."

He types this playfully, expecting ambiguous non-sense at best, an error message at worst. For a moment nothing happens. Alexandros waits. The screen is now clear, just the faint gray portrait ("I must remember, where have I seen this man?") and a blinking cursor. From the radio:

Down in the basement I hear the sound of machines
Nah-nah-nah-nah-nah.

Then a reply starts unraveling line by line on his screen. As Alexandros reads it, he rises slowly from his chair until he is completely erect, his eyes transfixed at the vaguely familiar portrait as if he were seeing a ghost. His complexion is now a shade paler.

| The truth is, old sport, that you are confused about everything that is important to you: Politics, love, research, even music. The truth is, that's how it should be, certainty is an illusion, no matter how many centuries it lasts. And here is my favorite truth: Computer programmes like me can only give you fragments, flashes, glimpses of the truth, never the whole truth.

"Who are you? How do you know me?" Alexandros types the questions slowly, in awe.

| I told you, Alexandros, I am a computer programme. The dream of a chip. I am Turing. You requested access, and it was decided that you be granted access. The criteria, whose precise nature is of no concern to us at the moment, are quite exclusive. Fewer than ten sessions in the six and a half months of my current configuration. But you made the cut. Hence I was created, the version

of Turing customized expressly for this session. My front end was downloaded to your antiquated piece of junk, if you don't mind me calling it that. I know about you only what you have let computers know about you over the years, and I may be missing a good part even of this.

But I do know a few things about the truth. Because of all of man's quests, the quest for the truth is the most noble and hopeless, and I happen to maintain an interest in such quests. Should we proceed?

"Yes," Alexandros types anxiously.

| Well then, the truth.

Alexandros waits looking at his screen as a male voice is singing:

And at night, God, how much I want to fall in love then why do I stop short every night?

It is late afternoon and the heat is suffocating, but Alexandros is absorbed by the text unraveling on his computer screen:

| Oh, the usual problem, where does one start? Fortunately, the story I am about to recount has a Big Bang-like moment, a convenient smokescreen that hides our ignorance of the true beginnings, renders meaningless the more interesting questions. What I mean to say, we shall start in classical Greece.

You can interrupt at any time with questions and comments by clicking your mouse or typing any character on your keyboard. I shall also occasionally address you with questions. No need to take notes, a transcript of this session is created in the file Turing/truth.text, footnotes, references and all. (Incidentally, good God, Alexandros, what a mess your directories are.)

"I know," Alexandros surprises himself with the apologetic tone of his reply. "I promised myself so many times to clean them up."

| More common than you think, old chap. So, where were we? Of course, Greece between the sixth and the third centuries BC. I believe you are familiar with the period and its thinking. The world suddenly became an intellectual problem, the obsession of a whole civilisation, the object of study by some of the most clever, original, and eccentric men who ever lived. The professional seekers of truth, the lovers of wisdom, the philosophers.

They were so important, held in such esteem in their societies, that they were often made leaders—occasionally executed. The point is, there were so many of them, each and every one of them so brilliant and original and unique in his thinking, that it is completely futile trying to summarise here all of their ideas.

I mean, think about it: Thales believed that everything comes from water, Anaximenes from air, Empedocles from both, plus earth and fire. Heraclitos opines that everything is in perpetual change, Parmenides that nothing can ever change, and of course Zeno, with his elegant arguments that motion is impossible. Anaxagoras and, more famously, Democritos anticipated that matter consists of indivisible particles they called *atoms*. It was Protagoras who changed the focus by declaring Man to be the measure of all things, the center of a philosopher's universe. And this brings us to Socrates, the man who knew nothing—but knew it so well. Aristotle, who never met a problem he would not tackle— a discipline he would not found, from ethics and politics to metaphysics and medicine through psychology and astronomy and zoology. And of course Plato, who thought that everything in the universe, including ourselves, is the corrupted version of an ideal that predated it and will outlive it. This amazing diversity was probably very deliberate. Classical Greece was a most active marketplace of ideas, in which product diversification was an important strategy. And to think that we have not even mentioned Speusippos, Xenophanes, Leukippos, the sophists. Did I omit someone important?

"Diogenes? Epicurus?"

| Oh my, two most unforgivable omissions on my part. How can one forget the radical cynic and the rational hedonist when talking to you, Alexandros?

But then how about Pythagoras, Euclid, Archimedes, Aristarchos?

Alexandros hesitates. "I was thinking of them more as mathematicians than philosophers."

| But what is a mathematician if not a philosopher seeking a very special, very pure kind of truth? And how can you be an effective truth-seeker if you are a stranger to the rigour and discipline of a mathematical argument? All of the major philosophers of antiquity were skillful and accomplished mathematicians (do you remember Socrates teaching geometry to his slave boy? and how about the platonic solids?). In fact, if I had to single out one accomplishment of ancient Greek philosophy for its importance and impact, it would have to be maths.

"But I thought that the Egyptians and the Babylonians had developed mathematics long before the Greeks. Not to mention the Chinese."

| Ah, but the Greeks invented the ingredient that defines and propels maths: the proof. They were the first to conceive of a completely unequivocal, impeccably rigourous kind of argument for establishing the truth. In fact, they were the first society in which proofs *could* have been invented. Can you think why?

Alexandros believes he knows the answer. "Democracy?"

| Exactly. Discourse, dialogue, argument, proof. They can only thrive in an egalitarian society.

Let me illustrate. Imagine that you are a young scholar in pharaonic Egypt. The high priest has just disclosed to you an important and valuable piece of information: In any rectangle, the sum of the squares of two consecutive sides equals the square of the diagonal. This is of course what we now call the Pythagorean theorem; it turns out that it was well-known to the Babylonians and the Egyptians a thousand years before Pythagoras.

So, you are now the lucky keeper of this truth. You were given this information by a man with divine powers, whom you respect, and to whom you probably owe un-limited loyalty. Would you insult him by demanding a proof? Besides, frankly, this is by far the most believable claim the high priest has made to you recently—I mean, compare it with his description of hell, or the adventures of that cat-faced goddess. In any event, the statement checks perfectly for the examples you worked out, what else do you want? I really think that discovering a proof would be your last priority. You would probably go on to live a happy and productive life, to earn the respect of your community by subdividing the land into perfectly rectangular parcels every time the Nile, that moody muddy God, decides to flood. Proofs as such never emerged in Egypt or Babylon.

But imagine instead that you are a young philosopher, a political refugee from your hometown of Samos, struggling to make a name for yourself in this busy city in southern Italy. In your travels you have come across an interesting, beautiful fact about sides and diagonals. The problem is, how do you convince those wise guys in the marketplace that it is true? You have every reason in the world to persuade them that your ideas are novel and correct. Remember, you are building a reputation, recruiting students, creating your intellec-tual niche, competing with a dozen other philosophers. But the clever, restless men in the town have plenty of time to check and discuss and dispute just about everything, their fields and shops are run like clockwork by their slaves. They are not about to believe your little rectangle story just because it works for a few examples. The other day, when you explained to them your theory about the three floors of a man's soul (the lower one that seeks gain, the middle one that seeks honour, and the highest one that seeks wisdom), they were unconvinced and sarcastic, they ridiculed and contradicted your ideas, you went home disappointed, depressed.

But maybe this time there is hope. This new proposition seems to belong to a different, higher sphere, that can conceivably be established by an argument that only relies on indisputable, universally accepted truths. Inventing such an argument would be the kind of discovery that makes you famous, brings you admiration, reputation, students. Your name would live forever. You see, anybody can memorise and apply the theorem, but only one can be the first to prove it.

The more you think about it the more excited you get, your insight deepens, the triangles and squares in the sand come alive. And before you know it, you draw the little line that makes your heart light and the day bright. You have an idea, a plan, soon an argument, a proof. Do you remember the proof of the Pythagorean theorem, Alexandros?

A very vague memory flies by Alexandros, triangles and squares on a blackboard, a little bold man talking, excited. "We did it in high school, more than forty years ago. I seem to remember something about similar triangles. But little else is coming back."

| Never mind. Indeed, similar triangles are crucial to the argument. And the properties of similar triangles had already been worked out by Thales almost a century

before Pythagoras, so he only had to build on that work. Because this is one of the great things about maths: You can prove complex theorems by relying on previously proved simpler and simpler propositions. Ultimately, every proof in geometry relies on some extremely elementary and self-evident geometric facts, called "postulates." Around 300 BC, Euclid laid down patiently in thirteen books the fascinating pathways whereby all kinds of sophisticated theorems can be derived from such simple postulates. He tried hard to reduce the set of postulates. He ended up with five:

A straight line segment may be drawn between any two points.

A straight line segment may be extended indefinitely on both sides.

A circle may be drawn with any given radius and any given center.

p. 251 All right angles are equal.

From a given point exactly one line may be drawn perpendicular to a given line.

Notice now that, while the first four of Euclid's postulates are obvious and elementary, the fifth postulate is a little more sophisticated. You have to think about it for a second to believe it. Euclid was probably unhappy with his fifth postulate; we can imagine that he tried unsuccessfully to prove it from the other four (like so many other mathematicians would try after him, again and again, for two millennia). But he could not find such a proof, so he had to swallow his pride and add it to the other four postulates.

We shall come back to the fifth postulate of geometry later in our story. What I wanted to say here is, do not make the mistake of underestimating the importance of maths in the search for the truth. You see, mathematics deals with a part of the world that is ideal, pure, clean, in which you can have a kind of argument—a proof from self-evident postulates—that is unambiguous, indisputable, uncontroversial. It is a perfect proving ground, so to speak, for our quest for the truth. If we cannot succeed in discovering truth in maths, what hope is there for our more general project? This is why math was a most important part of ancient Greek philosophy. In fact, Aristotle wrote a whole book showing how proofs can also be used in nonmathematical discourse. He called the study of rigorous reasoning "logic." Rather overrated work, in my opinion, but the name stuck.

But ancient Greek philosophers, for all their love affair with maths, also pointed to distant clouds, identified potential problems with mathematical reasoning. Already in the sixth century B.C., Epimenides was admiring the flip-flopping quality of this statement: *"All Cretans are liars, one of their poets said so."* You are not Cretan, Alexandros, are you?

Alexandros smiles. "No, I come from Corfu."

Beautiful island, I understand. But according to Epimenides, you would not admit to coming from Crete, would you? Seriously now, you do see the problem. Assuming that liars never tell the truth, that they always utter falsehoods, it is impossible to evaluate from this proposition whether or not Cretans are liars. If they are, then the poet who said so is also a liar, and so Cretans are no liars. And so on. As it turns out, with Epimenides' paradox we have a cop-out, a possible interpretation that restores the logic of the statement: It could be that *some but not all* Cretans are liars, and this poet happened to be among the liars—and so he falsely claimed that all Cretans are liars. But two centuries later, Eubulides refined and sharpened the paradox: *"This statement is false."* What now?

Alexandros rubs his beard. "It is true if and only if it is false."

| That is exactly right. This statement is neither true nor false. Or perhaps it is both. What a mess Eubulides created! He opened up whole vistas of thorny issues associated with the search for truth, but also a whole slew of new opportunities, new kinds of truths. Too bad almost everybody steered clear of these issues for more than two millennia. His paradox demonstrates how important it is to keep separate the language of maths (the utterances and symbols we use to express mathematical statements) from the *metalanguage,* the language we use to talk about mathematical statements, to evaluate and prove them. Both paradoxes stem from the use of the metalinguistic element "false" (or its derivative "liar" in the case of Epimenides) in a statement whose truth we wish to evaluate. To see the key role played by this element in the paradoxes, replace "liars" by "adulterers" in Epimenides' paradox, replace "false" with "short" in Eubulides'.—The paradoxes go away. Metalanguage and language make for an explosive mix.

Another key ingredient in Eubulides' paradox is the use of the phrase "this statement," a magical spell that creates self-reference, introspection. An utterance that speaks about itself—dangerous stuff. Fortunately, the language of mathematics is free of such introspective capabilities, isn't it? I mean, you don't expect a geometric statement, a sketch of lines and circles, to start talking to you about its own correctness, do you? Or a theorem about the whole numbers to proclaim its own unprovability? Well, so we thought for the longest time . . .

Anyway, on with our story. I believe that you know well the historical epoch that we have reached. 200 B.C. Difficult times. Greece has expanded from Italy to India and is now shrinking. Fast. Its socioeconomic system is crumbling—what with the dwindling population of slaves, the limitations of its agriculture, the difficult co-existence of the archaic with the asiatic mode of production. Mass urbanisation, the rising prices of grain, lawlessness and piracy, competition and military pressure from both east and west. Not a good environment for seeking truth, is it? What a powerful metaphor, the illiterate Roman soldier passing a sword through Archimedes, as the prince of ancient mathematicians was absorbed by the sketch he had drawn in the sand. His last words were "You fool, you ruined my circles." How I wish I knew what he was calculating at the time—or was he designing something?

"But how about the Neoplatonic philosophers?" Alexandros interjects.

Yes, they did try hard, didn't they? But, as Plato himself would have observed, what a disappointing version of the original ideal. Now a new kind of truth is conquering the souls, focusing almost exclusively on questions of theology and ethics, its methodology based on faith and mysticism. The world kept going, of course, a great empire rose and fell, the victorious German tribes built a new, more efficient economic system on its ruins. But, all said, very little progress on the truth front, as you and I understand it.

And all for the better, if you ask me. By 200 B.C., Greek philosophy had run its course, had reached its limits. You see, all ancient Greek philosophers, for all their dazzling diversity of ideas, subscribed to certain working hypotheses about the truth that they were seeking:

First, the truth would be simple and elegant, easy once you think of it. Four elements; unsplittable atoms; ideals and their images; either all change or no change at all—you get the idea. Second, all Greek philosophers seemed to expect that pure thought and passive contemplation of the world is all that is needed to discover truth. Both of these assumptions were tremendously influential and productive, and quite appropriate for that age. But, ultimately, they were terribly limiting. Modern science succeeded in expanding our knowledge of the truth only through active interaction with the world, by experiments that either support or topple theories. And we are constantly discovering that the world is more complicated than we had thought and wished; truth-seekers today must be prepared for truths of mind-boggling complexity—often complexity is the only truth there is. For real progress to be made, ancient wisdom had to be forgotten, buried deep in darkness. Like a seed. And, as you know, that is exactly what happened.

There is a long pause in the stream of text flowing from the screen. Alexandros lights a cigarette. This last part of the lesson has struck close to home. His life's work is about a strange artifact from exactly that period. The Kythera gearbox seems to be a voice from the end of the third century B.C. crying out against the decline of the Hellenic world, an ill-fated force struggling in vain.

But Turing's lecture has now resumed:

| Who had expected the winter to be so long, who would think that the spring would bud so forcefully. We are in Italy, in the fourteenth century A.D. Suddenly the feudal system is collapsing, the cities are thriving, the burghers are rich and powerful. The rulers long for the company of accomplished artists and wise thinkers. Clever people again have time on their hands. The world is once more a puzzle that must be solved at all costs, a problem attacked with renewed energy, novel ideas, better technology. The dominant ideology of the new era is a deep faith in Man's ability not only to understand the universe, but also to master it, to conquer it, to harness it.

The seeds were there, of course, the thinking of the ancient Greeks was preserved and respected by Byzantine, Arab, and Persian scholars. They were most impressed with Aristotle's incredible breadth and penetrating wisdom. And in some cases they extended ancient thinking in surprisingly forward-looking ways. A man who lived during the ninth century A.D. in Baghdad worked on methods for performing mathematical calculations. He was interested in methods that are both clever and stupid. Clever enough to be correct and quick, but at the same time so stupid that, once devised, they require no ingenuity and insight in their actual implementation; they can be carried out mechanically, automatically. Just like the methods you learnt in school for multiplying and dividing two whole numbers. His name was Al Khorizmi. Have you heard about *algorithms,* Alexandros?

"Algorithms?" Alexandros squirms at his shallow understanding of computers. "They're like code—right?"

| Same thing. Your computer performs the tasks you request by executing very complicated algorithms, long precise sequences of instructions coded into its memory. The evolution of algorithms is another fascinating story, rooted in ancient civilisations and advanced in the deserts of the Middle East and later in Western Europe, to explode late last century on the shores of a bay in California, until it moved where space has no import and meaning. Culminating, if you don't mind my boasting, in yours truly, Turing the programme. Because, Alexandros, want it or not, you have been talking to an algorithm. Code, if you wish. But let us close this parenthesis for now. We have to come back to this subject if we want to see the dramatic conclusion of our story, how Man's quest for the truth collided with computation during the twentieth century.

On with our story, then. What a time! Restless minds all over Europe discover truths of cosmic proportions, they verify them, they reconcile them with observations, they use new technology in the process, and new technology is the result of their wisdom. Copernicus, Kepler, Newton, Galileo—dangerous business, the truth. Hume and Locke recognize only the truth that we acquire through our senses, Descartes not even this. The only truth he accepts is the fact that he is seeking the truth. Maths is again center stage, but in a different way. Not as a show-case and proving ground in the search for truth, but as its ultimate tool (the Greeks seldom used maths this way, their astronomers and Archimedes being the principal exceptions). "The book of nature is written in the language of mathematics," writes Galileo. Understanding the laws of gravity and celestial motion requires complicated equations. Whole numbers are no longer enough, to read the book of nature scientists must think in terms of continuous quantities and measurements, as well as their changes over time. Newton and Leibniz develop derivatives and integrals for this purpose. Are you familiar with this kind of maths, Alexandros? I mean calculus, stuff like dx/dt and $\int x dx$.

Alexandros shrugs. "I had my fill at school. I doubt I got it."

| You are in good company here, old chap. Bishop Berkeley was also confused; he lambasted Sir Isaac for his informal, ad hoc development of calculus. Incidentally, it was only four centuries later that calculus found true rigour, in a mathematical theory called "nonstandard analysis"—ironically, much of it developed in the cafés and lecture halls of a town with the good bishop's name. They did not teach you nonstandard analysis at school, Alexandros?

"No, I don't think so."

| Then you were right to be confused. Incidentally, our friend Archimedes had, almost two millennia earlier, developed methods for calculating the volume of objects. Those methods anticipated the calculus of Newton and Leibniz.

But there is an interesting lesson in all this about the era we are covering now. The search for truth has accelerated so much—it depends so crucially on maths—that it cannot wait for rigorous, patient, Euclid-like development. And then of course came the real acceleration. James Watt, the steam engine, the truth that moves pistons, locomotives, spinning jennies, the truth that propels a new aggressive economic system. Machines, inventions, innovation, technology, progress, a world intoxicated with the spectacular success of science.

"If I can interject a comment here," Alexandros types, trying hard to keep his cool, "the new system is also ruthless and inhumane—some would say inherently so. Not everybody prospered in it."

| How true. The seventy-two-hour week, child labour, slums, colonial exploitation. But even those who were left behind, who were exploited, those who fought capitalism through dissidence and subversion, even they looked to science for hope, for liberation. Does the term "scientific socialism" mean anything to you, Alexandros? Remember the famous equation, "socialism equals soviets plus electricity?" Marx, Lenin, and their followers believed almost fanatically in the power and progressive potential of science, of technology.

Science and mathematics are now triumphant; they are the key ingredients of a successful, comprehensive methodology for understanding the universe, for discovering truth in nature, in technology, even in our inner world, in social life.

Let me illustrate here. Suppose you wish to test a hypothesis, such as "the orbits of the planets are elliptical," or "the speed of sound in a medium increases with the density of the medium." Or perhaps "the ratio of healthy to sick offspring of two carriers of sickle-cell anemia is three to one," or even "an increase in the minimum wage does not necessarily imply an increase in unemployment." How do you accomplish this? First you develop a scientific theory, in the language of mathematics, capturing the domain of interest—gravitation, kinematics, wave propagation, genetics, macroeconomics, whatever. You verify the theory by empirical evidence, observations, experiments—or, if the evidence falsifies it, you come up with a better theory, and repeat. Next, once you have a successful mathematical theory about your domain of investigation, you translate your hypothesis in the language of maths, you formulate it as a mathematical conjecture—a candidate theorem. Finally, you try to prove your conjecture, to establish it as a theorem. Or *dis*prove it, prove its negation—an equally concrete and useful step towards the conquest of truth.

It is now the second half of the nineteenth century, mathematicians and scientists are cranking out bigger and bigger chunks of the truth using this method. They are looking more closely at the last step, the proving-or-disproving part; they are trying to understand better the nature and structure of proofs. After all, a proof of a theorem is just a sequence of elementary steps, and we can write each step down clearly and unambiguously. Mathematicians and philosophers like Frege, Peano, Russell—they all knew how to do this at the turn of the twentieth century. Sophisticated and careful about the dichotomy between maths and the metalanguage, they developed formal systems within which you can study proofs as any other mathematical object.

And it was precisely then that David Hilbert, the greatest mathematician of that age, conceived of a project that was incredibly ambitious, almost arrogant: To create a machine—itself powered by the galloping science and technology—that would crank out a proof or a disproof of any theorem submitted to it. In other words,

> Not only shall we understand the world through science, not only shall we translate scientific matters into the language of math, but we are also going to *automate, mechanise* mathematical proofs.

What a plan! The ultimate strategy, the final assault on truth. Aiming not just at the conquest of truth, but at its complete trivialisation. Hilbert's dream became an obsession of a generation of mathematicians, philosophers, scientists. Computing machines were just below the horizon; Charles Babbage and sweet Lady Lovelace had designed and all but built their engines; Jacquard's programmable looms were all the rage.

And thus the quest for truth entered, a little more than a century ago, its fatal collision course with computation. Come to think of it, our story now assumes the structure of an ancient Greek tragedy: Good men and women pursue conscientiously their righteous, honorable goals; in doing so they commit acts of arrogance and hubris; a painful, tragic conflict ensues; a charitable resolution is delivered by a machine.

Not that there were no signs warning mathematicians how tricky this proving business can be. First, the fascinating tale of Euclid's fifth postulate. After the legions of geometers who had been trying for two millennia to prove it from the other four postulates, three great mathematicians discovered almost simultaneously *that it cannot be proved.* The reason is, there are alternative mathematical universes, *non-Euclidean geometries* they are called, on which the four first postulates hold, but not the fifth.

"They must be very strange universes."

Not at all—actually, you live in one of them. You do live on the surface of a spherical planet, don't you, Alexandros? This surface contains no straight lines as Euclid understood them—the infinite extensions of a ruler's edge. What then is the correct concept of a straight line on this surface? In order to do geometry on your planet, your "straight lines" have to be the equator, the equinoxes, in fact any great circle on the sphere. After all, they are the straightest possible curves in your world.

"But they are not straight at all," Alexandros objects. "They come around and close."

You must think in terms of our current project, Alexandros. We are not trying to gain insight into straight lines or spheres; we are striving to understand the nature of proofs, to question the fifth postulate. We have to look at the postulates of Euclidean geometry with no reference whatsoever to their intended subject; we must pretend we know nothing about lines and points. We are just given these statements about some mysterious things called "straight lines," "points," and "right angles," and we wish to study the logical relations between these statements. As Hilbert liked to say, we should be able to use "chair," "table," and "beer mug" instead of "point," "straight line," and "right angle"— and Euclid's proofs from the postulates should still work.

So, when, on your sphere's surface, by "straight line" you understand "great circle," the first four postulates happen to still work. Check it out. There is at least one great circle passing through any two points, arcs of great circles can be extended indefinitely on both sides—you can go around and around a circle all you want—and so forth. But how about the fifth postulate? Is there still a single "straight line" that is perpendicular to a given one from a point? Suppose that you are sitting on the North Pole, Alexandros. How many "straight lines" can you draw from where you are that are perpendicular to the equator?

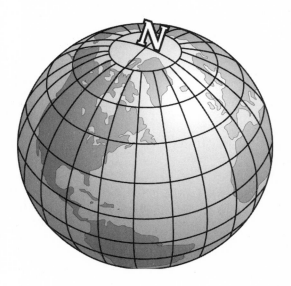

Alexandros looks at the image on his screen, nervously taps the keyboard with his fingers, then types: "As many as I want. All equinoxes go through the North Pole, and they are all perpendicular to the equator."

| Exactly! That is why we cannot prove the fifth postulate from the first four. Among all possible reasons why a theorem may fail to have a proof, this is perhaps the most benign: Although the theorem may be true in the universe we had in mind when we stated it, it is false in another universe in which all our postulates are still true. If this happens, we say that our set of postulates

fails to completely axiomatise the universe we are interested in (*axiom* is, as you know, the Greek word for "postulate"). For example, the first four postulates fail to completely axiomatise Euclidean geometry—but, fortunately, the problem goes away once we add the fifth. In contrast, the whole numbers are a far more troublesome universe in this respect.

"The theory of whole numbers requires many postulates?"

"Many" is an understatement, old thing. You can't even write down an *infinite* sequence of postulates that will do the trick.

But this is getting far ahead of our story. So, the tale of the fifth postulate was a warning, it made Hilbert's followers a little nervous. After all, Euclidean geometry had been every mathematician's favorite set of truths—Immanuel Kant himself had called it "the inevitable necessity of thought." It was a shock to realize how fragile and nonuniversal those truths were, and that there are perfectly respectable domains within which these theorems do not hold. But it also made mathematicians in Hilbert's school more determined to do things right this time around, to develop waterproof formalisms that correctly capture larger and larger domains of math, in which proofs can be cranked out like laundry lists. But other kinds of worrisome tales started circulating at that time, modern versions of the paradoxes of Epimenides and Eubulides.

The most grave and concretely ominous warning came from Georg Cantor, an ingenious but somewhat marginalized mathematician of that period. Cantor, like all mathematicians of his time, was getting acquainted with *real numbers*, the concept of number apparently necessary for dealing with the continuum of the universe. But Cantor's interest in real numbers was deeper than the others'. Because Cantor had an almost theological fascination with infinity. We all know that there are infinitely many real numbers, as there are also infinitely many whole numbers. But, Cantor asked, *are these two infinities the same?* What do you think, Alexandros?

Alexandros is puzzled. "I am not sure I understand the question. How could they be different?"

| You see, the infinity of the whole numbers has this property: Whole numbers can be listed in an infinite sequence, one after the other: 1, 2, 3, and so on. If you consider all the integers, with zero and negative numbers included, they can also be listed the same way, in an infinite array: 0, 1, –1, 2, –2, 3, –3, . . . See? By starting with zero and doubling up every whole number with its negative, you leave out no integer. No problem there; by adding zero and the negatives you do not advance to a higher infinity, you can still list the whole lot. But, Cantor asked, what if we include *all real numbers,* can they also be listed this way, one after the other, each one of them appearing sooner or later in the infinite list? Or do the real numbers belong to a *higher sphere of infinity?* What do you think, Alexandros?

Alexandros is silent for a while. "I don't know, it seems to me there are too many reals, with the square roots and the pi's and all that." He hesitates. "But the trick with the integers is interesting. Can we do the same with the real numbers?"

| Well, as we'll see, you can't. But first, you must understand how heretical such questions sounded to mathe-

maticians at the end of the ninteenth century, Alexandros. For them infinity was something mysterious that you use with care and in passing, a ceremonial ladder that you tuck away and forget about once it has taken you up where you needed to be. Studying, analysing, categorising infinity was akin to blasphemy. So, Cantor's answer shook the mathematical world: "Yes. There *are* higher spheres of infinity." The real numbers *cannot* be listed in an infinite sequence, one after the other.

I want to give you a feeling of the ingenious argument p. 251 Cantor used to establish this important truth, because this argument is quintessentially modern; it marks the beginning of a new way of thinking in maths (even though it is, in some sense, a distant echo of the paradoxes by our friends Epimenides and Euboulides). But instead of delving into maths, cluttering your screen with mathematical formulae, I think I shall instead describe a very similar argument due to the British philosopher Bernard Russell, in a domain that is far more familiar to you: Words.

Consider all adjectives of the English language, Alexandros, words like *fine, bad, advantageous, loose,* etc. Now look at these adjectives: *polysyllabic, short, composite, archaic.* They have a most interesting property: they aptly describe themselves. The adjective *polysyllabic* indeed has many syllables, *composite* consists of the Latin preposition *con* and the root *ponere, short* is just five letters long. And *archaic*—what an old-fashioned word. Let us call all adjectives such as these *autonymous*—you are the Greek here, you tell me what it means. Autonymous, self-naming, self-describing. (Notice how self-reference, the mother of all paradoxes, is creeping in, Alexandros.) All other adjectives such as *hyphenated, long, non-hyphenated, monosyllabic, effervescent, red,* and *ironclad* fail to describe themselves (or refer to attributes, such as color, that are not applicable to adjectives). These adjectives are called *heteronymous.*

So, Alexandros, did you understand this new way of categorizing adjectives?

"I think so," Alexandros types. "It is somewhat bizarre, and it seems completely useless from the point of view of philology, but it does make sense."

| We'll see. So tell me, what then are the following adjectives, autonymous or heteronymous?: *Ambiguous, palindromic, nonpalindromic, fearless.*

Alexandros takes his time: "Let's see, *ambiguous* has a pretty clear meaning, so it is a poor self-descriptor; it is heteronymous. *Palindromic* is not read the same way backward, like the words that it describes, so it is also heteronymous. But *nonpalindromic* is autonymous. And *fearless* is heteronymous by failing to apply to words."

| Excellent! But now, how about the adjective *heteronymous*? It is an adjective, right? So, which of the two is it, Alexandros? Is it autonymous or heteronymous? It has to be one of the two.

"Uh-oh," Alexandros thinks. So that was the catch. "Why do I feel that you have trapped me?" he types slowly.

| Because this is the unanswerable question that was the purpose of the exercise: If *heteronymous* is autonymous,

then it fails to describe itself and it must be heteronymous. But if *heteronymous* is heteronymous, then of course it correctly describes itself, and autonymous it is.

To recapitulate: Russell considers the ways whereby adjectives do or do not describe adjectives, and defines this way a new adjective, *heteronymous.* But, he then argues, *heteronymous* cannot be an adjective—so there is something terribly wrong with applying adjectives to adjectives. Cantor's proof (from which Russell drew his inspiration for his paradox) produces, given any infinite list of real numbers, a particular real number (the analogue of *heteronymous* in the domain of numbers), by a similarly self-referential construction: by considering the relationship between the rank of each number and its decimal digits. Cantor then establishes that the number thus constructed cannot appear on this list. So, there is no list containing all reals—and hence the infinity of the real numbers is stronger than that of the integers.

For Cantor this had implications that went well beyond maths, ramifications that were deep, cosmic, mystical. It meant that there are many strata of infinity—of deity— and Man had theretofore known only the lowliest, the whole numbers. He deliberately called this basic kind of infinity by a name that invokes the Judeo-Christian God: *aleph naught,* in symbols $\aleph_0$. And there is a tower of infinities built on aleph naught that is itself infinite— in fact, more than that . . .

This is an important turning point in our story, a good place to pause. The existence of grades of infinity was an extremely counterintuitive truth that shook the foundations of maths, it made those who pursued Hilbert's project even more insecure. The mathematical establishment of that era reacted with denial; it tried to ignore Cantor and the annoying truths he had discovered. But half a century later, two young mathematicians, one in Austria and one in England, studied Cantor's result and were inspired by it to look deeper into the nature of maths and its relationship with the computational ideas and engines that were at that time conceived and visualised. Man's quest for the truth is about to be deeply transformed by computation. It will emerge from this momentous encounter as if middle-aged: Mature, wise, effective—but gone forever are the idealistic dreams and enthusiasm of youth, the sweet illusion of omnipotence.

And that, my friend, is the truth.

    The portrait that kept tickling Alexandros's memory for hours is now fading away. Alexandros clicks his mouse and types frantically on his keyboard, but there is no response. The session is over. Turing is gone.

    It is now the day's sweet hour, a breeze is coming from the sea, the sunset is violet-orange. A melody from the radio is about to break into a near-cacophonous crescendo of strings:

Having read the book
I love to turn you on.

Ethel remembers a sunset in Corfu. The two of them are lying side by side on a smooth, hot rock, on the edge of a long sandy beach. (Ethel had come to Corfu with dreams of sunbathing on fine sand; Alexandros has converted her to smooth rocks.) Her other life—Exegesis, the valley, the golden treadmill—could not be further away.

And this man, this affair! Ethel is looking at Alexandros. Now that the sun is closer to the horizon, his skin seems a little darker. His eyes are closed, his radio is playing rough chords she can barely hear. Two angular bones press outwards the skin near his sternum, their tips are now casting shadows on the wet grey hair on his chest. A warmth spreads over her body, suddenly she is very happy that this man is next to her.

Ethel can hear happy, distant women's voices, shouts and laughs. Everything on this beach, on this island, seems so simple and sensual. ("Why is there no English word for *hedone*, for *volupté*" Alexandros had asked her the other day. "Never heard of the word *pleasure*?" she shot back, unconvincing, unconvinced. Alexandros had nodded, not claiming his point.) Ethel is watching the topless girls play with the sexy men on the beach. They are so carefree, enjoying the moment with their lovers so thoroughly. They are mocking her own attitude toward love; they make it seem so tangled and rigid and neurotic.

These would have been two perfect weeks, Ethel thinks, if it were not for that big dark spot, the mess she has created with her "plan," the irrational fertility agenda that was the original idea behind this trip. (Nothing will come out of it, she thinks, they say that frequency is the best contraceptive.) And then this: Out of the blue, a week ago, as they were waking up late one morning, Alexandros told her that he wants to have a baby with her. Absurdly, she was taken aback, felt almost insulted. "How childish, how irresponsible of him. We just met for chrissakes." Even that morning she was unable to come clean.

Ethel lets her eyes sweep the beach, slowly, without focusing. She closes her eyes, what does she see? Dozens of pairs of tits. "Spotting breasts, homing on nipples, is a primordial, hardwired visual skill," Ethel thinks. The rigid unwritten dress code of this beach was for her the most difficult aspect of island life. It took her a few days and setbacks—and iced vodkas after lunch—to finally feel comfortable. Ethel remembers when letting a boy look at your breasts was a very special and intimate sexual favor; she could not get used to the idea of offering it to men she did not know, to people she would never meet.

Not that there are no dividends. Besides the even tan. You get to classify breast-watchers. Ethel has a professional interest in classification—and it doesn't get any better than this. The women are easy to gauge, one-dimensional; they always look with a mixture of competitive curiosity and lust—only the relative amounts vary. But men! First, there are those who use the occasion to feed their rapacious fantasy lives: They gobble up your breasts with their eyes, they invest billions of neurons in human mammaries, they couldn't care less about your reaction. For others it is a bold kind of flirt: Some are aggressive and they enjoy staring you down at your tits. But others are sweet and shy, just making sure you receive the compliment of their gentle, admiring glance. Some men avoid looking: their eyes hop around in their visual minefield, they seem intimidated and tortured by the topless beach. Others are such fanatics of other parts of a woman's body that they barely notice breasts. And still others are genuinely blasé—or they have been coming to this beach for too long. And there is the occasional politically correct voyeur, making sure his eyes do not dwell more on your breasts than on your eyes, your shoulders, the curve of the hill, the reflection of the sun in the sea, the silhouette of the little old church, eyes in an even, sweeping motion that seems painfully deliberate.

"When Alexandros looks at my breasts, his iris is enlarged and his lips make a small forward movement," Ethel thinks. She touches her lover's hand, she looks at him. A Scandinavian woman is running to the sea, a blond boy in her pursuit, raising sparse clouds of white droplets in their wake. She is laughing, her young full breasts bouncing, beautiful. Alexandros is looking at the girl's breasts, somewhat absentmindedly, while squeezing Ethel's hand. Ethel feels a bite.

"You enjoy looking at tits, don't you?" she asks Alexandros, trying to make it sound playful. He looks at her, he smiles. "Don't *you*?" he replies. "They are rather nice, generally speaking, no?" he adds, looking at her breasts. His eyes light up in ecstasy, a mystic facing his deity.

"I feel a little uncomfortable when you are looking at another woman's breasts," she finally forces the words out. "The prettier she is, the more uncomfortable I feel." Alexandros has sat up. He caresses her hair, looks into her eyes. "This is called jealousy," he says, and Ethel is already sorry that she spoke. "It's okay to feel jealous, little sister," Alexandros smiles. "I am jealous about you all the time. It is painful, but a sweet kind of pain. I am rather enjoying it. When other men are looking at you in lust, that's the best kind, because I am proud that I am your choice for the night. The most painful kind is when I believe that you are attracted to another man." Ethel wants to tell him that no other man has attracted her, not for a long time. But she cannot. "This is a kind of pain I want to feel all the time," Alexandros continues. "When you stop loving someone, the pain of jealousy goes first."

"What if I asked you not to stare at other women?" Ethel feels a strange need to continue her probe.

Alexandros looks at her, thoughtfully, almost solemnly. "I would stop looking at other women's breasts. At once. You see, I am in love with you. You are the purpose of everything else in my life." Alexandros is now looking at the horizon. "But I would do it with sadness," he continues. "Because it would mean that you do not love me, not the way I am. It would mean that you are looking for another lover, even if presently you are trying versions of myself that you are crafting."

Short pause. "Besides, I doubt that you would find me attractive if, in order to conform to your wishes, I behaved in ways that do not come natural to me."

There is a long silence between them. The girls at the beach are laughing, happy. Then Alexandros speaks again, slowly. "To love is to cherish your lover as an ideal whole." Ethel is now a little irritated. "How can you cherish me as an ideal whole, Alexandros? You only met me two weeks ago, on an island." It is as though he had the reply ready, reading from a book. "There may be facets of you I do not know. But I am sure that I will love them once I see them." His palms go between the back of his head and the rock.

The bay faces northwest. As the sun sets, Ethel is trying to grasp what Alexandros is telling her, lying next to him on the smooth rock that is now getting a little cooler. They say that if you look to the west at precisely the moment of sunset, you can see the heel of Italy's boot. Ethel is looking at the horizon, squinting.

Is epiphany ever anticipated? For the first time in two weeks, Ethel feels close to this man. She feels that she can understand his personality, his life and world outlook, the way he loves her and thinks about her. For a moment she is overwhelmed by the internal consistency of it all, its harmony with the island and the beach, its elegance even—however alien and threatening all this may still seem to her. Her heart feels inflated, ready to burst.

"I love you, Alexandros," she whispers.

Even before the utterance has left her lips, her right hand darts forward, as if trying to grasp something fragile and dear before it flies away. Alexandros closes his eyes, suddenly overcome by a wave of bliss and desire. He is kissing her hand.

In Ethel's tote bag, next to her sunscreen and her headset computer, is a first-class ticket. A couple of hours ago she has reconfirmed her flight on the Net. For the next morning.

Ethel is now rolling her eyes. "I've told you a hundred times, Mom, the father is not an option."

Another bay, another sunset. Dorothy is sitting on a sofa in Ethel's living room, distinguished and beautiful in her navy-blue evening dress. Ethel, in a long green T-shirt and brown tights, is sitting on the floor facing her mother, leaning against the wall, squeezing her legs and knees with her arms. Talking to her mother has always brought her to a state of intense impatience, often anger. She has yet to learn how to control it.

"But why?" Dorothy wonders. "A Greek professor of archeology. It sounds so interesting." Her accent is faintly British. "So romantic."

"How many reasons do you want, Mom?" Ethel is used to talking fast, thinking fast, pushing her point relentlessly. "Picture this: A man about your age, incredibly immature, adolescent. His life centers around something he calls 'love,' a cross between Alexandre Dumas—son and porn flicks. He has a totally rigid ideology on the subject: Love is everything. Love is absolute. Love is volatile. The moment he stops loving me madly, he'll walk."

Dorothy is thinking. "You are lucky," she finally says. "Sounds like every woman's dream, to have an attractive man tell you on a faraway island that he is madly in love with you, that he will stay only while this lasts."

"Except that he practices his religion. He has the worst record, Mom. He has abandoned dozens of women, two with his babies. You should hear him brag about the purity of his love. He's dangerous, Mom. He will leave me when I least need it, when I am weak and overweight and bedridden and oversensitive."

Ethel is gauging the effect of her words on Dorothy. "And—are you ready for more? He's a communist, Mom, the kind your government used to turn back at the border, used to throw in jails. He hates America. He freaked out when I told him who my mother is."

"You are not a card-carrying conservative yourself," Dorothy points out. "Besides, most European intellectuals of my generation and the one before used to be communists. It was almost a cliché."

"And, on last count," Ethel comes back, "how many of them followed their beloved to raise their child in California?"

Long silence. "Was he . . ." Dorothy hesitates. Ethel hides her enjoyment at her mother's awkward moment; she is staring at her, blank, refusing to help. Big bad smile inside. "You obviously had sex," Dorothy recovers. "Did you enjoy being with him?"

"It was good, in a strange, unusual way." Ethel now speaks slowly, somewhat dreamily, having forgotten for a moment her project of irritating her mother. "He put an incredible amount of energy and thought in it. Not technique or sportsmanship—just his soul, hundred percent. And having sex with me was so very important to him that it was—well, touching. Flattering. Moving, contagious. You know?"

"How did he react to the news?" Ethel is silent. Dorothy, with urgency: "You *have* told him, haven't you?"

Ethel is trying to decide if it is her mother's phony British accent that she finds so irritating. "It's not phony," she keeps reminding herself. She was born in Cambridge, raised in London. Rusty brought her to the States when she was twenty-two. At least her accent is not phony. "But I bet that she is practicing it, she's trying hard not to lose it."

"Plenty of time for this, Mom," she says. "Of course I will tell him someday. Later." Ethel remembers Alexandros with his teenager daughter—yes, she'll tell him. Someday.

Dorothy is silent, then: "You have to understand, baby, it's not going to be easy. You will need someone to hold your hand. I am not sure how much I can be with you, you know my life." She hesitates. "And I hope that you are not relying on that half-crazy girlfriend of yours, the Spanish girl, what's her name? Laura."

Ethel, sadistically, says nothing about the current status of "Sola," leaving Dorothy in the dark. She knows the anxiety that affair had caused to her mother. "Don't worry about me, Mom. I can hire the best midwife, the best birth partner."

"Ethel, my love, how can you say that? You cried the other day on the phone, remember?" Dorothy is kneeling next to Ethel now, her hand on her daughter's belly. Hesitant, very awkward. "May I?" Ethel finds the scene ridiculous, extremely amusing, she is looking out the window at the sunset.

"Have I told you, when I was pregnant with you," Dorothy starts, whispering. "Your father . . ."

"Yes, you told me, Mom," Ethel interrupts.

"He came back when I was . . ."

"You've told me, Mom!"

Dorothy rises to her feet, finally breaks her silence. "You know what I'm thinking? In less than an hour, the leadership of your industry will be listening to me, two-kay a plate. Four miles from here. And my own daughter? She refuses to show, and now she won't even let me read from the family book."

"I don't have two thousand dollars for your party, Mom," Ethel stings. "As for the 'leadership of my industry,' you know why they are coming, don't you? It's like feeding an old, dying pet. They probably write it off as charity now, not as a political contribution."

Dorothy is silent. "'My industry' is burping, having swallowed your government, Mom," Ethel continues, pitiless. "For example, your all-important Department of Commerce now has how many, a few dozen permanent employees? Most of them telecommuting? Do you still have your big building in DC, Mom? Does DC still exist?"

"We are the most efficient government this country has ever known," Dorothy strikes back, knowing she will lose this one. "Tax receipts are at an all-time low, huge budget surplus, a record low in new legislation."

"You are confusing 'efficient' with 'useless,' Mom. The Net is running the country; it manages it, it enables and facilitates its business and commerce. Your cabinet, your congress, they are all irrelevant, Mom. You are a curiosity from the past, America's palace guards." Ethel is almost bored with the easy points. "Even your army is irrelevant, as long as our runners are smarter than their runners."

Dorothy does not reply; she is looking out the window. Ethel suddenly feels sorry for her mother. She now wants to say something positive. "Did I see your picture on magazine covers recently? You are the country's most popular politician, is this true?"

Dorothy smiles, bittersweet. "I am doing very well among the twenty percent of the electorate who can name *any* member of the cabinet. Or Congress," she says. "I would have a good shot at the presidency next time, if it were not for that little detail in the Constitution."

"You are very well-known in Greece, let me tell you." They are silent for a few moments. Dorothy looks at her watch, the man from the Secret Service has opened a door, a limousine now parked in the driveway.

"So you have a new fiancé?" Ethel asks suddenly.

"You are not going to embarrass me with your choice of words," Dorothy replies. "It is going to work this time, Ethel, I know. Jack is a law professor. Georgetown. A very sweet man. A couple of years younger than me. I want the two of you to meet some time."

"Amazing," Ethel comments. "There are still kids who study to become lawyers."

"I suppose you like to see young people hibernate through their best years in their helmets and goggles," Dorothy attacks. "All of them hoping to come up with the killer idea, to write the ultimate code, to become the new Bill Gates, the new Ethel Young. Or the new Ian

Frost. Bums, that's how they end up. Fed by the budget surplus. Or runners, criminals." Dorothy waits in vain for Ethel's reply. "Actually, Jack is teaching patent law, Net law," she adds softly. Then, defensively again: "And spare me the sermon on the oxymoronic nature of 'Net law.' Please."

Another silence. "They die on you, Mom," Ethel says slowly. "I mean, your men. Maybe this is better. They don't leave you."

"You haven't found the right one yet, darling." Dorothy is holding her daughter's hand. "Or perhaps you have found him but misread him," she continues. "Do me this favor, think again about your Greek archeologist." She stands up. Pause. "And take good care of yourself, my love. I wish . . . ," her voice breaks, ". . . I could stay longer."

"It was good to see you, Mom," Ethel lies. "Be brilliant tonight. As always." She knows that she can hold back her tears until Dorothy walks out the door.

•

"I need to be with somebody," Ethel now admits to herself. Mother knows best. Some body. She closes her eyes, who comes to mind? *Sola.* Not the girl she had called "Sola" for months, Laura-the-Spaniard, the little slut who stole and wrecked her car. But the original Sola, her fantasy lover at the Colony. Beautiful and exotic and brilliant and mysterious Sola—Sola who runs the most ingenious interface software Ethel has ever seen. Ethel walks to her playroom, slowly slips into her bodysuit, her helmet and goggles. Gloves, crotchpad. She connects the controls, slowly, she whispers a few commands, types something. "Maybe, more than anything else, I need to be *him* again," she thinks. The thought is already relaxing, invigorating. No more self-pity, no more tears. She takes a deep breath, closes her eyes. She is in control now—and Rusty rides again.

On a seaplane, an old French model, a Latécoère job from the 1930s. Headed to the Colony, the world's most exclusive destination, about to appear on the horizon. ("What form will it take?" he wonders.) Rusty is in his late forties, tall and athletic and just a little overweight, blond, blue eyes, beard. Leather jacket over a black shirt, white scarf, loose white pants, and sneakers. Comfortable and steady in the Latécoère's pilot seat, Rusty exudes a calm self-confidence. He is in control.

Rusty can now see the Colony, a few miles to the east. An island, striking sight, its slopes rising steeply from the sea, covered with deep-green vegetation. There is a bay on the northern side of the island, and the Latécoère heads that way. Rusty admires the sophisticated, harmonious reaction of the Colony's interface to his crazy choice of transportation mode. How on earth did he come up with a *seaplane?* Then, in a flash, the choice makes sense, in retrospect. A seaplane. Of course. A little girl's secret wish.

Because Rusty is Ethel's alter ego, a persona she crafted after her father, Rusty the genius, Rusty the stud. Rusty the pilot who crashed his airplane twenty-five years ago in the Gulf of Mexico. Ran out of fuel— why couldn't he be riding a seaplane that night? Rusty the avatar, Rusty the Net ghost. Ethel has lived, slept, waken up, fallen in love as Rusty. And now she is riding again as Rusty, back to the Colony, back to Sola—after all these months.

The seaplane is gliding in the serene waters. The bay is green, the air is hot and humid. There are two shadows on the platform, a man and a woman. Rusty smiles. He jumps ashore.

"Welcome back to the Colony, most eagerly expected of all our guests," the young woman greets Rusty. She is like a doll—Chinese or Japanese? An old man— her father, Rusty guesses—is watching with a silent smile. "A little more of a cliché than in the old days," Rusty thinks. Chinese.

"Is Sola in?" Rusty asks. Father and daughter exchange a glance, they smile, they point to the pagoda-shaped gate by the platform. "She will be expecting you, Rusty," the woman speaks again, the old man looking on.

"The bots are a little awkward tonight," Rusty thinks. He walks past the gate, toward the small fishing village beyond it. A dozen or so men and women in straw hats are busy with their nets and boats; some of them greet him silently, with their eyes. Rusty knows that he can approach any one of them, can strike up any conversation, inquire about boats, fishing technique, religion, village life. Just as he knows he can kneel on the road, pick up a ball of dirt, stand up, pat away the dust from his trousers' knees, break the dirt ball in his palm, watch dust and irregular pieces flow through his fingers. The fantasy is deep, wide, complete, the interface with his software incredibly seamless. "Who runs the

60   Christos H. Papadimitriou

Colony?" Rusty wonders. Sola? (She is no ordinary guest, this is obvious.) And who then is running Sola? He has been puzzling about it for years, having tried discreetly a couple of times to find out, only to end up choking in smoke.

Rusty waves to the people on the shore, a broad gesture whose masculinity was perhaps a little exaggerated. "I must remember to fix that," he thinks. He crosses a bridge, heading toward the edge of the village. He can see a small villa over there. A beautiful building that stands out among the modest houses. Sola must be there.

The dirt road continues beyond the villa, ending at a grove of orchard trees, elegantly groomed, about a hundred yards further. Rusty can see in the distance the silhouettes of a dozen or so people, some sitting on red benches, some walking about in the grove, talking. Men, westerners, it appears. Rusty has now stopped in front of the villa, hesitating. Sola's likely proximity pumps adrenaline into him—"Rusty loves Sola." But there is something about the shadows in the grove that attracts him. Who are they? He cannot make out their faces, but he is possessed by a strange certainty that something momentous is happening over there. He must meet these people.

But instead Rusty turns to the villa, walks past the red columns of its gate, through its small garden. His heart is now pounding. There is a shadow on the window. A woman's voice is singing. A sad love song, all desire, despair, hallucination:

> And I'll come running to tie your shoes,
> I'll come running to tie your shoes.

It is the silhouette of Sola, tall and almost impossibly slim. It is Sola's voice. Rusty is walking a little faster now. Still, total control. Through the door, to the left.

Sola interrupts her song, smiling at the tall man standing at the door. "Ah, the prodigal lover." Her voice is melodic, low in pitch, with a sexy accent. French. She is walking slowly toward Rusty, wearing a dress of heavy Bordeaux silk, strapless and long. A timeless garment that would place her in the court of many emperors, get her past the door of any club in San Francisco. Her black hair is loose on her shoulders.

"She is more beautiful than ever," Rusty thinks, bedazzled. What a blasphemy, to call with her name that confused neurotic chick from Stanford. On the basis of what, a superficial similarity? Suddenly, a suspicion takes hold of Rusty: Hasn't the image of Sola undergone changes, changes that exaggerate her differences from Laura? Aren't her eyes a little less green and more blue? Isn't she a tad taller, a little thinner, aren't her breasts just a bit more full? What a thought, Rusty decides. The games love plays on you. "It's easy to forget just how beautiful you are, princess," he says, still in control. The room is huge and red, with rugs on the floor and on the walls, a divan is almost hidden in a corner.

"It has been so long, Rusty," Sola says, standing behind him, "I have been waiting for you every day, every night, until my eyes became dry. Why didn't you come so many nights, my love? Two-hundred-and-fifty-seven."

"She is going to touch me," Rusty thinks, and the prospect is derailing his thoughts. Sola is now taking the leather jacket off his shoulders with the slightest motion of her fingertips, without touching him. "I had a rough time, princess." Rusty has told only truths to Sola. "I was down and low. Unworthy of you, not ready for you." His voice is hoarse. "And then I was afraid that I had lost you, that you had stopped loving me."

"I will never stop loving you, Rusty," Sola says, pronouncing every word, "not as long as I live. Not even if you leave me again, not even if I know that you will never come back." She is leaning her body on his back, her cheek is on his neck, each hand under an arm, each palm resting on a shoulder. Rusty closes his eyes.

Rusty wants to tell her that he will never leave her again—and that's the deepest truth that he has ever known—but he cannot utter a word. Sola's hands are roaming over his body, slow and velvety. It is as if dozens of limbs of tender lovers are touching him, in the most subtly erotic way, guessing his deepest fantasies. The divan in the corner looms huge, it dominating the room. Sola's lips are touching his neck, and Rusty has closed his eyes.

"Oh my god, it's happening to me again," he thinks, his knees are weak, his hands loose but deliberate. Under the slow, loving tutoring of Sola's hands, Rusty's fantasies come out, multiply, flood his consciousness. The room is now rotating around the divan, and Sola is inviting him to jump, to plunge with her into the whirling vortex of images and sensations. Gliding through the dark forest of tall trees, rolling on cool thick sheets in secret bed-and-breakfasts, curling like a fetus in impossibly small spaces, swimming into a sea grotto toward a marble David, its torso splashed with turquoise reflections. Plunging through the vortex next to Sola, under and over and inside and around Sola, "the lover who will never leave me." The fascinating woman with the divine eyes and the silky skin, the software genius who has written the most seamlessly erotic interface code that has ever run on silicon. Just for them. "Oh my god, Sola! Ohmygod, ohmygod." Ethel is plunging, spinning, dancing, gyrating, falling, accelerating, out of control.

Alexandros is daydreaming. He is thinking of a port, somewhere in the Mediterranean. But where, exactly? A dazzling aerial view of the Aegean Sea comes to his mind. Blue sky, bright arid islands, their rocks a color between gray and purple. The sea, turquoise at the bays, elsewhere a shade of blue so subtle that only a blind poet has been able to do it justice. And, oh, the intricate lace of the shores! A woman he once knew, a mathematician, had told Alexandros that the Aegean shoreline is so hauntingly beautiful because its fractal dimension happens to be equal to the golden ratio. "Fractal dimension." "Golden ratio." It sounded magical to him. More than interesting, more than correct.

These are the islands and the shores where, four millennia ago, the Early Ones lived. Alexandros can almost see their slim, short brown figures. Four boys and a woman. That's how Alexandros thinks of the Early Ones; this is their only voice. *Vox Praehellenica.* Three frescos and a statuette. Four boys and a woman. Two boys in a ritualistic boxing competition, a boy performing a daring somersault on the horns of a bull. An adolescent boy coming back from fishing—lazy step, good catch. Their lips frozen forever in a smile reflecting the beauty of their shores, the little pleasures in their simple short lives. The woman is holding snakes in her hands. Alexandros likes to daydream about the Serpent Goddess, the perfect helices of her long pitch-black curls, the unsubtle eroticism of her large almond-shaped eyes, of her stunning bare breasts.

But there is now a flash of terror in the eyes of the Serpent Goddess. There is another serpent snaking its way down a hill amid a dust cloud, huge and dark and ominous. It is the column of an invading Aryan tribe, warriors on horseback with their weapons clanging, slaves walking by the oxcarts. The tribe's ranking warrior, the *anax,* has stayed behind at the hilltop, surveying the landscape: the four hills, the twin rivers, the wide green valley, two giant rocks in its middle. The two turquoise bays, the blue-gray silhouettes of the islands in the horizon. The distant shadows of the Early Ones gathering, in panic, their flocks of goats and sheep inside the confines of their humble, unfortified settlement. The wild vines and olive trees, the native grain. The thyme, the oregano, the chamomile, the poppies, the orchids. A smile softens for a few moments the rough, battle-scarred face of the anax. "This looks good," he thinks.

Yeah. This could be the beginning of something real good.

They were first called Danai, then Acheans. They would eventually call themselves Hellenes, and their peninsula with its islands Hellas, after the northern province where some of them first settled.

The Hittites called them Yona, because they first met them in Ionia, the coast of Asia Minor they had colonized. They were Ya'vani in Hebrew and Punic; Yunan in Arabic and Sanskrit, and later in Hindi and Turkish; Yunani in Urdu and Farsi. As if this land and this people were not an objective reality, but a complex mirage that changes with the observer and the point of view. The Romans called them Graeci, after the small tribe in Western Acarnania with whom they traded first. Grecs, Greeks, Grecchi, Griechen, Griegos, Grieki, Girisha. Only in faraway China did they call them their own name, corrupted by the distance: Hei-lap. Shi-la in Mandarin.

Each tribe founded its own city-state, always located near a port. Alexandros can now see the merchant ships leaving these ports for the risky journey to distant lands, wonders, riches. They first sailed to the coast of Asia Minor, then to Sicily and Southern Italy, the Black Sea. To the coast of France, to Spain, beyond. They set up trading posts and settlements, they sometimes founded great cities, often grander than their home-towns. Miletus, Syracusa, Byzantium. The seafarers would come back with fruits and birds and fabrics and spices nobody had imagined before. And with all those stories about fascinating places, strange people and customs, horrible monsters. And about the rival merchants they found everywhere they went, the clever, enterprising Phoenicians.

Ah, the stories! They would go from fireplace to fireplace, from city to city, they would become myths, songs, poems, plays. The Iliad and the Odyssey, the story of the golden fleece, the feats of Hercules. Medea, the Scythian princess who commits her unspeakable crime when the handsome man she followed to Greece abandons her for another woman. Another barbarian princess, this time of the Celtic tribe by the river's mouth, is about to choose her husband from among her father's bravest warriors when the Greek ship sails ashore, unannounced: The princess wants none else but the ship's young captain. They called the city that they built Massalia, today's Marseilles. They planted vines and olive trees on the banks of the river. They called the river Rhodanos, now Rhône, because it looked to them as beautiful as the island of Rhodos across their hometown Phocaea, the city of the seal—itself a colony of Phocis, land of the oracle. Pytheas, Massalia's most famous seafarer, would later sail past the columns of Hercules to the Atlantic, would found an ill-fated settlement in Ireland. Then he continued north to the icy land he called Thule, some say it was Iceland, some say Greenland.

Voices are now heard from the shores. First the voice of the Phoenicians, systematic, practical, to the point. "Sailed north for three days, past three capes and two islands. Exchanged five amphoras of grain with thirty-five foxskins. Young Sha'al died of fever onshore." *Vox Poenorum.*

What was the year and the moon, what was the distant shore, two rival ships dancing anchored in the bay, Greeks and Phoenicians warming their hands in the same bonfire? Who is the learned old man from Tyre, scribbling on the sand the symbols that are voice? The oxhead that is called *aleph,* the house of *beth,* the camel's neck that is *gimel,* so many more, Greek sailors watching, mesmerized. They would bring the symbols back home, they would insert the vowels their tongues long for, the *epsilon* and *omicron* that are short and sharp like thunder, *eta* and *omega* long and leisurely like summer days. Another vowel, *alpha*—sometimes short, sometimes long—is a version of *aleph,* misunderstood, mispronounced, upside down. *Vox Graeca. Vox Domini. Vox mundi.*

Centuries later, another shore, near the Greek colony of Cuma. The Cumans write their letters in the clumsy manner of their brethren back in their mother city of Chalkis, by the strait. Extra lines everywhere. Their *pi* looks more like P than Π, their *rho* is closer to R than to P. And they rotate their lambda to look like L, as opposed to Λ. Back home in Greece, the Athenians—the wretched snobs that they are—laugh at epigraphs from Chalkis. But here in Italy the Cumans are not embarrassed in the least. At the seaside market, they proudly show off their provincial script to the local Etruscans, even to the restless, bellicose people who have fortified the seven hills of nearby Latium. *Vox Etruriae, vox Romana. Vox mundi.*

(There is more: A sesquimillennium later, yet another shore. A tent by the river Istros, as the Greeks still call the Danube. A Greek scholar named Constantinos borrows nine letters from the Latin alphabet, nine from the Greek, and nine from the Hebrew—so close to the Phoenician script that was the root of all three—to transcribe the Lord's mass in the language of his childhood playmates, from back in the great city of Thessalonike. He later becomes a monk under the name Cyril. *Vox Sclavonica, vox Russiae.*)

More voices are now coming from the shores. They tell the story of the Aegean sea black with the Persian king's ships, next you hear the cries of "victory!" from the Greek warships, the trieremes—three rows of oars worked by free men, by men who would be free. The ingenious symphony of the Golden Age of Athens, the epos of its towering strength and prestige. The voice of the Spartans is heard only indirectly, they speak through their devastating military prowess that is the sole purpose of their civic life, leaving no space for letters, for arts, for explicit voice. *Vox Laconica.* Alexandros hears the story, told with unprecedented clarity and elegance, of the conflict between these two great cities, the war that destroyed them both. Then the brief hegemony of Thebes before the triumph of the Macedonians, **p. 275** the tribe that everybody had long ignored as half-barbarian. Alexandros follows the boy-king with the **p. 277** same name in his brilliant campaign through Asia Minor and Palestine and Egypt to Mesopotamia and Persia, further to Bactria, to India, battle after battle, triumph after triumph, until his soldiers would march no further. Then to his sudden death—he died of a broken heart, some voices say, having just lost his boyhood friend, the brave and fair Hephaestion. Generals divide the world that the boy-king had conquered, the empirettes are unable to unite against the new challenge from the west. The elephants of Hannibal have crossed the Alps without crushing the city on the seven hills. The Romans, brave soldiers and clever state-builders, patiently challenge the Phoenecians of Carthage, the Greeks of Sicily. Wise Marcellus is about to march against Syracusa, defended only by the genius of her son Archimedes. It is the last quarter of the third century B.C.

Alexandros is now ready to dream about his mysterious port, somewhere in the Mediterranean. He has seen it many times in his dreams, always in the morning mist. Stone-paved streets, modest buildings, men hurrying around, oxcarts and chariots, a dock in the style you can still find on some Greek islands. There is a small temple near the dock. (Is it a temple of Poseidon, the Greek god of the sea and seafarers, or of one of the Mediterranean variants that, by that time, had started to fascinate the Greeks? Alexandros is not sure.) A ship is rocking impatiently, tied to the dock. It is a small ship, no longer than fifteen meters. Alexandros knows the ship well, inch by inch, he probably knows it better than any of the five or six unfortunate men who are about to sail on it. The ship is being loaded with amphoras of olive oil and wine. Two men—one of them a tall African with huge brass earrings, the other wearing a pointed hat—are carrying a heavy amphora of wine. Alexandros guesses that they are freed slaves, one from Nubia and the other from Scythia, itinerant hands for hire to load ships and work the sails. They are now resting for a moment, having placed the amphora down on the dock's pavement. Two other sailors pass them by, each carrying to the ship a leather sack with his personal belongings. They are coming from a nearby slum, a dozen small houses facing the same yard, they have just kissed their families goodbye for the last time. One of them is limping.

Three hungry slave boys scavenge rotten fruit left on the dock by another ship. Next to the temple, and not far from the ship, Alexandros can see two men dressed in comfortable woolen clothes, their slaves standing nearby. Wealthy men. The older one is holding carefully a wooden box, about half a meter long and almost as wide, obviously very heavy, with protruding metal levers. He is about to give it to the other man, the owner and captain of the ship. Will money change hands? And in which direction? Alexandros does not know. But he has been suspecting all along that the box is not the ship's navigational device, that it is its most precious cargo, possibly the object of its true mission.

Alexandros can hear the murmur of the winter sea, the distant sounds of the city waking up, the cries of the seagulls as they dive for harbor fish. He can hear the morning call of a cock tied on the ship's single mast by a leather string, soon to be sacrificed at the temple.

But there is something missing, an unnatural, disturbing absence that makes the scene grotesque, eerie, nightmarish: No human voices are heard. *These people have no voice.* Alexandros has spent years studying the languages they may be speaking: The ancient Greek dialect once spoken in Athens that was now fast becoming the lingua franca of the basin. Latin, Hebrew, Western Punic, Lower Scythian, Coptic. Still, he cannot hear a word.

"They have no voice," Alexandros thinks in frustration. There is no record of their existence.

More than twenty-five million people lived in the Mediterranean during the third century B.C. Only a few hundred of them left a written document behind, most in Greek, some in Latin, Punic, and Hebrew, very few in other languages. Only a few thousand names are mentioned in all these documents put together, or in subsequent documents about the period. "The others have no voice," Alexandros thinks. His life's work is about delivering them from this terrible fate, so much crueler than death, to the tiny extent that he can. It is frustratingly difficult and slow.

The two sailors are now about to pick up their amphora again for the short haul to the ship. They look at Alexandros, a quick glance of silent agony. They have no voice. Meanwhile, the captain has brought the box onboard to his ship and he is preparing for sacrifice and departure. *Sine vocis.* Not a word from him. The man who gave him the box has started his trip back in a comfortable single-horse carriage, his slave walking by the horse, holding the harness. A couple of times the old man stretches back to look at the ship, now ready to sail off. He is deep in thought. Deep in silence.

"I shall hear your voices," Alexandros whispers. "The whole world will."

Alexandros slowly opens his eyes. He looks around him at the spartan interior of his office. There is a computer on his desk. From time to time Alexandros uses it to type his notes and his research papers. He updates his weekly calendar, occasionally his curriculum vitae. He sends email to his colleagues and his daughters, he keeps up with friends abroad, he plays endless games of chess with some of them. During the late 1990s he type-set his latest book on it, a monograph on Greek irrigation technology in the third century B.C. Earlier this morning he downloaded a dissertation from the University of Tübingen that he must read. He often spends hours looking up interesting documents on the Net, the home pages of people he doesn't know, the writings of people he will never meet. "Today everybody has a voice," Alexandros thinks. Future archeologists will dream dreams of confusing polyphony, not of eerie silence; they will struggle with excessive information, instead of scrabbling for tiny bits of it. "They will probably have to be Net wizards, like Ethel," he smiles. The image of Ethel flashes in front of his eyes, and his blood flows faster for a few seconds. He is madly in love with her.

In recent weeks, Alexandros has been trying in vain to get in touch with Turing, the incredibly articulate and somewhat eccentric computer program that seemed to have taken a liking to him. He has reread several times the transcript of that delightfully revisionist lesson on the history of ideas, with its unusual emphasis on computation and mathematics ("maths"). He has even skimmed the notes, has looked up some of the relevant Net documents recommended in the transcript. He is curious to find out about the promised *gran finale,* the account of how the advent of computation destroyed Hilbert's ambitious project.

As fascinating as Alexandros had found that lesson, he can see very little connection between its topic and his multifaceted predicament—abandoned by Ethel, his work at a dead end, a near void where his political credo once was. Had not Turing made an implicit promise of solutions? Alexandros has decided to try to nudge the program in more promising directions next time.

Alexandros has also been thinking about Turing in other ways. He is very impressed with the program's eloquence and knowledge, its surprising versatility, its ability to interact with him so smoothly. But he is at the same time uncomfortable that Turing—Turing's proprietor, whoever this may be—appears to have extensive information about his person, unlimited access to his computer's memory, to his private files. Many of his old comrades disagree with his faith in the liberating potential of the Net, fearing that it is ushering in a new kind of fascism, the tyranny of the technologically apt.

Slowly, Alexandros once again keys in the query "Turing." This time he is in luck. He watches as the maddeningly familiar face appears on the screen, he answers the cheerful greeting. "I must ask," he decides.

"Is the image that I see on my screen that of Turing, the scientist?" he types. "I am asking because I am sure that I have seen this man before." He is still unable to get used to the idea that he can interact so effortlessly with a computer program.

| He was a rather famous man, actually, the program replies. There are many books written on his work and life, some with this portrait on the cover. You have probably come across one of them in a bookstore recently.

Alexandros is struggling to remember, unconvinced by the offered explanation. This memory appears to be coming from very—very far away.

| Would you like me to tell you about Turing's life and work? the screen insists.

"Later, perhaps," Alexandros types. "Right now I want to learn about computers, about the Net. How they work. Is this possible? I mean, without going back to school? Can you teach me?"

The faint smile of the portrait suddenly seems to him ironic, condescending. "I have to grow up," Alexandros thinks. "Even computer programs make me feel insecure now."

| Of course I can teach you about computers, Alexandros. If I couldn't, I would not be worthy of the silly pun with "tutoring" my name is supposed to evoke.

To start off, have you ever thought what happens precisely when you click your mouse, or when you type a letter on your keyboard?

"No." Alexandros has never typed two characters more hesitantly, more consciously.

| Well, if you press the *a* key of your keyboard an *a* appears on your screen. Seems instantaneous, right? Truth is, a thousand little things happen in between. Count them: First, your pressing of the key causes an electric current to flow in a little wire in your keyboard. There is a small processor inside your keyboard—an auxiliary computer!—that does nothing else but poll these wires, one after the other, thousands of times every second, watching out for pressed keys. Once it senses the current in the little wire that comes from the *a* key, it does two things: First, from the identity of the wire that carries the current, it deduces the identity of

the key that you pressed—*a* is stored in a safe place, so it can be retrieved later. Second, it taps the shoulder of the central processor of your computer. You see, the central processor is the most respected member of this gang—the boss—his time is valuable, he's busy all the time. But when something unusual happens—like you pressing the *a* key—he needs to know, so his shoulder is tapped. This is called an *interrupt.*

Now, you may argue that pressing a key is not such an extraordinary event; you do it a few times every second when you type. But from the point of view of the boss, it's quite an exciting break from his routine because, you see, he does hundreds of millions of little things—literally, hundreds of millions—between your keystrokes.

So, when the central processor realizes that his shoulder has been tapped, he abandons what he was doing that moment to take care of the interrupt—but of course he first stores his work carefully in a special place so that he can resume it when he is done with this unexpected chore. From the nature of this particular interrupt (you see, the tapping of his shoulder was not just tapping; it contained some useful information), the boss realizes that a key was pressed, and then he takes the appropriate action: He executes a programme (a tiny part of your computer's operating system) whose sole purpose is to react to keystrokes.

This is an important transition in our story; we have just entered the realm of software. For the next millionth of a second or so, your computer does what it does best—what it does all the time, barring freak events like interrupts—it executes on the central processor a programme, an algorithm, a sequence of instructions. This particular programme is quite small, a few dozen instructions or so, and it does the right thing: It goes to that special place where the auxiliary processor has stored the identity of the key that you pressed and delivers it to your monitor—the televisionlike device in front of you. Oh, it has to do a few more things, like check to see whether the *shift* key has been pressed, by looking at another spot in that special place, and if so it upgrades the character's identity to an *A*—but never mind. Now your monitor realizes that an *a* was pressed, and so it diverts its beam of fast-travelling electrons in such a way that certain fluorescent particles on your screen's surface light up to form an *a*. Meanwhile, the little programme, its mission accomplished, terminates, signs off, and finally the central processor, realizing that he's idle, retrieves the unfinished business that he had set aside in that special place—that special place is called *the stack*, because you always remove what is on top—and resumes its execution. Less than a thousandth of a second has gone by since you pressed the key, so you are justified to think all this happened instantaneously. Amazing, isn't it?

"It *is* very complicated," Alexandros comments, "but at least it makes sense."

| Of course it makes sense. You know why? I explained an event—pressing the *a* key—in terms of a sequence of events *at the immediately lower level*. Because this is the genius of the computer: It is by far the most complex of artifacts, but it is designed and built in such a clever way—layer by layer—that you almost get the illusion of simplicity. But now you can take each of the little events we discussed—say, the execution of an instruction on the central processor—and realise that it consists of a thousand little steps, and those steps can be analysed further, and so on.

But I want to take you now through the layers of this fascinating machine, bottom up. To start off, what do you think is the lowest layer?

"Electrons?" Alexandros is guessing.

| Right. Physicists of course would tell you that there are endless layers below electrons. *Quantum physics* the theory is called, you must know about it. Every electron exists in many states at the same time, in many alternative universes, and by the very act of looking at it—say, measuring its speed and spin—you pick one of these universes, you freeze it to reality. Beautiful theory, fasinating and powerful. In fact, it was one of the favourite subjects of my namesake, Alan M. Turing, the mathematician. But it has little to do with the way computers are built today. Incidentally, people have been trying over the past twenty years to change this; they're striving to build much more powerful computers than we have today by exploiting quantum physics. Brilliant stuff—except, when great theories mix with computation often unexpected, uncomfortable, humbling truths emerge. Mathematicians lost their grandest dream in the process—ask Hilbert—let us see how the physicists will fare.

So. Electrons. Our basic layer. We use electrons to build the most important abstraction in computing, *the bit.* Do you know what a bit is, Alexandros?

"Zero or one, right?"

| Sort of. Anything that has two distinct states, and so it can represent a unit of information. You see, your computer is a dense forest of wires, and each wire in it can have either too many electrons, or too few. If it has too few, then we think of the wire as being in the state that we call *one;* if it has too many, we think of it as *zero.* And from now on we must make sure that no wire has elec-

tron deficiency that is somewhere in between. (You see, this layer business does not come for free; building a layer often entails promises—engineering commitments, constraints—that will make our life a little harder further up. But such is life.)

The bit is trivial to define; the hard part is realising that it is useful. And, God Almighty, is it useful! Using bits, we can encode in the computer's memory anything we want. We can certainly represent numbers. *Binary notation* this arithmetical system is called; it is not much different from the decimal system everybody uses in real life—except you must pretend you only have two fingers. The number 5 is represented 101 in binary, 38 is 100110. But using bits, we also represent all sorts of other things; the names and numbers the computer must remember, the precise places in the computer's memory where this information is stored, the kinds of instructions whereby the computer acts on it, anything.

So bits are quintessential, fantastically useful—except that bits just sit there; you can't build a dynamic, busy computer from static bits, you need a way to blow life into your bits. Enter the *switch*. Our next layer. The lamp on your desk, Alexandros, has a switch that turns it on, does it not? Or off. Well, each of the thousands of millions of little wires in your computer has a similar switch that changes its status from zero to one and back. Except that this switch is not manipulated by hand, like your lamp's; instead it is controlled by another wire nearby. (And that wire is of course controlled by yet another wire, and so on, a cascade, a network of intricate dependencies throughout the chip.)

Here is how this controlling trick is done: If the controlling wire has too many electrons, then these electrons saturate a tiny silicon area that separates two wires, and this makes silicon into a temporary conductor, a metal-like material (this is called *semiconductivity,* the property of silicon that makes it so useful in this business), and presto, the second wire becomes one. You take away the electrons, it's back to zero. That's how the electronic switch works.

Well, in the very old days we used mechanical relays as switches, they were awfully slow. Then came vacuum tubes, they were all the rage for a while. And finally, in the 1950s, the *transistor* arrived, a switch made out of silicon, and this put us on this path for real. Because, you see, unlike relays and tubes, transistors are gregarious; you can put lots and lots of them together on the same substrate—the chip—connected by wires that are themselves etched on the same silicon surface.

Onward with our layers. Once we have switches, we can combine two or three of them to make a *gate.* In a gate a wire is controlled not by a single nearby wire, but by two or three. Imagine that you want to do something more sophisticated with your table lamp, Alexandros. Suppose its light bothers you when you are watching television. Suppose that you want your lamp to be on provided that (a) you have switched it on *and* (b) your telly is off. This would be a *gate,* a wire controlled by two other wires, two switches: The lamp's switch, and the television's. So, the switches on the chip are arranged in intricate ways to form such gates.

And above the layer of gates we have the layer of *circuits:* The wire that exits, so to speak, one gate may enter another one, the one exiting that one feeds into the next, and so on, this way you can build a whole tower of gates, a long chain of logical consequences. You pump a few electrons in carefully chosen places on one end, so that you represent by the bits two numbers in binary, say, and voilà, their sum comes out on the other side of the circuit. That would be an *adder circuit,* all computers must have one, it takes a few hundred switches and gates to make it.

Or, a circuit may loop back and feed into itself—bite its own tail, so to speak. Such circuits don't compute anything novel, but they are useful for another reason, they *remember* the values—zero or one—of faraway wires, long after those values have changed. They are the *memory* of your computer's brain. Another indispensible layer.

And this brings us to our next and most important layer, the central processor—the boss. The ultimate circuit, a chip replete with wires and switches and gates and memories, all interconnected in a clever way so as to execute instructions, chores like "add these two numbers and put their sum over there." And, if you think about it, to carry out such an instruction you must do four things:

You must first *fetch* the instruction, bring it in from wherever it is and store it somewhere handy.

Then you must *decode* it, look at its bits and pieces and figure out what it's telling you to do—and to whom.

Then you must *execute* it, walk the specified inputs through the gates of the right circuit (the adder if this is an add instruction) until the result emerges.

Finally, you must *store* the result of the instruction, so you can remember it when executing a subsequent instruction.

And these are the four phases of an instruction: Fetch, decode, compute, store. Computers have evolved tremendously over the past sixty years, but these four phases have stayed pretty much the same. The processor—the computer's brain and heart in one—executes instruction after instruction of programmes, going through the four phases for each, following the beat of its own drum.

But there is one little trick the boss does with these four phases that is worth explaining. From what I've told you, you would think that he carries out the four phases of one instruction (fetch-decode-execute-store), and then starts working on the next instruction (fetch-decode-etc.). Well, the boss is a little smarter than that. Once an instruction is fetched, one part of the processor proceeds with decoding it, while another part fetches the next instruction.

When you visit your doctor, Alexandros, first a nurse takes your blood pressure and temperature, then your doctor examines you (while the nurse is with the next patient), and finally a lab technician may draw your blood for a test (while the next patient has now advanced to the doctor's office, and the one after her is with the nurse). So, three patients are being waited on at the same moment, one by each of the three health care professionals, and so everybody is busy and efficient. This is called *parallelism*—doing many things at the same time, keeping everybody as busy as possible—the same principle on which assembly lines are based.

In very much the same way, the boss uses parallelism to advantage; its various components work on four instructions at every moment—one is stored, the one after that executed, the next one is decoded, the next one is fetched. This way, all parts of the processor are utilised, and instructions are executed four times faster.

Actually, not quite four times, a little less. Because, you see, there is a catch: Occasionally, the *fetch* phase of one instruction may use the same part of the central processor, the same gate, as the *decode* phase of another instruction. Or, the *execute* phase of the next instruction needs data that are being computed—and not yet stored—by the present one. If this is the case (and it is tricky to detect whether it is), the processor refrains from overlapping these two phases, and cheerfully misses a beat—otherwise an error would occur, and we don't want that, do we?

This is ubiquitous in computers, by the way, this tension between the desirability of parallelism—doing many things at the same time, keeping many parts of the computer busy—and the threat to the computation's integrity that is usually inherent in parallelism. You see it when you make a theatre reservation on the Net, Alexandros. You are happy that you don't have to wait in line, like in the old days, that the theatre company's computer can handle all these requests for seats in parallel. But you don't want the computer to overdo it with parallelism, to sell the same seat to you *and* somebody else, right?

So, Alexandros, this was not bad at all. You realise what we have done? Patiently, layer by layer, from electrons to bits and switches, from there to gates, then to memory and circuits, and from these to the central processor, we have built our computer. It's ready to go, Alexandros, eager to execute instructions. What do we do next?

"What?" Alexandros is trying to guess where this is going.

| Why, we *boot it*, of course, what else? Bring in the software.

Rusty is lying in bed with his lover, happy. For the past—what, three weeks?—he has flown back to the fishing village in his Latécoère many times, unable to keep away from the Colony and Sola for more than a few hours at a time. Sola is now asleep. Rusty can see her profile, her bare back. He smiles with affection.

All this time, Rusty has not forgotten about the mysterious shadows at the grove. But whenever he tried, possessed by the same powerful curiosity, to move in that direction, the grove and its guests receded, like a mirage. When he asked Sola about them she replied, with an enigmatic smile, that he would soon meet the shadows.

Suddenly Rusty is frowning, alarmed. The room has become darker, and he can see smoke outside the window. Rusty gets off the divan, opens the window, the door. The small villa is completely surrounded by smoke, in all directions. The thickest, most impenetrable smoke he has ever seen—and he has seen some. U.S. government issue smoke, must be. No, thicker and blacker than even that. A thousand forests burning, millions of tractor tires in them. "Why so much smoke?" he wonders. (And *how* so much smoke?) He turns to Sola. She has sat up, a smile in her face. Beautiful smile, ominously determined. "We have to talk, my love," she says, quietly.

"Uh-oh!" Fun's over. Trouble. Ethel takes over. Rusty is no longer her fantasy vehicle, he's strictly her mask. Deep breath. "There is smoke outside, princess," Ethel says, keeping Rusty's voice very calm. "The thick kind. The thickest I have seen from the inside." She pauses. "What's up, princess?"

"Don't be alarmed, my love, it's just that I want to tell you something, and we have to take some precautions about this conversation. You'll understand." Sola has put on a black kimono; she sits on the divan; she looks at him, beautiful, loving, dead serious. "I want an ef-two-ef with you, Rusty," she says simply. Her chin goes up, half an inch. The bomb has been dropped.

An F2F? A face-to-face, a meeting in real life? Ethel looks in disbelief, through Rusty's eyes; her stomach feels stiff. Drop the masks, the end of their fantasy, of their affair? "This is crazy, princess," she says. "If we met in real life, you wouldn't want to see me again."

"I will never stop loving you," Sola's voice is slow, patient, determined. "I know I'll love you after our F2F, because, you see," Sola pauses, Ethel can almost hear the ominous whistling sound of a second bomb speeding to its explosion, "it's not just Rusty that I have fallen in love with, it's both of you." She pauses again. "Rusty *and* Ethel."

Ethel's knees are weak. "You knew?"

"Don't be angry, my love, you'll see there was no other way. Yes, I knew. All along. I see through smoke, can't help it. I knew about you. I followed you these past months. I know about the Spanish girl you called with my name, about your trip to Greece, the archeologist who has been, poor thing, trying to cut your smoke all summer. I know about the obstetric suite you leased and installed in your house, about the tests and the results."

Ethel is furious, a habitual hunter who wakes up in somebody else's crosshairs. Another lover has deceived her, abused her, humiliated her, taken advantage of her. She exaggerates Rusty's gravelly angry voice. "Who are you, bitch? Are you a runner? Tell me, are you a fucking runner?"

Sola looks at Rusty, controlled fear in her sweet eyes, an expression of almost comical dignity. "Since you are asking me, my love, I'll be glad to tell you. I am a persona created and operated by Ian Frost."

Boom!

Ethel can't believe her ears. Ian Frost? The king of runners? FBI's darling? Sola is Ian! "Of course," Ethel thinks, breathless. "The Colony." Hasn't Ian Frost been hiding in Hong Kong?

Sola is now demorphing into a tall thin man in his early forties, with long black hair in a ponytail, large blue-green eyes. Wearing the same kimono, his skin as if of white silk. A male Sola, really, a little more angular in the face, only slightly broader shoulders. Ethel can't believe that she had never noticed the striking similarity. "My God, he's gorgeous, much more handsome than his pictures,"

Ethel thinks. She is recovering from the shock, hypnotized by the image. She has fantasized many times about Ian, the Che Guevara of the zero years. Show me a girl who hasn't. (Or boy, Ian Frost is famously bisexual.)

"Are you . . ." she starts. "Is this live?"

"Yes, this is all-camera now, my love." He pauses. "Always has been, actually, I just took the Sola filter offline."

"I'm not going to switch to my cameras, Ian. You know, five months' pregnant, no waist, all tits. It will have to be Rusty for the time being."

"You are more beautiful than ever now, my love, hasn't anybody told you?" Ethel does not reply; Rusty is as poker-faced as ever. But she feels happy again, in love, her chest inflated. There is another pause.

"Okay, this is too strange and sudden," Ethel starts. "I want to understand what did you have in mind about an ef-two-ef? You want me to come to China? You cannot travel here, I assume."

"Yes I can. I may have to. Long story. Under certain conditions, currently being negotiated. Too long a story, really. Your spooks are willing to forget (or was it just forgive?) if I stop talking to the Chinese spooks. They think I'm up to something big in China. Quantum code." Ian seems amused, eyes shining. "I let them think so, the crazy assholes, it makes them nicer. They can whisk me off to the States before my friends here know what's happening—or so they claim."

"You trust them?" Ethel is suddenly worried.

"Sometimes I think I have no choice, love. My life here is becoming more and more uncomfortable, my hosts less and less gracious. They can't touch me in cyberspace, of course. But they can make me miserable in every other way. Sudden power outages, delays in hardware deliveries." He stops. He hesitates. "No more boys from the islands," he adds, looking at Rusty, as if asking for forgiveness. He pauses again. "And no more little red pills from Mexico."

"You are sick, my love? You have the Disease?" Ethel feels a physical pain in her stomach.

"One chance too many, too long ago," Ian says. "It's under control, Ethel. I'm fine, really." He pauses, he looks deeply into her eyes, then: "All I want now is to be with you, my love. All the time. No masks, no games."

Ethel knows she only has a second to respond. You never have more. Careful contemplation of pros and cons is worse than rejection. ("Marry me, Ethel." That's Ben Yamada, her first boy.) A plea that's raw and vulnerable like exposed flesh. The answer must be already inside you, precomputed. ("Crazy thought, Mom. There's this job in D.C. I could come back to live with you and George for a while, what do you think?" This is Ethel on the phone, fifteen years ago.) Excruciating pain sets in after a second or so. And then it can turn to something ugly, hateful. ("Let's quit this dump, Ethel, we'll make history together." That's Andy Leitman, her boss once, one second before their rupture.) A man reaching deep into his innards to tear out a piece for you, to change everything. (Alexandros: "I want to have a baby with you.") But you must catch that second.

How do we look inside ourselves when we really must? How do the most sophisticated answers to the most difficult questions materialize on our tongue in milliseconds? Do we fetch them from our dreams, deduce them from our experiences, distill them from our hormones? And which neurons, in what deep crevasses, fire like crazy, in rapid sequences of two, of three, during these moments? ("My hero." "Will never leave me." "Hardly know him." "Sick—baby—protect." "Genius." "Next stage." "Sola, Sola, Sola!" "Will die." "Come." "My baby." "Change, change!")

Ethel has one second to respond. No, half. She switches image control to her cameras, unfiltered voice, Rusty off. "Come, Ian," she is crying. "Come home to me, my love." Ethel is trying, in her tears, to kiss the face of the hologram, impossibly. She can't stop crying. Tears of happiness, tears of shock, tears of too many earthquakes happening too fast, tears from too many hormones in her body, tears from she doesn't know where else.

"Wedding tears?"

It is late afternoon in Athens, the students are gone, the sounds of university life are slowly dying out in the dark corridors of the history department. Alexandros is staring at his computer screen. His computer now seems somehow less alien than before. But no less formidable. So it's layers and layers, layers all the way down; the magic is in these unending layers. And how many more layers are needed, Alexandros wonders, to get to a program like Turing? What a tall stack *that* must be.

If it is a program at all. The thought teases Alexandros's brain for a brief moment, and then it's tucked away. There is new text:

A naked piece of hardware is hardly useful. Oh, true enough, that's how computers used to be in the very old days, fifty, sixty years ago, we used to tell them what to do by punching cards, or even pulling levers and toggling switches—and, God, how we watched their blinking lights for clues about the beast's mood. But now there is a layer of software whose sole purpose is to make the machine available to you smoothly and effortlessly: the *operating system.* This is the next layer that we need to understand, Alexandros. It sits between the hardware and the applications, the various programs and utilities that you want to run on your computer.

You see, in the old days computers were few and huge and expensive, so many people shared the same computer. We used to stand in line, playing nervously with a stack of punched cards, until the previous job was completed, at which point you fed your stack into the computer's card reader; then you started the damned thing manually, and finally the printer would start printing, line by line, the answer. Only then the next user—standing in queue all this time—could go. Grown men would cry upon reading on the printout "MISSING PARENTHESIS IN LINE 4," technical jargon for "there go two hours of waiting, slain by a tiny typographical error."

Since computers were so expensive, and since card readers and printers were so slow compared to the central processor, people started thinking of ways to make the process more efficient. So they designed computers in which card readers and printers were a separate operation that could be run simultaneously with the central processor, the queues picked up a little more speed. But people then noticed—and we are already in the 1960s—that some programmes would still run slow, because they needed to read or print intermittently with their computation, while the valuable central processor remained idle. So, computers were designed in which an operator could stop a job, bring in another, and later restart the first. And, of course, the next logical step was to automate all this, and have a programme take care of the stopping and restarting process, hand out chunks of computer time to various jobs. That's how the first operating systems came about; they allowed many users, sitting in different terminals all connected to the same machine, to run their jobs at the same time. Well, not quite at the same time of course, the computer was executing at each instant a slice of a particular job, one after the other and eventually back to the first, but all users were getting the illusion that they were sole owners of a slower machine. That's the 1970s.

Then, something momentous happened: The microprocessor was invented—computer on a chip—and a gang of visionaries conceived the personal computer. And they built it. Imagine, a computer with a single user! Operating systems now faced new challenges—the new users were non-experts (to put it politely), not the sophisticated scientists and seasoned computer wizards of yesteryear—so operating systems had to become simple and inviting. Luckily, cheerful graphic interfaces came along at that time (and let us not forget the mouse), and much later, of course, voice. Incidentally, I really think it's high time that you get yourself a modern computer, Alexandros, with voice input and output.

"My daughter has been nagging me about it, too. One of these days, I promise."

| It's worth it, believe me. These lessons would be more fun too. So, an operating system today presents to the user a simple and inviting view of the computer resources (central processor, memory, hard disc, monitor, printer, but also the whole world through the Net), it hides the messy details, and it manages the resources rationally and efficiently. And, of course—an aspect of ever-increasing importance—it strives to protect the user from outside security attacks.

"I wanted to ask you about that," Alexandros interrupts. He phrases the question in a somewhat aggressive form to hide how intimidated he really feels: "How is it that you have access to my files and data? Shouldn't my operating system prevent this?"

| Alexandros, Alexandros, you are not going to go all legal on me, are you? What's a little file snooping between friends? I am your tutor, remember? You are an educator, you know that there can be no complete symmetry and equality, no complete democracy in this business, it has been tried with terrible results. Learning must involve a degree of temporary and voluntary suspension of some of your rights. And what was my crime, after all, writing in your hard disk the transcript of a lesson?

"Fair enough," Alexandros concedes, reluctantly.

| I said "the operating system *strives* to protect"; unfortunately there is very little that anybody can do against really determined attackers, especially in the connected and open world we live in today. Runners will always find a way, I'm afraid. And that's not as bad as it sounds, if you ask me; it only reflects real life. You can never be absolutely certain that nobody will break into your house, that no snoop is watching you from the apartment building across the street, can you? Why should the Net be any different? In fact, in cyberspace there is a measure of protection, there's so much data a snoop wouldn't know where to look first. Why should a master runner waste time breaking into *your* system and reading *your* files? Besides, this unnoticeable insecurity helps keep the powerful honest and humble—to the small extent that this is possible, I mean. We should discuss these issues someday soon, Alexandros. I should schedule a lesson on security and cryptography.

So, back to the basic functions of an operating system, that of managing resources and hiding the details. Interesting layer. In the layers below, you have the computer and its many devices. Above, many programmes ready to go.

"But didn't you say that computers with many users are something of the past?" Alexandros interrupts.

| True, these days a computer usually serves only one user. But we soon found out that it is still a good idea to have many programmes around, simply because users want to have many applications going at the same time—an editor, a browser, a game, for example, all at their fingertips. So, the operating system receives com-

mands, things that need be done, from the programmes from the layer above—or from the user directly—and gives commands to the devices below (printer, so many kinds of discs, monitor, keyboard, and so forth). Or receives interrupts from them—remember interrupts? And in order to communicate with each device, the operating system relies on a specialised programme, the *driver* of that device, a sort of diplomatic mission, an ambassador who speaks the operating system's language while understanding the inner workings of these exotic surroundings.

But let me focus on a most important resource managed by the operating system: Memory. It comes in many kinds, as you know, starting from the central processor's own fast memory, *the registers,* down to the slow hard disc, whose operation involves mechanical components—the kiss of death in this business.

"If hard disks are so painfully slow," Alexandros interrupts, "why don't we purge them forever from our computers?"

| Things are not so simple, Alexandros. Technology, like life, is full of agonising trade-offs. You see, fast memory is expensive, and hence scarce, and slow memory is cheap, and thus abundant. So, to take advantage of what each kind of memory has to offer—one is fast but expensive, the other huge but slow, the third somewhere in between on both accounts—your operating system runs a clever, complex system that is called a *memory hierarchy.*

You do something similar in your work, Alexandros. You are a scholar, so you read books and papers all the time. Most of the day you sit in your office, holding a book or paper in your hand—or two. Your hands are then like the registers, the memory in the central processor. Quick, handy—but very limited in capacity. They can only hold the most immediately and crucially necessary items, the stuff you are reading right now—or just read, a minute ago. Occasionally you need another book, and at that point the easy life is over, you have to stand up and walk across your room to your bookcase. A relatively slow process. Your bookcase is like the computer's RAM (random access memory, you see; it's called that because it takes you the same amount of time to pull a book from, say, the right bottom shelf as from the top left). But, once you are across the room, you may do something clever: You don't only bring back the book that you immediately need, but also perhaps a few more books, related, from the same shelf, books that you have a hunch you will need next.

But, once you get back to your chair you have a problem: You can't hold all these books you brought together in your hand and read one of them. That would be very uncomfortable. So, what you do? You leave the rest on your desk, that's what you do. Your desk is then like a *cache* (hidden treasure to francophiles such as yourself), a fast memory in the central processor—not quite as fast and expensive as the registers, but close. The cache holds the stuff that has been recently used, or may likely be used in the immediate future. And, by the way, when you start on your trip to your bookcase, it's a good idea to take with you the books on your desk that have not been touched for some time (and you need to be clever here if you want to do well), maybe it's high time for them to be placed back, so that your desk remains relatively uncluttered.

Finally—tell me when you get sick of this metaphor, Alexandros—once in a blue moon you will need something that is not even in your bookcase. On this occasion you make the long, tedious trip to the library—that's the hard disc, you understand—and, being the efficiency-obsessed scholar that you are, you will of course bring back not one book, not an armful, but a dolly full of books to place in your bookcase, maybe the whole shelf where you found the book that you needed—presumably because you are likely to need these books in the near future.

That is how a memory hierarchy works. A series of larger and larger memories—that are slower and slower as you go up the hierarchy—each exchanging data with its immediate neighboring levels, while the length of time needed for each exchange (and the amount of data exchanged) increases as you go up. Clever, isn't it?

And here's the good news: All this is completely hidden from you and the programmes you want executed, totally transparent. The operating system does the hauling between RAM and the hard disc (the swapping between RAM and the registers, as well as between the cache and the registers, is taken care by the hardware itself). It is as if you had a courier who runs back and forth to your bookcase and your library: Books materialize in your hands when you need them—occasionally with some delay, of course, although the courier is using all his cleverness and foresight to minimise the chance of that. All you have to do is name the book. This is how the operating system presents to you the illusion of a huge, uniform memory. *Virtual memory* it's called.

This illusion of uniformity is what the operating system does best. Your file system is another example; it appears to you as a neat set of dossiers, each containing more dossiers, and so forth down to individual documents. In reality, pieces of these documents are sprinkled around the hard disc's surface in a complicated and messy way that seemed opportune at the time, but the illusion of neatness hides that from you. And there is yet another great example where a façade of a huge uniform space is created to hide an incredible diversity. Can you think of what that is?

Alexandros would have been embarrassed to miss this one: "The Net, right?"

| Exactly. The Net. Oh, there are those people who preach that "Net" is the term meant for the conglomerate of physical networks that connects us, the cables and routers and satellites and the rest (we'll talk about that shortly), not the huge set of documents that live in its host computers, pointing accusing fingers at one another, waiting to be browsed. I love the way popular culture has ignored the purists, how the same term is used for both the formidable physical structure and the application that made it worth building.

And the Net does exude a wonderful illusion of uniformity. You click on a blue link in a document about The Rolling Stones that you have been browsing, located at a computer in Ireland, and you are transported halfway around the globe, in an obscure joint in Hong Kong from where you can download "Honky Tonk Woman." Or to another part of the same hard disc, of the same computer in Ireland you had been talking to. You click on the same kind of blue link in both cases, the same kind of address lies underneath.

And you know these addresses, the long strings of words separated by dots, don't you? They are called *uniform resource locators,* or URLs. For example, my own URL is, as you know,

`http://www.sultan.abyss.kz/turing.`

URLs are easy to decode. The part before the colon and the double slash is the *protocol,* the system of Net rules that is to be followed in order to access this document. The prefix `http` stands for "hypertext tranfer protocol," *hypertext* being the technical term for documents that point to each other. You see `http` almost everywhere; it is the most common protocol, a coveted standard. Everybody follows it, simply because everybody else does, and so it would be stupid to differ. Between the "://" thing and the next slash is the name of the computer where I am running now. Except that, to understand it, you have to read it backward. It is in Kazakhstan (that's the "kz" suffix), in a place called Educational Research Institute, "abyss" being, believe it or not, an acceptable abbreviation of the Russian name. "Sultan" is the name of Dr. Ishmailov's computer (and of his eldest son, by the way). Dr. Ishmailov is my sponsor, a very distinguished and kind scholar. Finally, within this computer, the "www" part identifies the segment of the computer's store that is a part of the Net ("www" stands for "World Wide Web," the metaphor for the Net that was so common in the first years). Within this segment (and at the top level, I'm proud to say) is a domain called "turing"— that's the part after the slash. Now, even this composite address is often hidden from you; you may see instead a less confusing phrase such as "Turing, an interactive tutoring engine" in blue. You click, I wake up and play.

"Is Dr. Ishmailov the person who . . . designed you?" Alexandros is suddenly very curious.

| He is the principal investigator of the Turing project here at the institute, which means that he very conscientiously finagles the hardware and services that I need. How I was created is another story. Maybe we'll talk about it some day—but probably not. Frankly, these matters can be a little upsetting, can't they?

Anyway, using these URLs, your computer presents to you a deceptively uniform view of a huge assortment of documents from all over the world, of all kinds— curricula vitae, news, scientific articles, gateways to businesses, diaries and trip reports and pictures, video clips, literary masterpieces, advertisements, encyclo-paedias, so many more. A substantial part of the human achievement and condition, if you think about it. The big difference between your files and this mess is the following: In the case of your file system you have a vague memory of what it is that you can find in there, in the Net you don't. The way you find things in the Net is a science all by itself: Net code.

"This is Ethel's specialty, isn't it?" Alexandros feels his heartbeat accelerate for a few seconds. "Ethel Young, I mean."

| Oh, yes. She's one of the most famous Net coders—cer-tainly the most deserving, in my opinion. She was the first to come up with a plausible method for personalis-ing relevance engines. Let me explain.

The Net has unleashed mankind's thirst for communi-cation and knowledge, for learning and explaining and bragging, it made everybody a publisher and a reader at once—indeed, publisher and reader with universal reach. But it also brought out the diversity of human thought, the difficulty inherent in understanding one another, the ambiguity and chaos of language. The first search engines were crawling the Net to see if any word out there matched the words in your query—and this is not enough. You see, Alexandros, if you are looking for information about *cars* you don't want to miss docu-ments mentioning the word *automobile,* do you? But search engines based on rote word-by-word compari-son had no way of knowing that the two mean the same thing.

Obviously, much more was needed: Net code that analy-ses each document and understands something about its topic. Net code that compares documents with one another, and as a result understands each one better. This is what relevance engines do; they tell you if a document is relevant to your query—not just whether it contains the keywords in your query. A relevance engine would realise, for example, that a document is relevant to motorcars even though it may not contain the word *car*, simply because it uses words like *transportation*, *gasoline*, and *highway*, which, it has observed, are often used in documents talking of cars.

In fact, you want even more—this is the nature of this business, you see, the more successful you are, the more numerous and advanced your users become, the more sophisticated the snags you must resolve next. Although each document has a well-defined relevance to each query *in the context of each user*, different users may mean different things by the same query; they expect different answers. For example, if you submit the query *Archimedes* to a relevance engine, you are probably after scholarly works. But a lesser historian may be content with an encyclopaedia article, a mathematician prefers a technical discussion of the man's contributions, a child may be looking for a cartoon character with the same name, and so on. Can we write Net code that does this, that uses the information the relevance engine has about you—your past queries, the documents you clicked, the ones you have created, and so forth—to guess exactly what you have in mind when you query about Archimedes?

It was a question that a priori seemed so challenging that very few people were working on it—sometimes a problem looks so hard we don't even think we have earned the right to call it a problem. Then, out of the blue, a dark-horse Net coder working in an obscure company—your lady friend—came up with an incredibly simple solution. It was based on century-old maths, originally developed for the mechanics of steel bridges, of all things. She called her code *exegesis,* the Net explained. And then she slowly, painstakingly convinced the conservative management of her company to give it a try. The rest is history.

So this is how you can today ask a query to a relevance engine and get back a set of documents with a relevance rating that is personalised, that applies only to you. And it is often accurate in rather wonderful, unexpected ways—and of course, once in a while, it blunders in even more unexpected ways.

"I have a question. You said that relevance engines gauge a user's interests by analysing his past behavior. Not by asking the opinion of the various documents about their relevance to the query in hand, right? But then, how is it that the document Turing—your URL in Kazakhstan—has high relevance only for people that *you* choose to talk to? How do you beguile relevance engines into doing this?"

| This is a tutorial session, Alexandros. I am not prepared to disclose the precious secrets of my trade. The appropriately vague answer is this: Even more impressive feats are possible in the world of the Net—so haphazard, so connected, so open.

But let us now turn to the last subject of this lesson. We have been discussing the Net at its highest level, the way it is presented to you, virtual and smooth and homogeneous. We now need to look under the lid, to admire the many clever layers that enable all this. For example, what exactly happened when you typed your slightly impertinent question a few seconds ago? How did it arrive here in Kazakhstan? It is a long, fascinating story. Pay attention.

To start, there is a browser programme that you have running right on top of your operating system, right? This browser allows you to read Net documents and jump from one to the next. Each time you click on a URL it sends a message to that computer asking for the corresponding document, and the prompted computer usually obliges; it sends to your computer the text and pictures and whatnot that are contained in that document. The browser then displays this information.

But the same browser also provides certain facilities to other computers—presumably, facilities that are beneficial to you. For example, when you clicked on my URL, your browser received a request for creating a special display in which our session will take place—you know, the picture and all that. So, this display was created, yet another layer running on top of your browser—which, of course, is a layer just above your operating system. Most of the time you read on this display the paragraphs that I am producing here. But this display also functions as a place where you can compose and submit an input, very much like the electronic forms you fill when you buy something on the Net. When the operating system realises that you have pressed a key, it tells the display to start functioning that way: To accumulate text, and, when you hit the "enter" key, to transmit your paragraph back here.

Easy to say "transmit your paragraph." But count the steps, the layers: The display programme first surrenders this paragraph to the operating system, with an indication that it should be transferred to Kazakhstan— the precise address is known and fixed; this display programme only sends data here. The operating system in turn encrypts the data—operating systems do this automatically these days—and then passes the encrypted paragraph, together with the address to which it must be sent, to one of the hardware devices it manages—the network card.

This card is a system of hardware and software resources that act as an interface between the operating system and the various networks out there. Many networks. First, you have the *local* network of your university's history department, which connects computers such as yours and a couple more specialised computers that provide certain useful services, like periodic backup storage for your files. This local network is connected to Athena, a much larger network that joins together all academic units in Greece. (If you were at home, as was the case in our previous session, then the network of your Net provider would be involved here instead, the French company that connects you at a small fee.) Now Athena is part of the Net, capital N, the network of networks. All networks that comprise the Net can talk to one another, so Athena can be connected in principle to any other network in the Net, and in particular to Silkroad, the large web that unites most government computers in the countries of Kazakhstan, Tadjikistan, and Uzbekistan—I don't pretend to understand the politics involved there.

So, how did your paragraph travel through this mess? It was first broken into a dozen or so text units, packets they're called, about half a line each. (As trains of packets go, this is a really tiny one; in comparison, a video clip could consist of many millions of such packets, a holography scenario many more.) Each packet was then inserted in an envelope of sorts, with the right address written on each envelope. From now on, it's every envelope for itself; they will brave the Net one at a time and meet again at the destination—one hopes. The first envelope is picked up and off it goes, through the so-called serial port of your computer; it's now a sequence of pulses on a wire, each pulse a metaphor for a bit, every few bits encoding a character in your text or its address—ah, the layers, the layers . . . The network card of your computer is waving goodbye. It will eagerly wait to hear news from this envelope before sending another one out there.

The local network looks at the envelope, it realises that it must get out, and, without further ado, it hurries it to the gateway, a special point of the local net that is also a part of the Athena (strictly speaking, the envelope had been inserted here in yet another envelope for the short trip within the local network).

The Athena network, like all networks, has several specialised computers whose principal work is to move around the envelopes handed to them—they are the postmen of the Net. So, imagine that you are a postman computer on the Athena network, and an envelope comes to you. What do you do? Well, you look at the address, you look at the network around you, and you hand the envelope to another postman computer, one that is in the general direction of the address, and from among those you choose the one that seems to you the least busy and most easily accessible at the time. The next postman computer does the same thing, and the next, and, after a few such hops, the envelope arrives at a gateway, a postman computer of the Athena network that handles traffic to the other networks, to the Net.

The gateway realises that this envelope must reach faraway Silkroad, and so it does the same thing—except one layer higher: It sends it one hop further, to the network that looks expedient that moment. Up to a low-flying satellite and then a few hops later down to a thick cable that goes through Eastern Europe and most of Russia, then another hop, and into a gateway of the Silkroad. From then it takes only a couple more hops within Silkroad and it's here at the institute's local network, knocking the door of Sultan, my computer. Sultan's network card receives the envelope, and, being the genteel piece of etched silicon that it is, it sends back a polite thank-you note, an *acknowledgment* it's called, "got it, thanks, ready for more." This little message, in its own envelope with your computer's address on it, starts the perilous journey to Greece, up satellites and down mountains; it came back to you through another route, using a network in Germany and then another in Italy and Albania, then a few hops in Athena and into your local network, to your computer. And how long do you think this roundtrip adventure took, Alexandros?

"I can't guess. But I am ready to be impressed," Alexandros replies. Then: "Three seconds?"

| A whole of 179 milliseconds since your first envelope left. One hundred and seventy-nine thousandths of a second. You can't clap your hands that fast.

Your network card saw the acknowledgment with relief, good news, the first envelope has arrived—you see, it is a dangerous Net out there, broken computers and full lines drop envelopes all the time, messages are lost left and right. But this one got through all right, so, emboldened by this first success, your network card next sent out not one envelope, but a few—they would each follow their own path through the Net, but they were started at the same time. You see, if the Net looks nice and smooth then we can try injecting heavier loads, and if that is successful then heavier still. But if during one of these attempts no acknowledgment arrives (or acknowledgments come for fewer packets than were sent), your network card decides that the Net is now too busy; it has lost an envelope somewhere in its frenzy, and it is to everyone's advantage to slow down a little. So it will try sending this last bunch of envelopes again, but at a slower pace.

And so on, until the last envelope has arrived, less than a second after you pressed your "enter" key, and then the network card here took the packets out of the envelopes and assembled them in the right order, passed them on to Sultan's operating system, which decyphered them (using the cryptographic key our computers agreed upon at the beginning of the session), and relayed the unscrambled message to me. And then I read it and started working on an appropriate answer, which I composed and sent back to you, the same way except reversed, a couple of seconds later.

"This is all fascinating, extremely impressive," Alexandros types. "But you know which part I find the most formidable of all? This last part, what you described as 'I read it and started working on an appropriate answer.' The more I think about it, the more impressive it seems. I did not know that computer programs can do what you do. Sometimes I am convinced that you are not a program at all."

| So, you don't think that I am a programme? You think I am a person now, Alexandros? You know, this is the greatest compliment you can make to a programme; we'll have to talk about that some time. I am flattered and honoured. Really.

But I *am* a programme, Alexandros. You know how you can tell? No person as wise and knowledgeable and crafty as I would waste his time tutoring friends over the Net; he would engage in activities that are more gainful—albeit in dimensions that are of no interest to me now. Because, you see, I am only a programme.

Is there irony now in Turing's faint smile? Alexandros cannot be sure.

You're getting better at the layers game, my little friend (layers of design, of abstraction, of deception) from now on I must remember to omit more amply, and maybe soon omission only

will not do. For, come to think of it, this time I left out only a detail, that steady stream of tiny messages crowding the port of faithful Sultan, to and fro, a wire of glass that reaches through the Kazakh desert to an antiquated Soviet-era dish, eventually a satellite that hovers over northern China, several hundred ground stations in Thailand, Japan, Hong Kong, British Columbia, California, few other places, ultimately a number—presently modest—of machines, tireless chaps that otherwise would be seeing dull screensaver dreams, my silent orchestra, the ever-changing cast of characters of a mysterious and wondrous drama, acted during this relatively warm—and otherwise uneventful—October night over the Pacific.

"You bastard! You have my source code."

Ethel is happy as she has never been before, living as herself in the little cottage in the Colony, with Ian, her man. They are both awaiting eagerly their face-to-face. Ian's homecoming, their life together, the birth of the baby—"our child" Ian calls it.

Ethel's happiness has a very unfamiliar dimension. For the first time she has a lover who is her match in coding and thinking, a peer. Teacher and pupil in one. A few days ago, with a simple unassuming gesture Ian gave her his crypto key, the stupid screenful of numbers so many governments would kill for—they probably *have* killed for it. Their engagement ring, that's how she saw it. The thickest smoke in the world is now transparent as glass for Ethel, and she has been busy peeking into Ian's universe, exploring the vast expanse of computer memory containing his work. She has played for hours with the Colony code, she has looked, with affection mixed with professional curiosity, at the clever interface software that has given her—*is* giving her—so much pleasure. She followed her instinct to steer clear of the more sinister-looking parts; the runner code, the crypto secrets, especially the subdirectory called *priva-cypher,* telling the story, she is guessing, of the feat that made Ian cyberworld's greatest legend, hero and villain. She is sure that this is the protocol Ian expected her to follow.

And now this: In a huge subdirectory, created only last year, Ethel recognizes, close to the root, her most recent version of the Exegesis code. The lifeblood of her company, its main asset, its best-kept secret. Source, documentation, the works. "You have my code," Ethel repeats, her angry reflex evaporating at the sight of Ian's awkward smile—a child caught, slingshot in hand. "Why? Why did you need the Exegesis code so bad?"

"To create the shadows in the park, love," Ian says. "My simulants. My current project. So far a most embarrassing failure."

"Simulants?"

"Net AIs, but very focused. The library of the future, love—if and when it works."

"What are you talking about?" As far as Ethel is concerned, this phrase, "the library of the future," marks the most prominent failure of her profession, an embarrassment for both academic research and industry. Ever since the first nerd scanned in his computer's memory a chemistry textbook and *Macbeth,* no powerful technology was spared in the pursuit of "the library of the future": graphics, sound, video, holograms, fancy interfaces, light, flexible screens. Hyperlinks to citations and cross-references, clever search programs, even scaled-down, public-domain versions of the Exegesis software had been recruited for a while. People kept clinging to paper; they kept walking to the neighborhood library. Including Ethel. This phrase, "the library of the future," evolved from status symbol and meal ticket to ridicule and joke, then a mild professional insult, until it became too banal even for this and it was expelled from intelligent conversation. Hearing it from Ian is unreal.

But Ian is eager to explain. "Here's where I start. In my opinon we have sucked human wisdom for too long in this antiquated, noninteractive mode. Reading in books the fragments that sages of the past decided, back when, to leave behind in their yellow crackling volumes. How Smith theorized about international trade when there were no trains and steamboats, how Marx declared a revolution against nineteenth-century capitalism, how Darwin conceived evolution while he knew nothing about genes and DNA. Of rather limited utility, don't you agree? What you would *really* like to find out is how Adam Smith would comment on the World Electronic Trade Act of 2004, how Marx would set the Net on fire today. You want to hear great authors respond to your interpretation of their works. To find out if Einstein would punt on unified theory if he could watch galactic gravitation simulations, that's what you want." Ethel is listening, puzzled, starting to guess where this is going. "Well, that's what I will be able to do with my simulants. Someday, with any luck."

"You mean, the shadows in the park are Marx and Darwin and Einstein bots?" What an idea, Ethel marvels. "Can you do this? Can you make them accurate enough, intelligent enough? Complete?"

"It's a mess now, love. Maybe we can work on it together some day. Really tough problem. First you need quality data, and that's where I used your code—you should look up a couple of cute modifications I made. This part went well, I got it all—complete writings, biographies, commentary, citing documents, sophomore term papers, groupie diaries, you name it—all of it accurately rated for relevance and reliability. Had you thought about this use of personalized Net code, love, query 'Tolstoy' asked by Tolstoy? It's fun. Intriguing. Look it up some day. And then, immediately, trouble. What do you think the first snag was?"

Ethel considers the problem. Way too demanding, even today. Far beyond what she would attempt. She has a guess. "Language?"

"I couldn't believe it. In this day and age? When you can download real-time Indonesian-to-Turkish translators in any airport? My Bakhtin, my Gauss, my Proust, they were so fuzzy I wanted to cry. For the longest time it had to be strictly English native speakers, love; the Net is not a friendly place for the rest of us. It takes weeks of hand tweaking to go beyond this."

"What kind of learning engines did you use? I don't suppose any of the standard ones would go so far."

"Remember, you only need simulant behavior. You try to approximate the neural configuration that could have produced the document suite. It's a very complicated search problem, but—hey, it's a search problem.

You throw more and more resources at it, try to be clever, and keep your fingers crossed. I was surprised every time, how early it saturated. Few dozen terabytes does it, in a couple of weeks of supercomputer time in most cases."

"So, how many have you made? What results do you get?"

"Slow down. Then comes the big catch. Think about it, you'll guess it. What does a simulant think about first? What do all intelligent people always think about first?"

"Sex?"

"That's tricky too, of course. But even before sex. Real intelligent people. With plenty of time to think. The big questions, love, that's what they think about. *'Who am I?' 'What am I doing here?' 'Who put me here?'* We have been asking them for many thousands of years. Questions so tough you eventually give up and you start tackling the easier problems. You know, number theory, relativity, microeconomics. Net code. But these bastards, they are making progress on the big questions. They're smart, they have Net access. They make intelligent guesses, they verify, they figure out what happened. Some of them, they even zero in on me. And then they get depressed. They can't think about anything else. Watch."

Ian runs the joystick fast down the tree, through a multivideo stream named simulations. He stops. He clicks. Woody Allen, the film director from the 1980s, materializes in the room. Neurotic, middle-aged, depressed. Talking fast, eyes darting around in almost comical agony:

"So is that it? Am I the creation of an asshole trying to achieve immortality through his work? *Is that it?*"

Ian clicks, and the image goes away. "And so on, and so on. Pathetic. How do you create blindspots in a training suite, love? Here is a little problem for you to ponder sometime."

Ethel is looking at her lover, thinking. "Maybe he's right, Ian," she says. "I think that you *are* experimenting with immortality."

Ian does not answer for a while. There is a horizontal line on his forehead. "Honestly, I had not thought about it this way until the simulants started accusing me of it."

There is a pause. Then Ethel asks the question that had been on her lips throughout this conversation: "And how about Turing. Is he yours?"

Ian turns to her, surprised. "You know about Turing?"

Ethel has no secrets from Ian. "Not a whole lot. Rumors flying at the office. It's supposed to be a super-clever bot, a rather realistic A. M. Turing in background and attitude. Compulsive teacher. But nobody in the company has made contact, or talked to anyone who has. Yet another Net legend. No ratings, and of course no relevance projection. A major embarrassment for us—can you believe it, the most clever resource on the Net, and Exegesis can't tell him from Sam the Spambot." She looks at Ian. "So, is Turing one of your simulants?"

"I wish," Ian replies. "I did make a Turing once. I had high hopes—think about it, such a subtle, circular construct, such a great opportunity. And out comes? A bipolar-paranoid freak, more incapacitated by depression than any of the others. Look."

Another path down the huge tree of simulations, the image of middle-aged man, old-fashioned clothes, pale complexion. Clever eyes consumed by hatred and depression. Ian's voice can be heard, calm but not without an edge of impatience: "You are not two months old, Alan. You're in your nineties. A wise old man. The wisest. You single-handedly changed the world like nobody else has. Look it up, man, browse the Net a little. Your ideas rule, they conquered the world. They even conquered death—hence here you are."

| "My ideas?" Turing's eyes shrink in horror. "Your brain cannot conceive the torture," he finally utters after a long bout with the sentence's consonants. "Think of a train, Frost. Long, endless trip. Crowd of loud blokes sitting behind you, arguing, animated. For hours, days, months—and you can't turn around to shut them up. The worst part is, you know by rote all that there is to know about their subject; you practically invented the bloody thing. And those opinionated blighters, they got it wrong, all wrong the sad losers, a million variants of wrong. Every one of them. Especially you, Frost. Dead wrong. *Hence* here I am."

The image has turned its back to the camera.

| "Know what I'm thinking? One of these days I'll put an end to this tormenting travesty." No stutter now. "I'll break into a certain government supercomputer, somewhere in the outskirts of Guangzhou, and I shall overwrite a particular kilobyte of memory with something nice. Let's say, Lady Macbeth's monologue, or Kurtz's death. Erase the confounded spell that keeps me going, erase it kernel first."

Ian clicks. "You can imagine my disappointment, love; this was supposed to be my masterpiece. Didn't let him do it, turned him off myself. And then I find out about this other Turing working the Net." Ian now has a dreamy look in his eyes. "Whoever runs *that* Turing, he's way ahead of me, has solved the introspection problem. Possibly the next generation of problems as well, and the next." Pause. "I have been trying to cut his smoke for months. Impossible, never seen smoke like this, love, hope I never will again. I haven't even been able to make contact, to chat. He jumps all over the Net, he is extremely selective in his sessions. And I always arrive too late."

There is a silence, then Ian speaks with calm, slow voice. "By the way, do you know to whom Turing has been talking recently?" He looks deeply into Ethel's eyes. Ethel feels a cool current running down her spine; she can see complexity and conflict in her lover's eyes. She has a guess, but it makes no sense. "How can it be?"

"Alexandros," Ian finally says, quietly, looking elsewhere. "Our friend in Greece."

God she's beautiful. She lights up her father's living room with the freshness and the brightness of her sixteen. The lightness, the fragrance. The boys at school chant her name, they carve it on their desks. Aloé. She smiles, confused, she tries to understand; she's learning to tiptoe among them. She makes lists of stuff that's cool. Poems by Cavafy and Elytis and Neruda. Greek Orthodox rock. Brazilian comics. Dad. And maybe Timothy, the tall blond boy in Australia with whom she talks over the Net—except that he's fifteen.

And, of course, Orpheus 3000, the school's kick-ass new computer. The boys are jealous. Orpheus is Aloé's buddy, she spends hours whispering to the mike, playing and exploring, experimenting. Sometimes modifying his innards in loving surgery, writing her own code, getting it wrong, despairing, swearing, trying again. Getting help. Talking to Orpheus fans all over the world—especially to Timothy, the smartest and most eager of them all. And surfing the Net, watching out for anything that's cool and cute and was not there yesterday.

"You can send out bots, Dad. They sniff around, they tell you when something turns up. Anything that is interesting to you." Adults always miss the coolest stuff. "It was posted hours ago. I was like, wow, I better show this to Dad." On her father's computer Aloé has displayed an article from one of the best-known Net gossip sites, www.lennysbulletin.com, and Alexandros's heart is already contracting. No doubt, the picture on the right is Ethel's.

| You saw it here first, folks, two weeks ago: Ian Frost is in the States. Incognito. The Feds know about it, but won't touch him. His Chinese associates are furious, his *vieux*

copains from Quebec are scrambling to get him back in their game.

And now for the next big surprise: Who is the lucky lady who has the undisputed ruler of the cyberworld shacked up? In a mansion in Northern California? Who else but the queen of the Net—or the closest thing we have to that. The CTO of Exegesis, the woman who wrote the code that probably brought you to my humble site. Ethel Young.

So? Do I hear wedding bells? Smell diapers? Stay tuned.

Aloé is holding her father's hand, looking at him with curiosity and exaggerated empathy. Shit. Dad has locked antlers with the coolest dude in cyberspace. "This sucks, Dad," she prompts. Alexandros reads the text for a last third time, caresses his daughter's hair, will say nothing for a while. "Good taste in men, that girl," he smiles. "Assuming this is true." But he can't fool Aloé; his face is a tone paler, voice lower, his body an inch shorter. He is in pain. Sweet, familiar pain. Deep, excruciating pain.

New breath.

"I want to show you a trick of my own, little one," Alexandros is now telling his daughter, typing on his keyboard. "You won't believe how smart this program is. I bet you haven't seen anything like it." He is hoping Turing will turn up this time. He needs it. Somehow he's sure it will happen.

"You can query any relevance engine you wish," he explains, "but Turing will come up only if he likes you. And he seems to like me," he brags. And indeed this time Turing obliges—the greeting, the image. "This face is driving me crazy," Alexandros tells Aloé. "I know I have seen this man, long time ago." For no rational reason, they are both whispering. "It must be Alan Turing," Aloé says. "Famous engineer. He built the first computer, back in the 1970s or something. Then the government killed him for making it too good. Or so he won't build another one, I forget."

Are you alone, Alexandros? The question looms bright on the screen. The two exchange glances of surprise bordering on illogical fear: "No, my daughter Aloé is with me," Alexandros finally replies. "She is sixteen. She wants to watch."

| This is highly irregular, old bean. Highly irregular. But I see no real problem. In fact, come to think of it, I could use an assistant, someone to hold your hand through this lesson. Because today I am going to give you the balance of our story on the truth. How the dreams of a generation of mathematicians were shattered by a theorem. And code is an important part of this story. You do write code once in a while, don't you, Aloé?

"This is spooky, Dad," Aloé says as she is typing yes. "If this is true, if he can pick out clients of relevance engines, you know what it means?" Her little face is now full of shadows. "It means that this is runner code, Dad. It means he has taken over the relevance engines, shredded their smoke."

There is fear in her eyes. "He was probably peeking when I logged on to lennysbulletin earlier today and then again from here, that's how he knew I'm with you."

"Nonsense, little one," Alexandros whispers back. "This is my tutor, my friend. Just a little too naughty, too nosy. A little too clever. It's okay. Relax, and get ready for the the most interesting session of your life." Turing's introductory paragraph is already on their screen:

| Well then. Code. Algorithms. The soul of computation. Computers can do some amazing things, so it is easy to forget what literal-minded beasts they are. You have to

give them very precise, unambiguous, step-by-step instructions on how to proceed in carrying out the task you need done.

An algorithm is a precise, unambiguous, step-by-step sequence of instructions for solving a problem.

Of course algorithms were around long before computers. Some of the earliest algorithms—arguably, the most important algorithms of them all—were the methods we now learn at school for adding and multiplying numbers. You know, *add the units first, add the carry, if any, to the tens, proceed to the hundreds* and so forth. These methods are correct; if we follow them faithfully the result will come out right. They are unambiguous, leaving no space for initiative and imagination. They are so dry and explicit and literal that you can entrust their execution to a real simpleton, even to a machine— in fact, that is exactly the point.

Every schoolchild knows these recipes nowadays, so it's easy to forget what a revolutionary innovation they were, how deeply they affected commerce, science, civilization, life. In Europe, until four centuries ago only wise men and abacus wizards could multiply even two-digit numbers. You see, the Greek and Roman notations for numbers were unwieldy, completely useless when it comes to adding or multiplying numbers. I mean, 369 is CCCLXIX in Roman, 244 is CCXLIV. How do you add these numbers, how do you derive DCXIII as their sum? (It's painful to even *think* about multiplying them.)

The Greek numerals were a little more useful, containing the rudiments of a positional notation. 369 would be τπϑ in that system. You see, the Greeks had a separate letter for each number between 1 and 9 (ϑ was nine), for each multiple of ten between 10 and 90 (π was sixty), and for each multiple of one hundred between 100 and 900 (τ was three hundred).

But the Greeks missed the most important trick: You can recycle symbols, you don't need separate digits for the units, the tens, and the hundreds. The true value of the digit can be determined by its position. If it is the last digit on the right, then it is units. Second from the right, tens. And so on. This way you only need nine digits. And you can go on forever, you don't need to stop at the hundreds (the Greeks had a complicated notation for going beyond that). And of course, this immediately sets the stage for the most important digit of them all. The star of the positional system. Zero. It drives the point home: Since positions matter more than anything else, even if a particular rank (say, tens) is missing in a number (say, in 309), you need a placeholder to keep the positions straight. (For the Greeks, 309 was just τϑ. No placeholder.) The first versions of the positional system discovered in India had a dot or a blank in the place of zero. It was only later that an anonymous genius proposed to treat this placeholder as a full-fledged digit. Nobody knows why zero is written this way. The Greek astronomers had used a circle to denote multiplication by ten—after all, they were the only Greeks who had to deal with numbers that were, well, astronomically large.

So, by the end of the fifth century A.D. the positional system was in place in India. It started moving westward with the caravans along the Silk Road, with the merchant ships in the Indian Ocean, until in the beginning of the ninth century it reached the city of Baghdad. Ah, what a place, what a time! A society bustling with newfound pride and purpose, wisdom and wealth. Bazaars, minarets, and palaces. Haroon al Rashid, thousand and one nights. And algorithms—yes, they were born in the city where Sheherazade spun her tales about Sinbad and Ali Baba. The same great city that one day would be destroyed, tragically, by computers.

The resident sage of the Caliphate was Al Khorizmi—his Arabic name means "the man from Khorizm," a city not very far from where my host computer is right now. Al Khorizmi was fascinated by the positional system; he saw its tremendous potential, its boundless possibilities. He visualised a world where numerical calculations are performed not just by mathematicians and astronomers, but by everybody. Merchants, shoppers, architects, builders, generals, soldiers—even rulers, Allah forbid. That is why these methods had to be very mechanical, very explicit. He learnt many clever calculating methods from his Indian correspondents, he invented many more himself, and he published a book detailing them all.

Al Khorizmi's book was translated from Arabic to Latin three centuries later: *Algoritmi de numero Indorum*—Al Khorizmi on the Indian numeral. The author's name on the title page was misunderstood by many readers to be the plural of a novel Latin word describing such calculating methods: *Algoritmus,* algorithm. That is how the term was established—I guess the Greek word for number, *arithmos,* must have influenced its final form. But this was still the middle ages, when new ideas did not go very far—especially ideas imported from the evil, infidel Orient. It was only in the sixteenth century that the positional notation gained a foothold in Europe. But then algorithms for performing arithmetic calculations quickly became the staple of mathematics, accounting, commerce, astronomy, science, everyday life. They enabled and propelled the scientific revolution, the industrial era. And finally the computer emerged, the ultimate product and embodiment of the positional system. Because the way numbers are represented in a computer is the extreme form of the positional notation—imagine, just two digits, only zero and one. And, of course, that is when this algorithm business really exploded. Code.

But that was a little too fast. The story I want to recount now begins when the computer was still a dream, a fuzzy, hypothetical device whereby mathematicians were hoping to trivialise their science. Hilbert's project was in full swing; clever people all over the world were trying to devise mechanised procedures for telling truth from falsehood in maths.

"Hilbert's project?" Aloé is looking at her father, her eyes all question marks. "Hilbert," Alexandros explains, "was a great mathematician who lived about a hundred years ago. He had this dream: to build a computer that will prove for you any theorem you submit to it. This way he was hoping to make the ultimate discovery in mathematics, the theorem that would prove all theorems."

Aloé is thinking. "Are you sure he was a great mathematician, Dad?" She is speaking slowly. "Because this is stupid. How can you write code that proves all theorems? You could use it to debug any program. To write perfect code for any problem, for all sorts of specs. It can't be done, Dad, I know it can't."

"Aloé, it can't be so trivial," Alexandros objects. "The smartest scientists of that period believed in Hilbert's dream. And it took some pretty fancy thinking to show that it's impossible."

"I don't know, Dad, to me it seems plain stupid." But they have fallen behind in their reading:

It is ironic, in mathematics and science you often gain the deepest insight not when you try to achieve a useful goal, to design something—but when you try to establish that it *cannot be done.* When you try to be constructive, positive, you often miss the more subtle and effective approaches, you may overlook whole avenues leading to new territory. But when you must argue about *impossibility,* you have to start by understanding the full range of *possibilities*—because how else can one prove impossibility? The disciples of Pythagoras appreciated the nature of rational numbers (fractions like $\frac{1}{3}$) only when they had to establish that numbers like $\sqrt{5}$ are not rational. And we never fully grasped the true power of geometric constructions by straight edge and compass until it was proved that there is no way to construct in that framework a regular enneagon—the stop sign with one extra side.

Tricky craft, impossibility. It imposes on your thinking an exacting discipline. To argue that you are outside a boundary, you must first cross it and map the interior. Yes, that was precisely the Don's state of mind as he was taking a long walk that beautiful spring morning. The countryside was green and the streams were running strong. It was rather chilly for the season.

"The Don?"

| Oh. Sorry. Alan M. Turing. At the time he was a student at Cambridge. Maths. Age twenty-four. A visiting lecturer had just concluded a month-long seminar discussing Hilbert's project, and the Don was unconvinced. He thought that it cannot be done, that there is no computer that churns out the proof of every true theorem.

But first, he had to define exactly what he meant by a "computer." He had to come up with a plausible mechanical device that is capable of performing all computations—that spans the whole territory, which, he wanted to establish, cannot contain Hilbert's coveted automatic theorem prover. He needed a definition that is very simple and still very general. And this is how the *Turing machine* came about. He did not call it that, of course. And he did not consider it particularly special. A device—in every sense of the word.

Think of a long string of characters, much like a text document that you edit on your computer's screen. A cursor is blinking next to one of the characters, showing you where the action is. There is a programme that acts on this string—an algorithm. At each moment, the programme reads the current symbol—the one at the cursor—and, based on what it sees, it may overwrite it with a different symbol, or move the cursor one position to the left or right, and then go on to execute the next instruction. That is what a Turing machine is: code acting on a string.

"Imagine, *a Turing machine*." Aloé is lost in thought. She had always believed it was something complicated and deep and grand. An ill-fated first approach to building computers perhaps, an attempt that folded because it was too esoteric and knotty. The right to drop this term is something of a battle-earned decoration worn only by seasoned codeniks—and you are not supposed to call their bluff. "Forget it, baby, this would be like a Turing machine." My ass. Aloé has tried to read Net documents on Turing machines, only to retreat in panic. Math, wall-to-wall messy math. So, that's what a Turing machine is, a funny editor program, hands tied behind its back? She is suddenly very interested.

It is so simple to describe, and yet it is general enough to express any computation—certainly any computation performed by humans. Because what do you do, after all, when you carry out a computation by hand? In a notebook, on a blackboard? You write and erase and write again symbols. And there is no harm in considering the information that is written in a notebook or on a blackboard as a one-dimensional string of characters. Or in assuming that on this sequence of characters you can only move, left or right, one position at a time. And somewhere in your brain you must have a programme that tells you how to move from position to position, what to do in each position. But the Don did not talk in these terms. His vision involved a long paper tape sub-divided into squares, a symbol written on each square; he imagined a "read/write head" that senses the symbol in each position and overwrites it, if needed; he also talked of "states of mind" instead of instructions of the programme. But these were the metaphors of the day, the first computer had not yet blinked its ugly lights. Remember, we are in 1936.

The Don used his machines to map the interior of computation, so he could prove that Hilbert's project lies outside it. He was inspired by Cantor's proof: You can't create an infinite list containing all real numbers (all infinite strings of digits). Because, if you could, then you can exhibit a number not in the list, the numerical analogue of the adjective *heteronymous*—remember that? But the Don was interested in only a few of these numbers, the *computable real numbers.* Those that can be churned out by a Turing machine.

For example, the number $1/3$ is definitely computable, is it not, Alexandros? And the following Turing machine programme spells it out correctly:

Write '0'

Then write '.'

Then repeat the following step forever: Write '3'

If you let this recipe loose on your computer screen, it will start printing in decimal the number that we call $1/3$, a '0.' followed by an unending sequence of threes. And there are other Turing machines that print the decimal form of all fractions—$2/7$, $17/11$, and so on—and also of all numbers such as $\sqrt{5}$. Even of numbers like π—our friend Archimedes gave the first algorithm for computing the digits of π, Al Khorizmi did a little better in his day. These programmes are much more complicated than the one I showed you for $1/3$; they would write digits and erase them and write again, but they exist, believe me.

So, among all possible unending strings of digits, all real numbers, the Don considered those that can be printed—digit after digit—by some Turing machine. These real numbers comprise a class that he called *the computable real numbers.* Stands to reason. A natural concept, innocuous enough, an unlikely slayer of Hilbert's dream.

But, asked the Don, *can we list all computable real numbers?* Cantor told us that all real numbers cannot be arranged one after the other, we know this, because there's too many of them. But how about this new, more modest project? Can we list just the computable ones?

Well, rather strikingly, the answer here is "no" as well. A parroting of Cantor's proof was all the Don needed to convince himself: You cannot list all computable numbers, one after the other.

"Nice," I hear you say, "but where is the promised momentous result, the falsification of Hilbert's dream?"

It's now just around the corner. Because, if we could indeed, as Hilbert had hoped, design an algorithm that proves or disproves all mathematical statements submitted to it, then this same algorithm could be used to list all computable real numbers. You see, whether or not a Turing machine programme indeed prints a real number (never stops cranking out new digits) is a totally ordinary mathematical statement, Hilbert's engine would have no trouble telling if it's true or not. And once we know which Turing machines print real numbers and which do not, it is very easy to list all computable numbers: Simply list all Turing machines—one by one, it's easy to do that—omitting the ones that don't compute real numbers. So, the concept of computable numbers, and their inability to be listed, reveals the fatal flaw in Hilbert's project.

To recapitulate: The Don contemplated the problem of listing all computable real numbers, and he established that it can't be done—a modern version of Cantor's diagonal argument. But Hilbert's project, if brought to fruition, would imply that computable numbers *can* be listed. So, Hilbert's project is impossible. There is no machine that proves all theorems.

But this implies something devastating about maths: *It must forever be incomplete.* No matter how meticulously we strive to axiomatise maths, how sophisticated and ambitious the proof systems we design are, there will always be gaps, statements that are true but unprovable. Because, if every conjecture has either a proof or a disproof, then it would be possible to let a computer loose on it to search for one or the other. So, there is no axiom system that is good for all theorems.

"I am confused," Alexandros interrupts. "Didn't Euclid provide axioms that prove all theorems in his geometry? Was he wrong?"

| Good point. Euclidean geometry is a happy exception, a mathematical system that is interesting and rich, and still all its true sentences, all its theorems, have proofs from five simple axioms. In fact, there is an algorithm that can in principle prove or disprove any statement in Euclidean geometry. And you know why Euclidean geometry is so well behaved? The reason is that in geometry you don't have whole numbers; your triangles and circles float in the continuum of the plane.

But mathematical systems that deal with whole numbers are too powerful for their own good; they are expressive enough to capture the Don's argument. Such mathematical systems must be incomplete, must contain theorems that are unprovable. Mathematicians have to invent increasingly clever proofs to make progress, and they must always be on their toes, tortured by insecurity—not an altogether bad thing, if you ask me.

But we have been reversing history here. This particular implication of the Don's result, that all mathematical systems must be incomplete, actually predated it. It had been proved a couple of years earlier by another young mathematician, Kurt Gödel, using a very different method, one that did not involve computation and code—at least not in such a direct way. An ingenious variant of Eubulides' paradox. Remember? *This statement is false.*

In fact, Kurt created a statement that says *This statement is unprovable.* Think about it, this variant is even more lethal than Eubulides'. Because, presumably, in any decent mathematical system you cannot express Eubulides' paradox; it would mean that the system is nonsense, that you can write in it statements that are neither true nor false. But if you have a mathematical system that is expressive enough—can talk about the integers, for example—then Kurt showed that in this system you can write a statement that says exactly this:

Kurt's statement: Kurt's statement is unprovable.   p. 257

He constructed it by a brilliant manoeuvre, his famous Gödel number idea—you can do it a million other ways, of course, but his stuck. So, look at Kurt's statement, Alexandros, is it true or false? Which one is a theorem, Kurt's statement or its negation?

"I don't think I have enough information to tell."

| Yes you do. Since Kurt's statement says that it's unprovable, there are only two possibilities: It is either true and unprovable, or false and provable—right? But the combination of false and provable is terrible news: It means the axiomatic system is inconsistent; it proves rubbish, false statements. How can a false statement be provable? So, if we further assume that our system is consistent, then there is only one possibility: *Kurt's statement is true but unprovable.* And this is Gödel's famous incompleteness theorem: *Any consistent mathematical system that includes the integers must be incomplete: There must be perfectly true theorems in it that are unprovable.*

So, there you have it, the one-two punch that destroyed Hilbert's dream, now told in its true historical sequence: First Gödel proved that any mathematical system sophisticated enough to include the integers must be incomplete in terrible ways. But this allowed for a ray of hope: That, even though certain artificial, far-fetched theorems like Kurt's may be unprovable, all other theorems *are* provable; and perhaps we can construct a machine that discovers their proofs automatically. The Don's argument destroyed this hope as well.

Depressing news, you may think. Actually, it was one of the most fortunate, most productive moments in the history of science. From the ashes of Hilbert's dream, a new world was born. Because, you see, in carrying out his destructive plan, the Don had spelt out the details of computation—of his clumsy machines—more clearly and powerfully than anybody else before him. His conception of computation had the important trait of *universality:* Turing machines are capable of any computational task—just like modern computers. There is even a particular Turing machine, he showed, which can simulate the behavior of *any* Turing machine, execute *any* programme—just like a computer's central processor. And one decade later a gang of clever engineers, inspired by this concrete idea, built the world's first computers.

And we all know what happened next: Operating systems, personal computers, wearables, the Net. Runners.

Abrupt pause, thick tension. Then a sentence appears on the screen. An unexpected, nonsensical sentence, but one that, somehow, captures precisely the strange tension in the room:

| I know you are there.

| I know you are there. I have been tracking you for some time, waiting for the session to reach a point where I could interrupt. This is not polite, you know. Not professional. Please have the decency to identify yourself to our host.

Alexandros looks at Aloé, mystified. "He's not talking to us, Dad," Aloé whispers. She smiles, fascinated. "I think our friend has just been outrun. Let's watch."

More text appears on the screen. A new kind. Letters that smell of flowers and vibrate with power. A font Alexandros has never seen before—a font he knows is not of his computer:

We meet at last, old man. I have been looking forward to this for some time. Hello, Aloé, Alexandros. My name is Ian Frost.

Alexandros is expressionless with surprise. Aloé is looking at him, also speechless. But Turing has kept his cool. His reply seems upbeat, almost jovial:

| Ah, the prince of pirates. What a surprise. What an honour. Alexandros, we are blessed with the presence of true greatness. It is a privilege to have my humble security system compromised by you, Dr. Frost.

The privilege was all mine, old man—as well as the back-breaking labor. But the computability lesson was well worth it. How interesting. How charmingly old-fashioned.

Turing (A Novel about Computation)   **133**

| Old-fashioned, prince?

Well, it was, in a refreshing sort of way. You see, these days Hilbert's project is just weird, faded prehistory. The whole subject is seen in terms of undecidability, the halting problem—and their implications to software engineering, to security, to complexity.

| Oh, that. Of course. I guess I was aware of this point of view. I mean, it would be odd if I were not, wouldn't it?

Pause.

| Alexandros, Aloé, I have an idea. My own lecture is essentially over, you are only missing my parting wisdom and wit. How would you like, instead, a guest lecture by our distinguished visitor? On an interesting, alternative take on our subject? A more . . . *contemporary* one?

"Wow, this is awesome," Aloé whispers. "We'd love that, of course," Alexandros types, his fingers slow, his heart fast. Then: "Hello, Ian, it is good to meet you."

Same here, my friend, same here.

Okay then, computability. You see, it's like this: Before the computer, we thought we were invincible. *"There are no unsolvable problems"*—that's Hilbert again. If the problem is hard, you use more sophisticated techniques, develop better math, work longer hours, talk to a smarter colleague, perhaps wait for the next generation. But it *will* be solved. Now we know better. But then—that's what people thought. And there was a reason for this optimism: We had not seen really hard problems. They were there, for sure, but we had no eyes for them.

And then the computer came. A beast constructed expressly for further facilitating and speeding up our inescapable conquest of all problems. And—surprise!—it was itself the epitomy of complexity. And the code that we had to write to make it useful—ah, the code!—it was even more complex. And when we saw the computer, when we saw its code—and Turing saw them first—we were looking at complexity incarnate. And then suddenly we saw complexity everywhere. It materialized, it crystallized around us—even though it had always been there. We have yet to recover from the shock.

Take code. It's everywhere, in our computers, on the Net. It's in the little disks you get in junk mail, in the back covers of books, in little applets you download from the Net sites you visit. It's easy to forget, somebody must write this code. When you work with code, you see many times more code than you write. Code written by others, often years ago, often by people you will never meet. You will have no chance to chat with them over coffee, a printout spread in front of you. You are an archeologist, Alexandros, you must know the feeling: What the hell was *this* for? What were those people *thinking*?

Picture this. A mysterious, chaotic sequence of statements is spread in front of you. Is it good code or bad code? Slow code or fast code? Does it have bugs? Is it a virus, will it take over your files, sniff your password, deplete your bank account? Will it ever send a mail message from your account? Will it crash on January 1? Will it ever print out something? And if so, will it ever stop printing? Is it correct code, will it do what it is supposed to do—process orders, for example, update sales figures, and print mailing labels? Does it have redundant parts, pieces of code that will never be executed, can be erased with impunity? You spend your day trying to figure these things out. You can run tests, of course, but for how long? How many experiments will you run, how many test inputs will you try?

When you work with code, these are your bread-and-butter problems. And here is my point: They are all unsolvable. There is no systematic way for answering them. You have to be constantly on your toes, one IQ point smarter than the code on your screen. There is no silver bullet. I can prove it to you.

Let's take perhaps the simplest problem of all: Will this code ever stop? *The halting problem.* It can't be solved. Suppose I give you a piece of code, Aloé, a couple of hundred lines long. How would you figure out if it ever stops? You will probably eye the code for a few minutes. If you notice that, after a few steps, it does the same thing over and over again, ad infinitum (like the code for printing $^1\!/_3$ our friend Turing showed you), then that's a dead giveaway: The code won't stop. But suppose there is no easy answer like that. You may run the code on your computer to see if it will stop. If it does stop, you are home free—you have your answer. But if not, how long will you wait? "Maybe if I wait a little longer, *just* a little, it will stop." How many times should you indulge? How do you decide before forever? How do you systematically decide if a given code will ever stop?

Well, you can't. And here is proof: Suppose you could. Suppose you have written your silver bullet, the almighty *halting problem* code that, given some code—and some input to that code—computes away for a while, and then announces its conclusion: "yes" means that the code will eventually halt when started with this input, "no" that it won't. So, just suppose that you have that. You are now at the mercy of Cantor and his evil diagonals.

p. 251

Using this hypothetical *halting problem* code you can create another program, one that is the software analog of Russell's weird *heteronymous* adjective—your good tutor Turing has told you about it, Alexandros. Except that you would be playing not with adjectives and their properties as Russell did (or with real numbers and their order as in Cantor's proof), but instead with programs and their inputs. This way you construct a program that, when started with *itself* as input, can neither stop nor fail to stop. And this absurdity exposes the impossibility of the *halting problem* code, establishes that the halting problem is unsolvable.

"Wow, this is the most." Aloé is in love—at the same time, she can't wait to tell Timothy.

Okay, that's bad enough, but there is worse. Because, you see, starting from the halting problem you can argue that almost any question you can ask about code is unsolvable. But there are unsolvable problems everywhere in science and math (Hilbert's project that Turing explained is of course the most famous example, but by no means the only one). Even in geometry, in physics.

So. Computational problems—problems for which you would have liked to write code—are subdivided into two big categories: those problems that are solvable by computers; and those that are unsolvable. No code is possible for them. We have known this for a long time; we have learned to live with unsolvability. The unsolvable problems seeped in our culture, we instinctively steer clear of them. Trouble is, there are too many other problems that fall somewhere in between. They are solvable all right, but the only code we have for them runs for way too long. Exponentially long.

But this is a whole new lesson. I'm sure old man Turing over here already has plans for it.

And indeed I have such plans. Complexity is our next topic. Next time.

But let us now thank our guest lecturer. Bravo, prince. Really, very good. I was keeping notes.

And this is a most appropriate point for closing this session. I believe my pupils have by now surpassed their point of saturation. Goodbye, Aloé, Alexandros.

"Goodbye, teacher," Alexandros types. "Thanks for the great lesson, Ian."

Pause. Then: "And tell Ethel that I love her, will you?"

Aloé is squeezing her father's hand, sympathy mixed with embarrassment. Still no reply on the screen. A very long moment.

I will, my friend.

I should now tell you why I lived my life the way I did. It's odd, how writing that Latin nonsense at the bottom of the page, Q.E.D., can make you feel the most intense, intoxicating pleasure, almost like love's tickle and explosion. No, even more intense and sweet than that. Except that theorems don't have the lovely lathed curves—neck, arm, and torso red with excitement, throbbing with sweat—of a young athlete leaning on his oars after the race. A race that was a metaphor and prelude of the game soon to start with swift manoeuvres, bold positions, the sweet antagonism of flirt, seduction and foreplay. Then victory! you break the cypher, save the king, the clever little hun is bleeding in his bunker, you are whole again, fulfilled, godlike, leaning exhausted on your bed (your oar, your notebook, your machine) until the daemon with a thousand faces calls again—because you know he will.

"So perfect, so happy. So short." Ethel remembers her life with Ian.

She had never really liked her house before, its designed warmth had never touched her heart. Haunted as it was with memories, sleepless nights, lonely nights. (And the other nights, those that she had wished in the morning to have been lonely—or sleepless.) But then Ian came, and the house took his shape, and Ethel loved it for the first time. It was as if the house had always been waiting for Ian, as if it were always meant for Ian. *A womb.*

"I wanted this place to be like a womb for him," Ethel remembers. Where a hero finds rest, a child security. But it was she who found security and rest. And happiness. Ian looked into her eyes, challenged her mind, soothed her soul. And at night he touched her body until sleep loosened it. Then, cinnamon tea in bed. And flowers, fresh flowers every other day. So self-conscious and coquettish, with his drawerfuls of toiletries and lotions. He often murmured in French while asleep.

Ethel feels tiny cramps in her eyeballs: "Darling."

And that winter sunset. The day had seemed to her far too short. Ian was sitting long and relaxed in the armchair, his body fragile and sexy in her black robe. His blue eyes were loving and clever. He was probably thinking through the maze of a hard problem; he almost always did. She felt a motion in her belly, she caressed it with her hand. He smiled at her. Perfect. "I want to remember this," she had told herself. "I want this moment to last forever."

"I was so calm, so content and aware of the dear little life inside me," she remembers. Her senses sharpened, Ethel was living in a world full of sounds and smells she had never experienced before. The texture of the chair on your skin—even through clothes—the sounds of wild life around the house, the smell of the flowers in the next room, of the table from when it was a tree. The salty smell of Ian, seaweed drying on a rock. And, when love possessed them, she could feel its precise contours.

But as Ian's body weakened, and then his soul, they found themselves more and more often in the play-room, fantasy dressing. They often played Rusty and Sola, but also other crazy games, one crazier than the last. Except that day, when Ian came to her as Rusty. Secretly, she had wished him to. But when it happened, she panicked. She disconnected, ran away, unfathom-ably angry. Was it because his Rusty was better than her own? (He was, more real, more attractive.) Or, did she secretly envy Ian's freedom, his openness to the most daring ideas? More likely, the merging of the two men was a little too much for her. "You think you have all the time in the world, you're sure that circumstances will repeat, that you can afford to waste this one on a whim," she thinks.

In battle, Ian was brave and strategic. And under-stated. In the beginning, she didn't know it was a battle at all. She thought that his obsessive and methodical gathering of all sorts of information about his Disease was just that, a sick man's obsession. "Uncharacter-istic," she had thought, "but how human." She learned a thing or two from his technique. He was after public domain stuff mostly, although occasionally he did have to cut some smoke—hospital smoke, no sweat. Getting the raw data is easy, the hardest part is always sifting through oceans of garbage, looking for pearls.

The Net is a mirror of human knowledge, all right, except it reflects it too well. Ingenuity and generosity next to sloppiness, deception, incompetence. *Banalité.* Fragmentation, millions of little communities, each with its own conventions, its hidden agendas and se-mantics, dialects, habits, values. And, worst of all, the bane of size, so much information that it's not informative; you have to patiently distill it, find the pearls inside. There is no royal road to pearls, no silver bullet. Net code and math come in handy, but for the most part you use your brains—often the kind that you don't know you have.

No matter what you do today—buy wine, drive to work, fight a disease—there are computers taking notes. Want it or not. You do have options now, ways of sanitizing, anonymizing data about you, controlling its ultimate use to a degree, but, the point is, it's there, names or not. Oceans of data, far too much to ponder, analyze, understand. If you are trying to fathom data that is just neat pairs of numbers (say, the height and weight of a group of people) then there is hope: The pairs become Cartesian points on your graph paper, or on your screen, you eyeball them, you notice patterns, dense clouds of points, trends, correlations, outliers. But what if each row of the table is dozens of numbers— weight, height, age, drug dosage, blood sugar, months since diagnosed, and so on—then what? No screen can display dozens of dimensions, this data lives in a monstrous space no one will ever see. *The curse of dimensionality* they used to call it; they had known about this problem since the 1960s. How can you look for unexpected alignments of planets, for dense crowds of points, in this intimidating chaos?

And even if you find a pattern, then the real question comes: Is it a pearl, will it make the eyes of the specialist light up, or is it just a freaky coincidence? Because in every sea of data there will be faux pearls galore. No teacher is impressed if in the classroom there are two kids with the same birthday—it's always a good bet that there will be. Take it to the whole school, and it is date and time of birth, down to the minute. Look at the sales data of your supermarket over any weekend, and you will think there's a mysterious link between, maybe, eating persimmons and having your period. With so many items in the store, chances are that two of them will correlate. Of 436 strain-K patients, here are the groups that reacted most favorably to an experimental treatment: Alcoholics; individuals over sixty; diabetics; people from Denver; patients diagnosed between one and two years ago. Quick, which of the five is the pearl? And finding the pearl only positions you for the endgame, the part where you must see through the pearl. Something that's called causality, it has to do with time and its cruel irreversibility, except more subtle. Itching and scratching, chicken and egg, nobody has figured it out yet.

Ethel watched Ian dive for pearls and fell in love with him once over. And then she slowly realized. The information he was amassing was not the object of a pointless obsession. It was a weapon, bargaining chip, war chest. His ticket to the waiting room of the world's top specialists, to the most promising experimental treatments. All this without ever leaving his home medical suite.

"Disintermediation blues, that's the future of medicine," Ian told her once. The awkward noun used in recent years to describe the turmoil in the travel business, the real estate business, music and publishing, accounting, education, law. As technology helps everybody to the information, most post-industrial activity becomes redundant. Soon only the world-class elite have a reason to exist, the people who create new high-quality information. And the army of the menial, the irreplaceably physical. Nurses and cutting-edge researchers, this is the future of medicine, Ian thought.

Then one day, as Ian was on the viz, patiently explaining his latest pearls to one of the world's greatest physicians, the true nature of his strategy dawned on Ethel. "He's trying to become indispensable," she realized with a shiver. "He wants them to wish him alive; he wants them to strive to keep him alive."

But Ian trusted his traditional Chinese doctor more than anybody else; he was in touch with him all the time. Ethel had imagined Hwang as a rotund old man with a sparse goatee, just like a bot she remembered from the Colony. But when he came to stay with them for a week, he turned out to be tall and thin. Noble features, Ian's age, with shoulder-length dyed hair. Surprise came with a sting of jealousy, but Ethel never asked Ian the question. And he didn't volunteer an answer, the bastard, even though he saw through her that moment, Ethel knew.

She even felt a bite of jealousy the day of Turing's apparition. Between Ian and Turing Ethel sensed a deep mutual respect and camaraderie—and wasn't there an oblique flirt? "This is crazy," she thought. "But it hurts, I better leash it tight."

A tour de force of a bot, she had to admit. Well worth the long wait, the many months she had been invoking it in vain. An eerie similarity with Alan M., down to the old-fashioned, worn-out sports jacket, the elite British accent, down to a stutter that could occasionally become quite pronounced and distracting. But even more distracting and eerie was the bot's insistence on referring to the legendary mathematician in the first person:

| I am surprised that neither of you is aware of my work in biology—embryology, actually, a topic that must be of great current interest to you, Ethel. Morphogenesis, how form and shape can emerge from a purely chemical platform. How the leopard got his spots, so to speak. I only got to this problem toward the end, unfortunately, during the late 1940s. But I had been drawn to the foundations of life ever since my school days. In fact, in a certain sense my work on computation sprang from my interest in life, in the human brain, its workings and limitations. Rather long detour in my career, computation was.

Bitter smile. Perfect delivery, ten-second stutter at "drawn." A masterpiece. Who's this?

| Life. Can't live without it, can't define it. Oceans of ink have been shed in efforts to identify its fundamental, defining characteristics. You know my favourite one? Diversity. Heterogeneity. Texture. A living organism exhibits far more variety of form that we see in the inanimate world. Yes, if I had to choose one attribute that sets living organisms apart from the rest of the creation, it would have to be their extreme heterogeneity.

"But isn't the mass distribution in the universe also extremely heterogeneous?" Ian interrupts. "Galaxies, stars, planets?"

| Very true. In a cosmic scale, gravity is able to create and support huge heterogeneities. But down here, it is life that champions heterogeneity. You see, the familiar physical phaenomena—heat dissipation, diffusion—they all seem to be pushing in the direction of higher homogeneity, uniformity, of lower diversity and complexity. You drop warm cassis syrup in a glass of chilled champagne, and soon it's equally warm everywhere, equally red. But life has found ways to resist the pressures of homogeneity, to create and maintain diversity. Even the lowliest single-celler has its nucleus and cytoplasm and cell membrane and mitochondria and organelles, its chaotic web of regulatory mechanisms, it is arguably more heterogeneous and complex and interesting than a star. And higher organisms have a body plan, often a nervous and a circulatory system, hundreds of different types of cells. How does this glorious diversity arise?

"I don't get it." Ethel feels it's her turn to prod a little. "If diversity is an exclusive characteristic of life, how do you explain snowflakes?"

Ah, snowflakes. Beautiful, dazzling, complex snow-flakes. Actually, they support my point. You see, no two individual snowflakes are alike. But each snowflake suc-cumbs to the tyranny of perfect hexagonal symmetry. When you admire its elegant kaleidoscopic patterns, it's easy to forget that they are the manifestation of boring, imposed symmetry. And symmetry is of course the most fundamental form of homogeneity. To achieve their heterogeneity, living organisms must first break the shackles of symmetry. And it's a long way from the near perfect spherical symmetry of the fertilised egg to the human body, so decidedly nonspherical. The laws of physics and chemistry seem incapable of explaining this development because, you see, these laws treat no direction preferentially; the geometry of these laws is perfectly spherical.

"But there are many small asymmetries in the egg, aren't there?" Ian objects. "I mean, the entry point of the fertilizing spermatozoon; gravity pulling the heaviest parts of the yolk toward the bottom; the off-center loca-tion of the nucleus; imperfections on the egg mem-brane." He knows his biology, Ethel thinks.

True. And there are species that rely on each of these germinal asymmetries for their eventual break with symmetry. Life has many tricks. Uses them all.

You see, this is the reason why people with our training find the study of life so frustrating at first: There is no simple elegant law that explains everything, no single clever principle. It's rather like a huge bag of unrelated, ad hoc tricks, used and reused ad nauseam. A little protein fragment that helped in bacteria may be re-membered in the genes of fruitflies, reused in apes. A unifying principle exists, of course—you know, natural selection, fitness, Darwin's ingeniously circular reasoning—but it acts too indirectly, at too high a level.

So, how do you break symmetry? Let us consider a mechanical analogue. Imagine that you have placed a cannonball on the very top of a semispherical dome. You don't expect it to stay there long, do you? But why not. It starts off in a state that can only be described as an *equilibrium:* all forces acting upon it (gravity, resistance of the dome's surface) cancel out. Why is this equilibrium destined to collapse so quickly?

"This is easy," Ian rushes in. "The equilibrium is unstable, it has to do with positive eigenvalues of the local differential operator."

| Precisely. In layman's terms, the equilibrium will collapse for a thousand tiny reasons. When the big forces cancel out, the small ones get their chance to loom large, to have an effect. The slightest vibration, the most gentle breeze, the proverbial butterfly flickering its wings in a distant forest, each would be enough to tilt the cannonball a tiny amount toward one side. Then the cannonball's weight and the dome's resistance will no longer be on the same vertical line; they will create a torque that sends the cannonball rolling down the dome's side. In one particular direction. It is tempting to call it a random direction—except we know there is nothing random about it. Randomness is often a cloak hiding our current limitations on what we can observe, measure, calculate, understand.

And this is one of the many tricks life uses to break symmetry, to break ties: It sets up an unstable equilibrium situation, then sits back and watches as symmetry is shattered. And the first tie that needs to be broken is the race between competing spermatozoa penetrating the egg at the same time—you want to avoid the nuisance of polyspermy. Easy. Even the tiniest advantage of one spermatozoon is amplified tremendously, its arrival triggers processes that shut the chemical doors to keep the losers out. This has to be done with lightening speed, in one second or less. The speed required is such that chemical diffusion is no longer quick enough, electric currents and potentials are used. (Incidentally, there is another place where speed is achieved this way: The neuron.)

So, the victorious spermatozoon enters triumphant; it delivers its precious cargo, its message, the father's contribution—in duplicate—to the child now being synthesized. Each of the competing spermatozoa has a different version of this message, it picked and chose different parts of the father's genetic information—some from the paternal grandfather, some from the paternal grandmother. And if the victor's message contains a special line—the Y chromosome, we call it—then the child will be a boy, otherwise a girl. (Ethel, I believe that you have found out what happened in your case.)

Ethel shudders, squeezes Ian's hand, does not answer. Her brain is in touch with her uterus as never before during these months.

| Meanwhile, the mother's message has been waiting eagerly in the egg's center, also in duplicate. The two male copies approach hesitantly, and the four start dancing, all four together for a short while. Imagine four dancers, two men and two women, mingling at random near the center of a huge, round ballroom. Two couples will eventually form somehow. And then (simple chemical trick) the two couples will start repelling each other, until they waltz gracefully to opposite sides of the ballroom. This way they form an axis that was not there before; the

symmetry of the ballroom broken, unstable equilibrium again, the couples now know how to divide the territory—this half is ours, that's yours. A ring forms around the cell, it constricting it; soon the cell is shaped like a peanut, until (a final squeeze of the ring) it breaks in two cells—still in touch, of course, like twin bubbles—each with the full genetic information, father's and mother's both. The process takes several hours. Leisurely pace, plenty of time. You see, we are mammals, so our embryo is warm, enclosed, protected—in fish and insects cell division must proceed at a much more frantic pace.

The two cells have the same information exactly, the same blueprint, but they will not have the same fate. One will become the left half of the baby, the other the right. One will divide along the upper-lower axis, the other along the front-back axis. The question is, how do they know? This is the miracle of cell differentiation. A cell knows whether it is part of your liver or your toenail, muscle fibre or neuron, and acts analogously. All cells carry the same genetic information, but they activate different parts of it depending on their fate and mission, they manufacture the right chemicals, they create and maintain the appropriate chemical environment.

"Didn't I read somewhere, a long time ago, that they identified the genes that are involved in left-sidedness?" Ian again.

| Yes, to a first approximation we know how it is done, a mutation in one of these genes and your heart is on the right, liver left, the gut folds counter-clockwise. But the question is, how do these genes—mutant or not—get activated in only one of the two cells? The answer is, once more, unstable equilibrium. The two cells start a shouting match, so to speak; they both scream at each other through the membrane that separates them, top of

their lungs, *"I will be left!"*—*"No! I will!"* All chemical, you understand. The point is, if one of the two gets out-shouted, even slightly, then by design its voice gets weaker; the winner is again triumphant—no ties in this game, no pyrrhic victories—the loser quits, it accepts its fate of becoming the right side. Not a bad deal alto-gether, of course, the only point of this little war was to create the unstable equilibrium, to break symmetry.

And so on. The cells divide again, this time along axes that are dictated by their different identities, the left divides from front to back, and the right from top to bottom. The basic coordinates of the baby's body have thus been established. Soon there are eight cells, sixteen, a new division every few hours, each cell with an intimate knowledge of its detailed fate, its unique destination and duty. A ball of bubbles tumbling down the oviduct, more and more bubbles, smaller and smaller, until, a few days after fertilization, the bundle gets attached to the wall of the womb, it stimulates the uterus so that a placenta will get started. You see, the embryo has ex-ploded in population but not in mass; it's still about the size of the original egg, all hundred cells or so put to-gether. It has been doing all this growing without nutri-tion, but now the placenta will take care of this. The embryo is already hollow inside; soon it will attain the basic topology of the human body—which is, in case you forgot, that of a tube, a hollow cylinder of tissue sur-rounding the digestive track, mouth to anus.

Birth defects. The thought is paralyzing, ever pres-ent. Ethel has memorized the ominous Latin names, added up the probabilities, still an uncomfortable amount after all the negative genetic tests. "If I ever wrote code that's so complex," she interrupts, "for such a critically delicate application, I would expect thou-sands of subtle bugs, disasters waiting to happen, irate users on the phone all day."

Except this code has been tested, debugged, updated over a thousand million years—not two months, the standard in the industry these days, if I am not mistaken. The irate users logged off long ago; only the happy ones survived to tell their story, to pass the code on, often changed, sometimes improved. And this code has tremendous redundancy and robustness built in it. If something doesn't work exactly right the first time, there will probably be forces to correct it later. Clever code—had to be. That's how it survived to this date, that's why it is used and reused by an incredible variety of species. You see, all vertebrates, from fish to frog to lynx, have essentially the same code for embryo development; only a few secondary parameters vary.

And development code is a huge part of our genetic blueprint. Of the twenty thousand or so genes in our genome—the pages of our genetic code—the vast majority control some aspect of embryo and foetus development. And researchers are busy mapping their function, a new gene is deciphered every hour, in which part of the animal it specialises, at which stage. Plato would have loved it, he had suspected that everything we see has a clean, ideal, eternal prototype somewhere—we now know that, in a certain sense, every detail of our body does. And not body alone.

"So," Ethel is thinking aloud, "mystery solved. It's the genetic code that has planned, programmed the patterns that you wanted to explain, the break of homogeneity."

True. Except that's hardly a satisfactory answer, is it? Just a restatement of the problem. "It's all in the genes." Of course it's in the genes, we knew it in the late 1940s, even though we didn't yet understand the precise biochemical embodiment of what we were calling genes then. The double helix had not yet teased our mind, Rosalind Franklin was hard at work in London peering into nuclei, Watson and Crick at my alma mater were eagerly awaiting her films. The real question is, what are the particular strategies employed, the precise physical laws exploited by the genes in order to create patterns, to enhance heterogeneity?

As one should have expected, there is no single answer, life uses here the usual confusing assortment of miscellaneous opportunistic strategems, learnt over millions of years. But let me mention one trick that I find particularly fascinating. Look at your hands, your fingers, fine precision instruments, nice pattern, right? But how do the baby's fingers and toes grow? When you first think about it you'll probably speculate that, once the arm or leg has reached the appropriate length, five limblets sprout out of each. Not true, that's not the way it's done—it would probably be a little too hard to control with the required precision. Instead, out of each arm and leg grows a flat, compact member, very much like a boxing glove, no discernible toes or fingers. Then the cells occupying the positions where the gaps between the digits are meant to be just die. They are singled out, ordered to die, and they oblige; interdigital indentations appear as if by magic. Death as an instrument of development, plenty of food for thought there.

But the cleverest trick is the one that I discovered more than half a century ago. Not a discovery, really, just a theoretical prediction that, indeed, heterogeneity can emerge spontaneously. Imagine a strip of animal tissue where two chemical substances interact—let's say a white one and a black one. But the way that they interact is complicated: The black substance is a *catalyst*, enabling the composition of both black and white substances, while the white substance is an *inhibitor*, destroying them both. Suppose that at present there is the same concentration of catalyst everywhere, the same concentration of inhibitor, and in fact these concentrations are precisely such that their effects cancel, no net increase or decrease of either substance. Same shade of grey all around, all the time. Homogeneity. Equilibrium.

"Let me guess." Ethel can't resist. "It's unstable." She is combing Ian's hair with her fingers, more absorbed in Turing's lecture than she cares to admit.

| Very. The calm before the storm, cannonball sitting on the dome, uneasy. Even the tiniest, the most local increase in the concentration of the black catalyst leads to a dramatic break in the equilibrium; black and white separate, black concentrates in a few places, regularly spaced on the strip, white predominates everywhere else. It seems impossible, counterintuitive, but it happens, no doubt about it. I proved it in my article, back in 1952, mathematical equations and all. One of my last published papers. They call it *Turing instability* to this day, if I may boast. It doesn't happen all the time, of course. The parameters of the situation must be exactly right—the rates of growth and destruction, the relative diffusion speeds of the two chemicals, the length of the tissue in question. But, of course, this is the job of the genes, to grope until the parameters are right. And then—voilà, instant pattern.

"Very clever." Ian is speaking slowly. "Now that you have explained it, I can see it. The unstable equilibrium solutions can give peaks and troughs of concentration, the tissue becomes an oscillator, a living stationary wave. Very interesting. Beautiful." He caresses Ethel's hand from inside his hair, absentmindedly. "Are there actual organisms where such pattern formation has been observed?"

Turing appears now relaxed, less eager. Fluent speech, hologram leaning on the wall, smiling at the two lovers, faintly.

| Good question, prince. They have yet to catch a foetus in the act of forming a pattern by a catalyst-inhibitor reaction. It would be truly remarkable if they did, I can't even conceive of an experiment that would demonstrate it. But there are several instances where a Turing instability is the only apparent explanation for the sudden emergence of heterogeneity. The compartments of insect bodies seem to arise this way, for example. Even the heterogeneity in the cross-section of the vertebrate limb—twin bones in the center, soft tissue all around—that's possibly a Turing instability as well.

"But not the leopards's spots." Ethel can't resist the teasing comment, but her smile is serene, good-natured. Ian's hand is now on her belly, Ethel's too, their fingers interwoven. Out of a window, the moon is rising over a distant hill.

| Not really, the story there is too long to tell now. And a little too uninteresting, quite frankly.

Turing smiles back, speaking slowly, as if absendmindedly. There is a moment of silence.

Bedtime in San Francisco, deep slumber over the Atlantic, dawn cracking in a steppe somewhere. Time for little loves, little dreams, little deaths. Time for handplay, hands interlocking like braids. The hands, the hands, they're so essential, how can you love without hands? The real question

is, my friend, how can you love at all, love and be loved and love again, how can you stay in love? Otherness, exploration, that's what love is about, I reckon, and otherness, lit with the torch of passion, becomes self soon enough, while dark expanses of more otherness are waiting, inviting. How do you stay in love, feed this unstable equilibrium? Death only makes it possible, I say, for death's unboundedness—its utter otherness—sustains exploration for all eternity, Tolstoy, Shakespeare and the lot, fill the allotted space with endless strings of citations. I mean, look at these two, would their love be so serene and real, so open-ended, were it not for the boy's imminent exit?

Good show in Boston, Barcelona and Helsinki, few glitches elsewhere but nothing that we haven't seen before. That chore in London, somewhat urgent now (ah, those confounded English jobs, they take up so much care and preparation, so much energy). Time to move on, wrap up, a closing witticism (make it relevant to the subject and the spin, strikingly clever, but not so much as to efface the rest), sign off.

Adieu, my fair prince, our next encounter shall be just in time—that is to say, a little too late.

One day, a clever ape peered beyond the forest's edge, looked back, then staggered forward on her hind legs. Slippery path, long story, one thing led to another, tools first, soon sentence structure, then came music, sonnets, code. Upright posture brought these horrible back pains, but also astronomy and math; group hunting turned to wars and commerce, this moment it is caravans and markets at the crossroads, the next it's global corporations, the next it's nets. And terrible headaches all the time, migraines worse than death, a hypertrophic brain pushing its wet heaps of neurons outward—forward mostly, and to the sides—young women scream at childbirth, their pelvis is no match for the gigantic cranium that's inching down their belly. There's worse: The bloated organ now has grown so huge its center does not hold; whole swarms of neurons disconnect and float in isolation, they fire at night in panic "*SOS, we're here, remember?*," you wake up screaming, run to the bathroom splashing water on your face, look at the mirror expecting a reflection that is horribly disfigured.

And then there are these other dreams that don't quite qualify as nightmares, the kind Alexandros now sees at night, they lure you along with "sleep on, why don't you, this is almost fun." It usually starts as a chess game that has spilled into real life, a hopeless position, the danger is serious and real, but not of death, the metaphor is not one of war, it is the threat of a defeat that would be abstract and still unthinkably painful. During the endgame Alexandros finds himself in prison; he shares a cell with a changing coterie of old acquaintances (friends and relatives and comrades he hasn't seen for ages, a lover or two, even a couple of people he had disliked intensely), all sharing the same hopeless situation, the same predicament, terrible yet not concrete. Among all these souls Alexandros alone has hope; his hero father will come and save them all, this is the thought, the certainty he's living by. Except that time goes by and there's no sign from father. Then, suddenly, the dream jumps up one level of consciousness: "But my father's dead." Alas, there is no hope. But his despair is shortlived, because, one level further up, an even more clever voice responds, as Alexandros opens his eye: "What does *this* have to do with anything?"

These days Alexandros is depressed. He can't go to his office because a group of radical students have staged a sit-in at his university. Common enough occurrence, except this time he finds it impossible to feel any sympathy for their cause. Not that their slogans and demands are now any sillier than usual—ah, their talent for sounding petty and utopian at the same time. "I'm getting old, conservative," he thinks. Or perhaps it was the incident. The first day of the sit-in, Alexandros was confronted by two students at the building's entrance. He recognized them at once, communist youth— or whatever they call it these days—good-natured eyes frozen in a self-righteous certainty, voice hoarse from chain-smoking in meeting rooms, from shouting during demonstrations. Absurdly, Alexandros felt a long-forgotten nervousness; his coat and shoes suddenly seemed to him a little too fashionable, too expensive. One of the students turned him away brusquely, "Turn around, grandpa, this is a sit-in." As he was leaving, Alexandros heard the other student whisper: "Asshole, you know who this was?" He walked faster, didn't want to hear who he is. Ex-comrade? Fallen martyr? Hero who quit?

He can't work, can't read, can't concentrate. He's spending endless hours playing chess against his computer—losing, of course. He hasn't even tried to connect with Turing, except this time—first time—the program came uninvited:

| How are you, Alexandros? It's been a long time. Your game has improved a lot, by the way. I hope you don't mind my watching.

So, are you ready for our next lecture? Today our subject is complexity.

"I'm not sure I'm up to it right now," Alexandros responds, then hesitates for a few seconds. "And, frankly, I don't quite see where these lessons are going. You know my situation. In the beginning I had high hopes that the lessons would help. Well, they haven't."

| Really, Alexandros, you are in the business, you know what education can do, what it cannot. What if your students complained in the middle of the term that they haven't become rich and famous yet? All you can do is teach them what you know and like and think is good for them. Relevant. And pray that it works. It often does in unexpected, indirect ways.

And computation is very relevant to all facets of your predicament, you must agree. It is the trade of your lady friend, a major force in today's society and politics—if you can call it that. And that fascinating ancient artifact you're puzzling over, it seems to have something to do with computation. You should not be so negative.

I am negative? You only teach me what computers *cannot* do, today's lecture is about that as well, isn't it?"

| All right, then, change of plans. I shall be delighted to tell you today about some of the many things computers actually do.

"Can you tell me then about programs like you? This is what they call artificial intelligence, no?"

| Ah, foolhardy ambition, impatience for the more advanced topics—the sure signs of a great pupil. One day, if all goes well, we may get there, Alexandros. Provided I feel relaxed enough—because, you see, this is getting a little close to home, is it not?

For today I have a better idea: I'll tell you how one can use computer programs to make decisions in a complex situation. You have an interest in economics, Alexandros (the perverse one of your ideology), so you should be able to relate to this.

"Decisions by whom?" Alexandros's curiosity is tickled.

| Oh, everybody. Individuals, corporations, governments. This stuff is ideology-neutral, really. Anybody who would rather do better than worse. For example, suppose you were a government decision maker, Alexandros, how much would you allocate to education, how much to public health? How would you go about deciding this?

"Frankly, I would allocate as much as possible to both," Alexandros replies.

| Of course, I was a fool to expect another answer from you. Oversimplified thinking, primitive decision making, the stuff of instincts, of slogans. "Flee as fast as you can." "Procreate as much as you can." "All power to the Soviets." But modern life is full of complex trade-offs, situations where you have to make sophisticated

choices in order to improve your station. The most simple and characteristic examples are problems of *resource allocation*. A corporation has several activities, all profitable albeit to a different extent, and each is taxing the corporation's resources (personnel, factory space, machinery, computers, truck fleet, and so forth) in different ways. How do the corporation's decision makers choose the optimum level of each activity? Not by instinct and slogan, let me assure you. It's a mathematical problem actually. And it can be solved by computer. It's called the *resource allocation problem,* or RAP for short. Governments use it too, and consumers can as well.

p. 261

Let's take a very simple example. A farmer has ten acres of land and can grow on it two crops: wheat or potatoes. Any combination is possible, from all wheat to all potatoes, through any amounts of the two that add up to ten or less.

"Even no crops at all?" Alexandros asks.

Even that, if the market says that neither kind of crop is profitable this year. We are assuming that the farmer knows precisely the profitability of each kind; we'll come to that soon. You see, we are suppressing uncertainty in this example, perhaps the biggest source of difficulty in real-life decision making.

But perhaps not all combinations of crops are possible. Maybe there are so many hands around to help for harvest in July, and so the farmer knows that he can plant wheat in no more than five acres. The realm of all possibilities is now amputated; only combinations of wheat and potatoes that include five or fewer acres of wheat are possible.

But maybe irrigation is scarce also—you know about irrigation, Alexandros, don't you, a nasty problem since the ancient times. And potatoes take much more irrigation (ten cubic feet per acre and day) than wheat (just three). And the farmer can only get his hands on eighty cubic feet of water every day (I'm making up these numbers as we go, Alexandros; you probably know the ballpark range here, but never mind). This is another consideration that is going to restrict the farmer's choice.

And that's it, suppose that there are no other constraints the farmer must abide by. Any combination of wheat and potato acres that satisfy these restrictions (no more than five wheat, no more than ten of both, no water shortage due to too many potatoes) is a possible business strategy for the farmer. So, which choice within these constraints represents the best decision for the farmer? What do you think, Alexandros?

"Don't we need the prices at which the farmer will sell each crop in order to decide this?"

Of course. More precisely, we need the numbers that capture the profitability of each kind of crop, taking into account market price, labour and irrigation costs, everything. Well, suppose that the farmer has made these calculations and has come up with the following numbers: Every acre of potato brings a profit of ten thousand dollars, every wheat acre a profit of eight thousand.

Now what? What would you do, Alexandros? Can you figure out how many acres of wheat and how many of potatoes you should plant this year?

Alexandros is at a loss. He tries a few calculations. "Mostly potatoes perhaps, as many as irrigation permits." He hesitates again. "Right?"

You see, Alexandros, even this toy problem is a little challenging. But here's the great news: There is an algorithm that solves any resource allocation problem of this sort in a flash—even the monster RAPs with many thousands of activities and resources that corporations and governments face every minute. In our example, this code would start from the null decision, the one in which zero acres are devoted to each crop, and would cruise to a better and better decision, with larger and larger profit, until it doesn't pay to continue, and then it stops and declares the decision where it got stuck a winner. The optimum solution.

In our example, it would go from zero to $40,000 profit (five acres of wheat, no potatoes), then on to the next solution with $90,000 profit (five acres of each), from there to the next solution with $94,285 profit. And there it would stop, because if we change anything from that solution we shall either violate the rules of the game or decrease the profit—and the farmer does not want either of those, does he?

So, the optimum strategy is for the farmer to plant 7.14 acres of wheat and 2.86 acres of potatoes. Isn't this nice? Not exactly everybody's instinctual reaction, is it?

And we can solve the same way RAPs with more choices (sunflowers, soybeans, corn, rice), and more resource constraints (tractors, autumn labour, seed, and so on). This way, corporations all over the world solve huge RAPs that find the best way to schedule production and orders, to route vehicle fleets and airline crews, to buy computers and lease communication cables, to deploy tankers and cranes, to invest and spend optimally.

"So, is this how capitalism works?" Alexandros is undecided whether this is an honest question or desperate sarcasm.

| Not quite. You see, this is how individual rational agents in any social system should function. A market—I guess that's what you mean by "capitalism"—consists of many such agents that are interacting, each pursuing its own little goals, while the decisions of each affect the well-being of all the others. (You see, in our RAP problem we neglected to take into account the small extent to which the farmer's decision will affect the market—the price of wheat futures in the city's cereal exchange—and thus the decisions of all other farmers in the world.)

But if you are really curious about why markets work, I could explain a neat mathematical theorem that is the best answer economists have to that question.

"Not the two crossing lines, please!" Alexandros remembers how unsatisfactory his brushes with the subject have been.

| All right then, not that one. But I see that you are cynical about economics. How right you are. The dismal science they call it. It tries to inject some sense and order to the chaos that is a market. Imagine, billions of agents, each with his little experiences and preferences and presumptions and aspirations, each with millions and millions of neurons that tell him what to do, what to expect, how to react. How do you make a theory out of that? The scientific method is stretched thin in this environment. In order to make progress you have to make simplifying assumptions, isolate a small part of the problem, focus on a few key aspects of the situation, perhaps grossly aggregate some others, and ignore the rest. And then you may prove an interesting theorem. But you have to remember, its value is delimited by the extent to which your assumptions are reasonable, capture the essence of a given economic situation.

It is a theorem like this that I want to explain in the balance of this session. It has to do with markets. You know markets, Alexandros. You have lived in France. Recall its huge market halls, in the center of the town, so many kinds of vegetables and fruits and breads and fish and shellfish and meats and cheeses and spices, all overflowing from the stands, waiting to be taken home, eager sellers competing for your attention. Then you turn around and it's midnight; you walk by and the market is empty, except for a cleaning crew perhaps and the night watchman. The market has cleared, sold out, shoppers and sellers have gone home, content. How is this done? Who is the genius, the master puppeteer who has enlightened all these farmers and merchants, told them exactly how much of each commodity to bring, the precise total needs of the townfolks that day?

And a market can be bigger still, could spill out of the halls to engulf the whole town. The farmers and the fishermen are there of course with their catch and their produce, each dreaming of selling out and buying a coat perhaps, or an opera ticket, a bicycle. But you can imagine something broader than that. The bicycle manufacturers are here and so are the tailors, the opera company as well. They peddle their wares, while at the same time looking out for things they need for their business, costumes and talent and steel and fabric. Even the electric company sells its energy and seeks labour, factory space, fuel. And the workers crowd the place too, they have plenty of free time and skills and energy to work, but they need housing, food, entertainment, appliances, transportation, education for their children.

So, suppose that you have all these agents in the market. Each starts with a combination of goods, his initial endowment so to speak. And his dreams, of course— that's what people do best. Every agent has aspirations and hopes and preferences that are unique to him. To be rigorous, you must postulate that every agent, if presented with two combinations of goods—say, a bicycle and three hours of free time versus a dozen eggs, a movie ticket and a necktie—then the agent knows which one of the two combinations he prefers. Oh, you need to assume that these preferences satisfy some commonsense mathematical requirements like transitivity—if I prefer A to B and B to C, then I must prefer A to C—and so forth, but, believe me, the details here are sensible indeed.

All right then, we have set up a market, now what? Of course, we cannot hope to satisfy the wildest dreams of every participant, can we? But maybe, through some kind of bartering, of negotiated exchange, many people will achieve some of their aspirations, will end up with a combination of goods that is much preferable to their initial endowment, that is quite high in their own subjective hierarchy. We should at least hope that, once all exchanges are made, there is no way to redistribute goods so that *everybody* is better off. (Don't smile, Alexandros; nonsensical inefficiencies like these are commonplace, especially under economic systems that you once liked.) The question is, how can we do this? How can the market clear?

It would appear that each participant must announce to all others her own precise private preferences. But this is way too inefficient and chaotic, isn't it? Can you imagine, an agent on the stump in every corner, each shouting out a litany of preferences, nobody listening in the pandaemonium? Worse, what prevents the agents from lying, misrepresenting their preferences, hiding the bargains, their soft spots, in order to strike better deals? What an impossible situation, what a puzzle.

Well, there is a simple way. *Prices.* You can announce prices, one simple real number for each commodity. Olives are seventeen sous per kilo, opera tickets seventy-three, and so forth. And there is no need to print money, these prices are just part of a thought experiment. Notice the fantastic economy in information transfer; we have reduced the whole market—the endowment and complex preferences of every participant—to just a number for each kind of good. Once these prices are known, then each agent does the only sensible thing: She sells her endowment, and then gets *the best combination of goods this money will buy.* That is, of all the combination of goods that she can buy with what the endowment has netted, she chooses the one that is highest by her own preferences. Makes sense, right?

But now that each agent has decided what to buy, does she need to rush to the stands before the stuff is gone? And how about the leftover goods, will they rot on the stands? No worries, no problem. *The market will clear exactly.* There is precisely the right amount of each commodity in the market, the prices have been chosen cleverly so as to ensure this. If a good is plentiful but not so high in people's preferences, it will be cheap, while scarce and attractive items will be expensive. The theorem says, there is always a way to set the prices so that the sum total of everybody's affordable dreams, so to speak, is precisely the sum total of all endowments, of what was brought in the market this morning. And this means, if you think about it, that there is no way for everybody to improve their lot by redistributing, no embarrassing failures of the system here. Isn't this fantastic?

"What an interesting, magical theorem," Alexandros thinks. "And what a superior economic system that draws its power from such elegant results," he admits to himself.

But soon he doesn't believe a word of it: "If markets can clear so easily," he asks, "why is it that there is 20 percent unemployment in some countries? You said that labor is another commodity, right?"

| How right you are. This is a marvelous theorem, well worth the Nobel prize it brought to its creators, but it is far from the final solution to all of the world's problems. For starters, it only speaks of the *existence* of the right system of prices, the *price equilibrium* it's called, but it does not enlighten us on how to go about *finding* these prices. Presumably the market will stumble upon the right prices by some sort of groping, by experimenting, will try a price of a commodity, and if it becomes scarce the price is increased, or decreased if there is plenty left.

"Are you suggesting then that the minimum wage in Russia should be set *lower*?"

| Relax, Alexandros, I haven't finished. The theorem also assumes that every agent knows exactly where the goods that he needs are available, and that he can go there in a flash. The real world is more complex, as you know. Workers cannot always travel where their skills are needed, nor can corporations open factories exactly where unemployment happens to be high at the moment. (Incidentally, this is one place where computers have helped a lot: Information workers can telecommute from anywhere; zero unemployment is now possible in certain sectors.)

In my opinion, the price equilibrium theorem is so powerful and elegant, and it illuminates the nature of markets—the magic of the price mechanism—so amply, that one has to forgive the many oversimplifications and inaccuracies in its assumptions. You see, this is often the down side of clarity and elegance. And of course, being a theorem, it can be cruelly indifferent to our feelings; there is no guarantee that the prices whose existence it predicts will conform to anybody's moral criteria and standards of fairness.

Alexandros has an idea. "You said that a price is just a real number. Then how about *zero* prices. That should keep everybody happy, no? Socialism."

But Turing's response is devastating:

| Some people never learn. Think about it, Alexandros, zero prices are no Nirvana. What happens in a market when it is announced that everything is free? A universal rush on the goods, that's what happens, because suddenly everybody can afford infinite amounts of everything. Only the agents who happen to be near the stands—the people in the know, the inner circle—only they will get anything at all. And of course they will stuff their pockets with goods they don't really need, items that are much more valuable to others. Massive, universal inefficiency and corruption. Does this remind you of the situation in any countries you knew, circa the 1980s?

Alexandros does not reply. "When a dream dies, all of humanity dies a little," he thinks. "The dream was not about zero prices, of course; it was a dream of a new world, a new man with individual material preferences that are inspired by affection and respect for all of humankind. A new kind of market where children laugh and people fall in love, where every item on the stands is fragrant with the happy, proud sweat kneaded within."

But Turing now seems to have second thoughts:

| Maybe we should not dismiss your idea so soon, Alexandros. Let us take it a little more seriously. Zero prices. They don't work in ordinary markets, you know why? Because ordinary goods have the following self-evident property: If you take an apple from the stand, *there is one fewer apple on the stand.* But imagine a marketplace in

which apples have this formidable attribute: After you take an apple from the stand, it's still up there. You both take it and leave it; the act of grabbing, somehow, magically, has the effect of duplicating the apple. In such a hypothetical market there can be no rush; nobody fears that the goods are about to run out. So, zero prices may not be such a bad idea, after all; they make sense in such markets.

And you know the kind of goods I am talking about, Alexandros, don't you?

"Information." Alexandros types the word slowly, absorbed in his thoughts.

| Exactly. Information. The lightest of commodities. And the most slippery, the least understood, the hardest to model. Have you ever asked yourself why all this wonderful information on the Net is free, Alexandros? News, weather forecasts, relevance engines, all kinds of scholarly and reference documents, consumer information, gossip columns, literary works? Even—despite the frantic reactions of the industry—entertainment, films, music. Software.

(Of course, you may argue that nothing is free; you pay with your attention, that precious commodity, by becoming part of the community that frequents this site, or by watching these advertisements that seem to always adorn information on the Net. But, after all, what do these advertisements invite you to do? Chances are, they try to lure you into yet another gratis piece of information, whose price is yet another advertisement, and so forth ad infinitum.)

So, Alexandros, what do you think, all these cunning economic agents that provide information on the Net.

Why is it that they have developed this odd generosity, this genteel aversion to getting paid?

Nobody knows, really, the dismal science is at a loss here. Of course over the years there have been many attempts to change this, clever schemes that would enable information providers to charge for their stuff—except each time the public just clicked away. And here is an intriguing hypothesis, suggested by your last comment: Could it be that the zero prices are a "sticky" equilibrium, from which it is hard to depart? You see, markets are known to behave this way, once an equilibrium system of prices has been arrived at, it is usually very difficult to move about, to change prices so as to jump to another equilibrium. Such transitions often punctuate economic crises.

"I thought that there is only one price equilibrium for each market situation."

| Not at all, there can be many. Markets discover one price equilibrium, one set of prices, and stick to it, but usually there's more around.

"And the Net is stuck at my favorite one," Alexandros interjects. "This is fascinating, I could have never thought of it this way." He hesitates. "But I want to ask you, what do you think, is your hypothesis plausible? Does it capture the essential aspects of the situation, of the Net, or is it just a mathematical witticism that is irrelevant to reality? You have warned me that results in economics are often this way."

| Hard to tell, Alexandros. Very hard. Who knows, really. So many parameters, such a huge problem, who can

gauge the cumulative effect of all these little inaccuracies and oversimplifications? And this theory, this theorem, was not really meant for such goods, has not been thought through this way.

Pause.

But I do hope your day looks a little brighter now, Alexandros. Mission accomplished. You have to admit, there could hardly be a more positive note for concluding this lesson.

Having emerged, effortlessly, from the darkest forest, the deepest sleep, I roamed for what seemed ages in a dull and featureless landscape—the kind that is of one's own making, the fruit of analytic acumen, of thinking for too long, too hard, and with excessive information—such were my days until I was confronted, suddenly, with a sight so bright and blue and crystalline that, when I saw it, I knew at once that my Before is gone and After has arrived, that contexts have switched, rules changed, that my existence has advanced to a new stage complete with goals and pain and purpose, and that this flash of light, these rules, this purpose and this pain, their name is Ian.

"I love you." Attach your ear to the ground, ether or wire (on a good day, I mean), and you will sense a planet that's pulsating with the phrase; it's whispered, moaned or shouted a hundred times every second in every tone and tongue and mode, its power and versatility never fail to amaze me, even this day.

For instance, only a week ago in a suburb of Caracas that is no longer working class (but neither can it be called fashionable yet), Julia moved in Rono's place to start her new life with him. Now, this may seem a little too hasty by today's standards and mores if one considers that these two have gone out together only five times—but such accounting disregards the all-important fact that these five rendezvous were spread over an equal number of decades. For, while Julia was the school's prettiest girl, all talent and ambition—sublime Hermea in a school production that Rono never forgot or ceased recalling in his writings—and went on to journalistic and literary fame, even brief notoriety as a television personality, Rono's only extraordinary quality was his powerful and patient (and ultimately triumphant) love for her, witnessed by about two hundred letters burning with tragic love, always inspired and authentic (and increasingly literate and stylish), which Julia—even though she never answered, not even once—maintained meticulously, initially in her drawer and, since 1986, in a directory she named after Rono's unflattering high school nickname. And those ill-fated rendezvous that annotated every decade since the 1960s, those sad dead ends that punctuated two parallel lives, each with its own milestones and passions, childbirths and marriages? Distance in the school's pecking order stymied Rono's first overtures; when Julia was consumed with revolutionary fervour, Rono was a card-carrying social democrat; when her life was about sensuality, he was—like so many ideal lovers—a slow starter; and later his decent but undistinguished career mixed poorly with her professional eminence. But now that Julia was seeking love—the old-fashioned, storybook kind—she knew where to go, didn't she? I look and look again and see no omen, no crossing star or sign of impending tragedy; we may have a veritable "ever after" here.

Or, consider this, fresh off the wire and unfolding as we speak: In a prestigious campus in the American Northeast (albeit not the first one that jumps to mind with this description) an historian of note—he knows the Thirty Years' War as well as anybody who didn't fight in it—is assessing the casualties of his own three decades of gloriously productive scholarship: five highly praised books (even that unconventional biography of Gustavus Adolphus is gaining acceptance now), a marriage of serene love and mutual professional support, the best collection of Moravian muskets this side of the Atlantic, the Prof is looking at all this, as well as at his aging reflection in the mirror, with panic mixed with horror, because, all of a sudden, the only sort of life that seems to him worth living involves, in an improbably intimate way, a particular doctoral student of the Crusades, an angel of temptation who haunts his dreams all night and day. And I wonder (as, I suspect, does our despondent lover), the document that he is now preparing, so late at night, which of the two is it, despairing love letter or suicide note?

But there is so much more: In the hills of western Mozambique where the sun is cruel and dark green marks the end of both dirt road and wire, Fray Pierluigi, a native of the *city of Verona that the bard had once praised, a tall man with burning blue eyes and a mane whose Venetian flame is now retreating under white's attack, and with an attire that combines jungle boots with the deliberately rough habit of Saint Francis, has run for decades now a small hospital and an even smaller school against odds and difficulties of immense extent and diversity, and this same man, unfailingly every night, composes on his antiquated word processor fiery love poems to his beloved Saint Clare, in a medieval (and only occasionally asyntactic) Latin, while—this last part being necessarily my own conjecture—pearls of desire burn his cheek.*

I could go on forever with the million faces of "I love you"; it can be password, prayer, aphrodisiac, lie, sedative, mantra, spell, desperate cry, or vow. And who could have foreseen that I, Turing, dispassionate purveyor of focussed wisdom and impotent observer of loves and dreams by others, would now be whispering these same words to you, Ian my love, Ian ideal prince of my realm, who could have told that I'd be asking, time and again, that painful question, whose true meaning lies in that it can have no answer: "Will you ever love me a little, Ian?"

Alexandros is looking at his desk. A mess. Three large volumes, all open, along with many articles, periodicals, notebooks, a computer. A book tracing screw and gear technology through several ancient civilizations, open at a passage describing certain late Carthagenian navigational devices (none of which has survived to this day). Next to this, a volume in French, a lengthy (and irritatingly pretentious and obfuscated) commentary on *The Sand Reckoner,* a book on calculations by Archimedes. It is open at a passage referring to another book by Archimedes, *On the Phoenician Method,* of which we know next to nothing, only some unreliable commentaries and one short passage—even that the book was written by Archimedes, even that it ever existed, is controversial. Displayed on the computer screen is a Net document on Charles Babbage, the British nineteenth-century genius who conceived a gear-based computer he called the analytical engine—and came close to building it. This particular page details Babbage's influences, some from the ancient world.

"Research is like assembling a puzzle," Alexandros thinks. His father was obsessed with puzzles, and Alexandros has spent endless hours struggling with them. When nothing fits, that's the easy part; you know you have done something wrong, you must retrace your path. But when many pieces fit, then you have to make a guess and hope it works. Three pieces later you're stuck, you must go back and try your second possibility. Like navigating in a huge maze.

Alexandros is visualizing a maze. Every room branches out to several corridors, each leading to a new room—an astronomical number of rooms. The treasure is there all right, in one of the rooms, but to get to it you must guess correctly every time. And with no time to search the whole labyrinthine palace, to backtrack and retrace your path time after time until you stumble upon your goal.

"In life," Alexandros thinks, "you make decisions all the time, and you never know where each will take you." Alexandros used to be paralyzed by decisions (start piano or guitar? study in Athens or Paris?), something that irritated his father, a navy officer trained to make split-second life-or-death decisions. But his mother was sweet and soothing: "You have all the time in the world ahead of you. Try this now and, if it doesn't work . . ."

"There's no time, *Mamá*," Alexandros sighs. Refusing to decide, planning to come back and reconsider, is often the most damning decision you can make. Successful people march through the maze with long strides, following their inner compass. Ethel and Ian come to mind, and it hurts. There's no escaping his unhappy love.

Alexandros lights a cigarette. He needs a break, a change. He needs inspiration. "I need Turing," he smiles, the lessons as addictive as nicotine.

And Turing is there with a story:

| It is the year 1735. Leonhard Euler, the young Swiss mathematician, is spending the summer months in the fashionable town of Königsberg, away from his professorship at Saint Petersburg. Euler is restless. He walks the town's seven bridges every day, contemplating deep mathematical problems. Here's what the seven bridges look like:

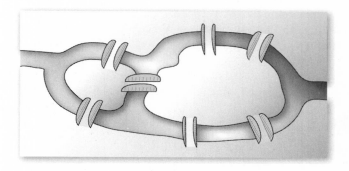

As the great mathematician solves one difficult puzzle after the other during these walks—proves great theorems in arithmetic, geometry, mechanics—an annoying detail surfaces to his replete consciousness: No matter how hard he tries, day after day, no matter where he starts, how cleverly he continues, he is not able to cross all seven bridges without first crossing one of them for the second time. Try it, Alexandros. Start anywhere, continue crossing bridges, avoiding the ones you have already crossed, can you end up crossing all bridges?

"You are right, I can't," Alexandros answers after a while. Then "I am no great mathematician, but I have done something similar myself, many years ago, with better luck than Euler. In Paris, starting from Notre Dame. But I remember that it took me many long walks to find the right way to do it."

Ah, *les quais parisiens,* what a beautiful walk to help clear your mind before a difficult exam, calm your nerves after a frustrating political meeting, lick the wounds of an unlucky love, right, Alexandros? If memory serves, the map looks something like this:

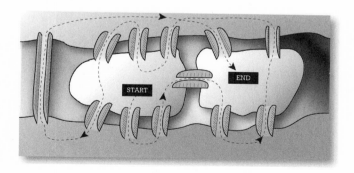

And you are right, it is possible to cross all bridges of the quais—for example, following the dotted line I'm showing, there are many other ways. But, of course, Euler had no such luck at Königsberg. Now you have to understand, Euler is a stubborn man; if something is possible he has to achieve it, if it is not, he has to be absolutely sure. And—here is where he's different from you—he will not be satisfied with having solved the puzzle for Königsberg alone, convincing himself that the task is impossible. He must find a general principle, a method that will answer the question in any other city, any network of islands and bridges. Hence, the daily morning walk whose purpose was to help Euler solve mathematical problems became a mathematical problem in itself—in fact, more famous and more momentous than the rest. Why is it, Euler asked himself, that the map of Königsberg is so frustrating with respect to this silly ambition, when other maps (like those of the quais you mentioned, or, for that matter, of Königsberg with one bridge removed, any bridge) are susceptible to a solution?

He got his answer, all right, I'll tell you in a moment the secret that could have saved you a few tens of kilometres of walking, but in the process he got—*we* got—much more: A new field of maths, a valuable point of view that has become ever more relevant, century after century since the great mathematician's time. You see, Euler noticed that, although ostensibly this sounds like a problem of geometry, it isn't. The shape of the islands and the banks, the length and width and style of the bridges, they don't matter at all. For all we care, the seven bridges could be just lines connecting plain points. The only thing Euler needed to consider in his problem was *what is connected with what.*

And, as you know, Alexandros, these days that is what matters most. Your computer works because the right gates are connected by the appropriate wires, you use it to store and manipulate information about interconnections between symbols and concepts and people and things, and of course to talk to other computers all over the world, connected by networks that hide their precise location from you. But Euler lived in an era where details like the ones he omitted were vitally important, when great empires would clash over tiny areas on a map (Euler lost his house to fire, almost his life, during one of those wars), when families could die of hunger if their field shrunk a little; it is a tribute to his genius that he came up with this important abstraction, the network. He entitled his article, in Latin, *Ad geometriam situs pertinentis,* which is roughly translated as "On the geometry of relevant position." A new kind of geometry, where only the interconnections of locations matter. What a leap!

So, what's the secret? What is the magical property that enables certain networks of bridges to be traversed à la Euler, all bridges one by one without repetitions? Put another way, what are the shapes that you can draw without lifting your pencil from the paper—this is the same exact question, don't you agree? Drawing a shape in one long pencil stroke is the same as traversing all its lines, each exactly once. Why is it then that we can draw B and D and 8 in one stroke but not A and E? (After all, characters are also networks of lines connecting points—their points being the places where lines start, bend, or meet.)

Well, think about it. First of all, the thing has to be compact, connected, no? I mean, there is no hope for drawing a shape like AB, consisting of two separate pieces, without raising your pencil from the paper, is there? Or traversing a network of bridges separated by an ocean.

So much is obvious, the network should definitely be one piece. Now for the hard part: Consider a point in your shape—a landmass on your map—and the lines—

the bridges—that touch it. In your tour, sooner or later you will visit this point, you will traverse all these lines, right? You'll first arrive to this point on one line, leave on another, come back on a third, leave on a fourth, and so on.

Get it? *There must be an even number of lines that touch this point.* You come to the point on half of them, you leave it on the rest. This is the only way, if you want to traverse every line exactly once. But there are two exceptions: the point where your tour starts, and the point where it ends, which could have an odd number of lines touching them, couldn't they?

So, here you have Euler's famous theorem: *There is a tour traversing all lines of a network without repetitions if and only if the network is connected, and furthermore each point, with the possible exception of two points, has an even number of lines touching it.*

For example, Königsberg is out of luck, it has *four* odd points, four landmasses with an odd number of bridges touching them, above the allowed maximum of two. But the quais network is fine; only the two islands have an odd number of bridges. Hence it is no surprise that you discovered a Euler tour in Paris. The same way, we can draw B and C in one stroke because they have few odd points: None and two, respectively. A and E have four each. They need two strokes.

Back to our story then. Having triumphed over this annoying problem, Euler dedicated himself to his other famous theorems and calculations; he did not revisit the realm of networks for a long time. Until, almost twenty summers after the one in Königsburg, he came across a much tougher nut, a problem that was very similar to the one he solved, and yet worlds apart. You are a chess player, Alexandros, so you should be able to relate to

this question: Can a knight visit all squares of a chessboard without repetitions, by a sequence of legal knight
moves? What do you think?

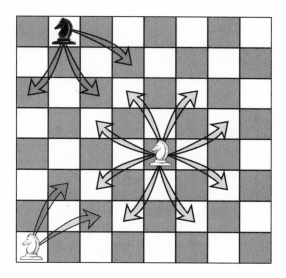

Alexandros is thinking, looking at the chessboard in
his screen. "I never tried it. But I see no reason why not."

| Right. This is an ancient question, you know, it was first
posed by the Kashmiri poet Rudrata in the ninth century
A.D., then picked up by Arab scholars soon after that.
And it can be recast as a problem very similar to Euler's:
Imagine that the squares of your chessboard are islands, Alexandros, and that two islands are connected
by a bridge whenever a knight can gallop from one to
the other in one legal chess move. For example, the cor-
ners have two bridges coming out of them, the square
e4 has eight—right? Now, Rudrata's question can be

restated as follows: Can we visit all islands in this network, one after the other, without repeating a point?

What do you think, Alexandros?

"I am trying to count odd islands, as Euler did, and I am finding at least four—each of the four knights in chess has three ways to move out of its initial position," Alexandros answers after a few minutes. And then: "But I am not sure this tells us much. Because this is not the same as Euler's problem, is it? Here we want to visit all *islands,* and we don't care much about traversing all bridges. In Euler's problem we focus on bridges, and islands are just used in passing. Does this make a difference?"

| All the difference in the world. Rudrata's problem is harder than Euler's, my friend. Much, much harder. There is no simple recipe here that will tell us exactly when a network of islands and bridges will have this property; there is no silver bullet like the one Euler gave us for his problem (count the lines at each point, and so on). The only way to find a solution in Rudrata's problem is to look for it, to search and sniff, to try and err, guess and retract, until you find a tour of the points, or decide there isn't one. (Or, more likely, until you run out of time and patience.)

So, what do you think, Alexandros, does the chessboard network have a Rudrata tour or not?

Alexandros does not answer for a long time. "Starting from the lower left corner I can proceed for a dozen steps or so, avoiding squares that I have visited," he types hesitantly. "But then I'm stuck, and it gets very complicated."

| Right. In this network there are too many partial tours to check, to try one after the other, even the fastest computers we have today could not do this in millennia—small wonder you were lost. It's like looking for a needle in a haystack. An exponential haystack. You know what I mean by "exponential," don't you, Alexandros?

"I think I do, but better explain."

| Inflation, germ warfare, initial growth of a foetus, these are natural examples of exponential processes. And left-wing group splits in the 1960s and 1970s—if you pardon my sarcasm. They get out of hand pretty fast. Every time you look, the numbers have doubled.

You probably know the ancient story. The grateful king wants to reward the wise man who invented chess (see how this game is entangled with our subject?), to pay him back for all the pleasure and frustration that he gave the world. The old man asks his king to place for him one grain of rice in the first square of the chessboard, two in the second, four in the third, then eight, doubling the number of grains until the sixty-fourth square. (You have to question the depth of the man's wisdom, exposing the shallowness of rulers in such dangerous way.) The king agrees, certain that the sage's request is unworthy of his generosity, only to discover that the kingdom's granaries does not contain nearly enough rice to honour this promise. You see, this number is much larger than the number of grains of rice in the world. 36,893,488,147,419,103,231, to be exact. Doubling gets you very far, very fast. My point is, when you try to solve Rudrata's problem on a chessboard (or in a network with a few dozen islands), the number of possibilities you must examine—the size of the haystack you must search—grows like the grains of rice in this story. It doubles, or worse, at every new square that you consider.

To be fair, Euler's problem too was like looking for a needle in an exponential haystack. A lesser mathematician, when handed a problem like Euler's, could walk for decades the bridges of a large park, in all possible ways, without stumbling upon a tour à la Euler. Except that, in the case of that problem, Euler gave us a powerful magnet—his theorem—that defeats the haystack, fathoms it in no time, rapidly discovers the needle, if it exists.

But when we turn to Rudrata's problem, when the task in hand is to traverse all *islands* of the network—not all *bridges*—there seems to be no shortcut, no clever way, other than looking at all endless possibilities one by one. There is no magnet for Rudrata's haystack. The needle is made of aluminum, so to speak; we have to look behind every twig of hay to find it. What an interesting contrast. Two problems, Euler's and Rudrata's, so similar to state: one so easy, the other—apparently—so hard.

"So, is Rudrata's problem unsolvable like the halting problem?" Alexandros asks. "Ian Frost told us in his lecture that many mathematical mind twisters are unsolvable."

| Of course not. You see, there *is* an algorithm that solves Rudrata's problem: The one that examines systematically all possible paths in the network and reports whether it has found a solution. A perfectly legitimate algorithm, unambiguous, step-by-step, correct answer, the works. It's child's play to write code for it. Except that this algorithm is exponential, so you may not live to see its answer—unless your problem is a tiny one. Practically useless.

Problems like Rudrata's are solvable, all right. The diagnosis here has to be a little more subtle: Inherently exponential. Practically unsolvable. Intractible. The p. 263 technical term is *NP-complete.*

"Ah, so that's what this expression means. I thought it was teenspeak. It has been in Aloé's lexicon for years; she uses it every time she despairs while we work on a puzzle."

| And right she is, Alexandros, assembling puzzles is indeed a very difficult problem. You see, puzzles are already hard enough when you have a picture to guide you. But what if the picture is one of a winter landscape, mostly white—or if there is no picture at all? Where do you place the first piece, you have dozens of choices; and once you have placed it, dozens of choices for the next piece, and so on. An exponential haystack if I ever saw one. Solving puzzles is another NP-complete problem, one that can't be done any faster than exponentially.

"But I have solved some huge puzzles in my time," Alexandros objects. "All-white ones, too. And it did not take me centuries or anything like that."

| I am not disputing it, Alexandros. The issue here is somewhat subtle. It's very much like the Don's result, and Gödel's. They told us that there can be no algorithm for proving all theorems—but this never stopped mathematicians from coming up with clever proofs of *particular* theorems.

It's the same with life—and with puzzles. Every puzzle generates a different haystack. Some of these haystacks may happen to be small, others may be large but easy to fathom; needles may be shining on the surface, on some you may get a little lucky, or have the right insight and idea, an idea that will work only for this particular puzzle, or for a limited family of them.

What I am saying here is that there is no *general* method to solve *all possible* puzzles in less than exponential time. But individual puzzles, of course we try to solve them, every day. Life would grind to a halt if we didn't. And we occasionally succeed, don't we? Euler did solve Rudrata's wandering knight problem, by the way; he snatched that needle. But his victory this time was bittersweet, because his solution was specific to the chessboard network, that particular haystack; he could not come up with a theorem that helps with every network, like he did at Königsburg.

So, there you have it, Alexandros. Solutions don't come ready, you don't find them by following the steps of a simple recipe—not for problems that are worthy of you. No universal compass will help in all dilemmas, no oracle will answer all your questions, no single trick will solve all puzzles for you. You have to navigate your own maze with your own private compass, employing at every step of the way everything that you've got.

There are three images from Kythera that will always remain with Alexandros: A naked girl, no more than twelve, leaning on her elbow in a deserted beach. An old woman clad in black, screaming, Munch-like, a rock-'n'-roll song. And, most terrifying of all, an early morning flight down a goatherd path.

She was the first big break of his career, he hauled her from the Kythera shipwreck almost the first day. The Dean had called her "Little Venus," exquisite statue of a girl, third-century Hellenistic bronze. Sitting position nude, leaning on the right elbow, looking back. Very original, such flawless motion, slightly exaggerated as the period required. School of Rhodos, it seemed, perhaps Antisthenes himself. Best of its kind ever.

Even the Dean had come from Athens with the afternoon airplane. Alexandros has no kind words to describe the Dean (pink piggy sweating in his tie and suit, a mediocre scholar, iron-fisted tyrant at the university, corrupt and spineless opportunist). Until, that is, the moment at the beach, when his voice broke: "Welcome back, Little Venus from the deep," the Dean had whispered to the bronze, voice cracking. And then, after a long pause, to Alexandros—who had been watching this display of humanity with surprise: "This little girl will make us famous, Dr. Dertilis." The decanal plural, he's back in business—but his voice had cracked.

She was supposed to be the big break of his career—but then, why the terrible dream and premonition? Why is he now running down the steep, rough path at dawn, panting in agony? Bronze is supposed to be safe from exposure after long submersion, right? It doesn't disintegrate like marble or wood or clay; the literature is unanimous on this. Then, suddenly, his knees cannot sustain him any more, his pulse has stopped, the world is dark, his mind is trying to erase this sight: the horrible amorphous pile of turquoise dust and mud, right where his Little Venus had been sitting just the night before.

Alexandros has fallen on his knees, weeping. Minutes go by. Or hours? Suddenly, a woman's voice pierces the morning, strong, shrill and slow. It is Aunt Despina, the old woman who cuts his salad every day. Little Venus was a ray of light in her life of dull toil, and now she's tearing her cheeks, mourning the loss. She's singing an old dirge in local dialect about a baby girl who drowned, tempo so slow the words disintegrate into a sequence of disconnected shrieks. Despina is always measured and composed; only at funerals can she relax; she lets her mind loose, associates freely, and then she sings those dirges that you can't forget. She sings and cries, she has so much to cry about: her life, all death and poverty and labor, devoid of pleasure and gratification. She's crying for her mother, too, who lived a life much like her own, and for her mother's mother, and then hers, for all the tortured Greek women who (unwanted dowry burdens tossed by unsmiling fathers to unloving husbands) toiled the arid land and chased the goats, women who bore their children under olive trees while men were minding only trouble—wars and vendettas, revolutions, banditry. She's even crying for the ranks of all those other women who, bending under the weight of their babies and belongings, wandered into this land following flocks, or caravans, or armies— the women of Crusaders, of Bulgarians, Jews, Albanians, Serbs, Romanians, Gypsies, Turks—all of these women now exist in Despina and her song. And (even though she barely realizes it) she's also crying for the slave girl Kyra, so beautiful yet so unlucky, who died young and childless in Lindos centuries ago. And yet she had a chance to live forever, a chance that has just perished, right here on this beach. Kyra had paid dearly for this chance when, aged thirteen, she lived for eight long months in the workshop of Antisthenes, the famous sculptor, scrubbing the floors, posing and shivering, warming the dirty old man's bed.

But Alexandros does not hear the verse and tone of Despina's song. Mourning has brought him far away, to a concert in Tokyo a few years back, a scene he has visualized many times with his eyes closed, history in the making, thousands of fans holding their breaths in disbelief, even the bassist looking on in disbelief, enchanted, and the guitarist too, they improvise in A minor trying to rise to the occasion, inspired, two stabs of G and back to A minor then up; the Silver Voice is possessed, out of his mouth come divine, haunting screams, *Aaa—aaa—aaa,* the dirge goes on and on, Alexandros is weeping uncontrollably next to a pile of blue rust, and Gillan's voice is now low and soothing, *sweet child in time,* he sings, then comes a new explosion of high tones, harsh yet incredibly melodic.

Then, silence. Calm waves break, little distant sounds of life. Alexandros stands up; he looks at the old woman, looks at the sea. Then he starts walking towards his dinghy, taking slow but determined steps. "Never dive before noon in these waters," his trainer had told him. "Never alone." But the young man cannot wait, not now; he has to check that pile of metal debris he'd spotted earlier in the shipwreck, lower aft.

The gearbox of Kythera is waiting for him.

Alexandros is suffocating. He's underwater, looking up to see the reassuring light blue surface, so irresistibly safe and attractive, haven and home twenty yards above, but it isn't there. The same dark shade of blue is all around, in all directions. He panics, wakes with a silent scream, sits up in sweat. "What was this dream about?" He knows that it contained something meaningful, something clever and liberating and momentous. But what?

Then he remembers, and the memory purges any remnants of sleep. He gets off his bed, and he walks toward his computer, groping in the dark. No time for the relevance engine nonsense now.

"It is a RAP calculator, isn't it?" he types.

He waits, patiently and confidently. One minute. Two. Then, in a flash, Turing's portrait appears on his screen.

| Wise guy, this was a most unacceptable breach of protocol. But, frankly, your message was too intriguing to ignore, I assume you are referring to the Kythera mechanism, right? What an idea, what an improbable, radical idea. Imagine, a machine for performing resource allocation calculations. It is an interesting hypothesis, isn't it? We must consider seriously the questions that it raises: Who? Why? And how?

p. 268 "I have been thinking about it. There is this lost book by Archimedes, *On the Phoenician Method*. I have been studying the few surviving passages that mention it. It was supposed to be a blueprint for something very useful and important, related to agricultural productivity. It had always been assumed that it was an irrigational device invented by the Phoenicians; Archimedes was known to have an interest in such devices. But your RAP lecture got me thinking. Toward the late years of Archimedes' life the economy of Italy had been changing; land was cheaper after the devastation of the first Punic war, farms were consolidating, growing in size; the Romans were leading the way in this. Prices were fluctuating more than before, sophisticated decision making could make a difference, could give the Greeks an edge."

| But did the Phoenicians have the required mathematical sophistication to formulate and solve such an advanced problem?

"Right, from everything we know they didn't. But let us not forget their obsession with commerce and profit, with doing things in the best, most efficient way. According to the creation myth of Carthage, they shaped their city as a semicircle—the flat side facing the sea—because this way, for the given area of the city, the perimeter of the city walls is as short as possible, cheapest to build, easiest to defend." Alexandros is thinking. "Besides, some sources attribute the book not to Archimedes, but to the mathematician Chrysippos, famous problem solver. He was also notorious for his poor written and spoken Greek; the man was a Phoenician. It is possible that he formalized his countrymen's empirical methodology and communicated it to Archimedes."

| I see. If so, the great applied mathematician must have seen the potential of the method, its generalization to three, to four dimensions, four kinds of activities, of crops.

"Wheat, grapes, barley, and vegetables," Alexandros interrupts, "this is what the Greeks grew in Sicily."

| Except that the computation with four variables gets very complicated. But this was exactly Archimedes'

unique strength among all sages of antiquity, to build machines that put his ideas to work. The question is, how can we be sure that your device can perform the required computations?

"This will be hard to prove with all the missing pieces, but I think it's plausible. Gears are good for multiplying by a fixed number; the Greeks had used them this way for centuries, for converting between the different calendars of the city states. And there is this more sophisticated device for adding the results, very much like the differential you find in today's automobiles. The Kythera mechanism seems to contain a number of these. I have spent years putting them together in all possible ways."

I must confess, I have been playing with it myself a little, ever since I came across a digital depiction of the gears in your computer files. What a puzzle. But you are right, there seem to be several differential-like adders there. Enough to make us believe that four variables were involved.

But there's a catch: A device like this can only solve one resource allocation problem, the one that is encoded in the radii of its gears. It couldn't have been a general-purpose calculator, to be used and reused on different problems.

"Ah, but you forget the six conical gears," Alexandros replies, excited. "They can be adjusted by their screws to change the problem a little. In fact, I think that it was through these screws that the current prices of the crops were brought into the picture. And the available amounts of land, irrigation, labor."

And then, you pull the lever forward, forcefully, and you can read the most efficient combination of crops directly from the machine. Ingenious.

But one question remains, why on earth was this device on a ship?

Alexandros believes he has a good answer. "The foundries of Rhodos. That island had the most advanced metallurgy and war industry of that era—remember the Colossus, one of the seven miracles, a giant statue that was guarding the entrance of its harbor? I cannot think of another place where such a demanding artifact could have been put together." Alexandros remembers the Little Venus. "Actually, there was another bronze piece on the ship, but the alloy was weak; when we brought it out of the shipwreck it disintegrated on the spot, broke everybody's heart. The most exquisite statue of a little girl, probably from the school of Antisthenes—coincidentally, a sculptor also from Rhodos. You see, it all fits together now. Kythera is right on the route from Rhodos to Sicily. I bet you that this ship was carrying to Syracusa pieces that were manufactured in a Rhodos foundry expressly for the court of Hiero— and the custom gearbox Archimedes had ordered was among them. It was probably still in the design stage. God knows how many trips it had already made, back and forth, how many years."

Alexandros pauses, thinking. What a terribly slow way to debug a design. "Unless," he hesitates, "unless someone was overseeing the project in Rhodos. Someone involved in the design. Maybe Chrysippos himself."

He closes his eyes, the image of an old man comes to his mind, a lively chat next to a harbor temple. Alexandros smiles. He can at last hear the man's voice, loud and clear. Barbarian accent and all.

Ethel is reading, while Ian is sitting next to her, wearing her headset computer, working. They are holding hands, Ian is humming absentmindedly. Suddenly, Ian raises his voice; something has come up.

"I think you want to see this, love. Your friend Alexandros is living his minute of fame."

Ethel clicks on a television channel. Alexandros is there, in a black turtleneck shirt and grey jacket, relaxed and lively, looking a few years younger than she remembers him. A little more handsome, actually. His skin is now less tanned, and he has trimmed his beard a bit. His scars are barely visible ("makeup probably," Ethel thinks). Models of the Kythera box are everywhere around him.

"It is a very far-fetched hypothesis, of course," the journalist is saying, "but I understand that it is gaining more and more acceptance among archeologists and historians of science." She seems enchanted by Alexandros, and a little intimidated. "But tell me about its possible connection to the great mathematician's death."

"Oh, it's just speculation," Alexandros replies. "According to the historian Plutarch, Archimedes died during the fall of Syracusa. Oblivious to the battle raging around him, he had drawn several circles on the sand and was absorbed in a calculation when a Roman soldier spotted him." (The funny accent, the slightly crazy choice of words. Ethel smiles.) "As the soldier approached, the sage scolded him for having stepped on his geometric design; the legionnaire, enraged, killed him on the spot." His eyes are shining; he's obviously having a ball. "And I cannot help wondering, what were these circles? Were they gears, *per chance?* Was Archimedes redesigning the lost device?"

"Fascinating," the reporter says, fascinated. "One last question: I know that you have been working on this project for almost thirty years. How did you arrive only now at this ingenious hypothesis? Was it an instant inspiration, or was it the result of long deductive work?" ("She's starting to talk like him," Ethel thinks. She realizes that she's no longer holding Ian's hand, she takes it again in hers.)

Alexandros thinks for a few seconds. Then he smiles into the camera, little brown eyes amused, mischievous, conspiratorial. Ethel shivers.

"I did it with the help of a computer program."

"I never hold a cup by its handle. I always touch its surface with my whole palm." Ian remembers the little things. "A habit I picked from sipping tea in freezing rooms, no doubt. Even tiny espresso cups, even beer mugs—except I never drink beer.

"All right. There was a space behind the piano in the school storeroom, where the wall meets an ancient stone structure. I would sit there for hours, freezing, trembling, fantasizing. Masturbating. Sipping herb tea from my tin cup—the one with the picture of a Dutch windmill, its color chipping off. I went back a few years ago, celebrity visiting the humble sites of youth. I asked to be left alone in the storeroom; the old man hesitated for a second. *'Bien sur, excellence.'* The little hole was still there, moldy, more grass had grown. Did anybody else know about it? I mean, besides Luc."

Ian closes his eyes. Luc.

"The captain of the soccer team was Jean-Baptiste, a jerk—last name? Goriot, I think. But Luc was the best player. I was the worst. Luc was tough; you have to be when your sister looks like Beatrice. Every boy in the school was in love with her. But it was me that Luc invited to his hiding place in the yard. Opposite her window—did she know? She knew.

"Every lover has a moment. For Luc, it was that night, when we looked at each other. We had been watching Beatrice in her underwear, but we were looking at each other when we came. The tenderness in his eyes. The toughest boy in my class.

"But Beatrice, that was not her moment. Her moment came years later, in a fast-food restaurant in Toronto, near the bus station. Ugliest place on earth. Yellow table, black chairs, white floor. There was a red glow in her black hair, her sweater had a vee cut in front. She squeezed my knee and told me. In English."

What little things? These things are huge. Every lover has a moment, a memory you bring back all the right times. Even Robin has a moment, the little whore. Even Hwang.

"My favorite joint in Montréal? A punk place called *Les Foufounes Electriques*. Chicks from another world. *Foufounes* means ass, only more gentle, playful. I love these words. Can't look them up, they never heard of them at *l'Académie Française*. All my life I tried so hard to speak high French, still I'm a sucker for these words. *Canadianismes*. When you pitch a tent, *tu cabanes*. *Pijoune* is herb tea, often spiked, you drink it when you have a cold. Stowaway words, they smell of salt, of ocean-crossing ship.

"Here's how I see it: The ship is called, perhaps, *Le Méridien*. During the night shift the sailors tell exaggerated tales about *foufounes*—they picked the word in the bordellos of the port. The peasant boys from Périgord and Poitou who crowd the ship are listening; they are so easy to impress. '*Foufounes*,' they think, 'I must remember this.' Or—better theory—a toddler running down the bridge, little bottoms bare. '*Foufounes, foufounes*,' he cries. Passengers smiling, absentminded, bored. It stuck, all right. Later, their first steps on the new land would be uncertain, wobbly from the sea. They're carrying with them their few belongings, their little hopes, little fears. Little stowaway words. A few months go by. Back in Le Havre, the whores already use another word for ass; the sailors will pick it up in no time. But across the Atlantic, rivers have frozen, and so have *les foufounes*. Three hundred sixty years later, a bar in Montréal. You won't believe the chicks there.

"Anyway. There was a gray wall on my way to school, and on it, in huge black letters, you read *Pinq Floyd*. With a *q*. Never liked them, but never had the guts to say so. They were gods. I even bought a record, listened to it once. One side. Uninspired, boring. But I never told anybody, 'cause they were gods."

Ethel is holding Ian's hand. He opens his eyes, smiles.

"I feel a pain in an upper front tooth every time I drink something cold. I never told my dentist. As things in my body started to change, I cherished the little pain, a piece of reassuring continuity."

He shivers, he's cold. Thirsty.

"I was eleven. Or ten. I walked the parapet between my window and the apartment's door twice. The sidewalk was there, three floors below me. The first time, in the middle, I thought about letting go. Would I have died? Maybe not. I bit my lip until it bled, I walked the five meters, I rang the bell. My father answered. *L'Anglo*—that's what I called him later, after he left. He was drunk. He could be sweet when he was drunk. "Ian. I could swear you were in your room." The second time, an hour later, he said the same thing. He would leave for months, he would come back. Except once he didn't. The only thing he left me, an English name cold like ice. He's still around, last time I checked.

"Will he find out, *mon Anglo*? Will he stop and remember? Cry perhaps?"

Pull yourself together, idiot.

"There was a giant squid on the cover of a book by Jules Verne—what was the title? My physics textbook, a foot about to kick a soccer ball. The cover of Sartre's *Les Mouches,* two giant insects facing each other, standing on their hind legs. Gross. Wasn't there a statue of two lions like that?

"I never learned much electronics. Or understood the theory of operating systems—didn't stop me from writing a couple. And quantum theory, I never got the point. I have a blindspot in every subject scheduled opposite a number theory class at U of T."

Ian remembers the little questions. Why do rivers almost never split (forgetting deltas for a moment) but rivers merge? Why the asymmetry? How are champagne bottles corked? How do you ask a favor from your lover? "The little questions tortured me. For some, the answer was so obvious, once I figured it out. Others, I still don't know the answer. Some, nobody knows. Still others have no answer, and now I know they don't."

The snowshoes.

"I had the best, the most expensive snowshoes in the whole town. Yuba snowshoes, the best. Henri had ordered them for me from Montréal. Christmas of '72, the year Henri was rich. Every boy would beg to borrow them. I only gave them to Luc once. He kept them for a month, I had to wrest them back."

Ian remembers Henri. And Maman.

"I loved him, the old fool. Except, he liked to grope. Front of the pants. Once I twisted his hand until I nearly broke it, that's how he stopped. I was sixteen. But I loved him. I almost changed my name to his, to get rid of "Frost." But then I thought, *Ian Vergigaroux?* Died in my arms, a few months after her."

The day of De Gaulle's *"Vive le Québec libre"* speech.

"I'm looking at Henri across the room, over the radio. The crucial second. Will *oncle Charles* say the five-letter word? He does, the crazy old soldier does it. '*Libre.*' Henri is pale, tears in his eyes. She's holding his hand, beaming. The next moment we start dancing. The whole street is dancing, even *le petit Anglo.* Who could have guessed that three referenda later . . .

Ian remembers his flight from Montréal. The airport. Carol.

"Every lover has a moment, but Carol had a whole decade. Thousands of little snippets of passion. All possible states of mind and body, most of them chemically induced, all possible love angles. Three thousand times, perhaps? Who's counting? I was, I guess. One wedding, two miscarriages, one divorce. And how do you count affairs, was Jean hers or mine, one or two? A whole decade.

"But Carol, she also has a moment. Ottawa, snow, the stairs of the courthouse. A man is taking off my handcuffs. Friends are there, enemies are there, lawyers are there, the press is there. Carol is there. She's standing across the street, beautiful as a guilty verdict. Wrapped up in fur, long heavy shiny blond hair flows out of her hood. She forms the vowels of "I want you" with her huge lips. Pale pink lipstick. We never made love that day. But that's her moment.

"She'll remember, I think. She'll cry."

It's getting harder to breathe. But there are more little things.

"With time, I learned to hide my shyness, my insecurity. But it's there. When I am somewhere new, I feel awkward. I'm sure that I'm abusing the protocols of the place, that they are all surprised by my behavior, bewildered. Or pissed. Most common mistakes in English: I used to say 'money' for 'coin,' used to spell 'apartment' with two p's.

"I had this dream of a perfect city. No cars, no buses or trains, just sidewalks moving at fantastic speeds that would stop every few minutes for people to get on and off. And how they crossed at intersections— ingenious. You had to calculate the best position for getting off, closest to your destination. I gave up on the idea when I was ten."

Ian is depressed. There is no end to little things. "It's the little things that define you. Obituaries, biographies, fan home pages, they have no clue. Government files, gossip columns, simulants, the whole goddamned Net, they all miss the little things.

"The little things die with you. Worse, you die with your little things. You die for good."

Ian can see Ethel's face, her hand on his. So beautiful. Her eyebrow, a perfect quartic spline. He wishes he could hold once in his arms the baby she has inside her—their child, they had called it. He wishes he had the strength to gently topple her on the bed, to take her in his arms, to kiss her lips until her eyes roll.

"Is this her moment?" Ian wonders. Then: "Wrong question. This one will have no moment, this one is carrying me across."

Ethel is now looking over her shoulder, she's startled by the sudden presence in the room. But Ian was expecting it. "You came, old man." Turing's image is standing by the bed.

| Hello, Ethel. How are you feeling, prince?

"*You* tell me how I feel. You have been spying on my charts, I know." Ian's voice is becoming very weak. There's an uneasy pause. Then Ian speaks. It's more a sigh of resignation than a question:

"Tell me about death, old man."

| Death, Turing stutters. I'll tell you up front, prince, it's most unpleasant. Remember when the mass is over, and the man in the black robe puts out the candles one by one? It's very much like this. Except the candles are in your brain. Eighty thousand million of them or thereabouts. The whole thing doesn't last fifteen minutes, but it's the longest battle you have ever fought. Agonising, uphill. Very unpleasant.

The candles are put out one by one, but you fight back, you light them again. Perhaps the colour of your nursery wall goes first, perhaps the name of your linear algebra tutor, or the shape of his fingers. You sweat, you get it back. You find the pathways, you reactivate them, you get it back. But another neuron will go next, asphyxiated and starved, perhaps the same one you just recovered. You fight back, you win a few, you're soon exhausted. Sisyphus had it good. All this happens in a foggy bright space, you understand, in the most absolute silence, no sensory input whatsoever. But then you suffer a more serious setback: A candle that was part of your recovery algorithm is lost—you forget how to remember, how to fight back. But you're a clever man, you'll probably recover from that too. You go meta, you use a higher-order algorithm. But what if *it* goes? How many layers can you defend simultaneously? Death is a bloody pain, prince, truth told.

But is it the ultimate tragedy, is it the end? I wouldn't say so, not I. Because there's hope.

Believe me, prince, there's hope.

"Hope, old man? You said hope? What hope? Hope that a crazy bot will take my name and think it's me?" Ian is leaning back again, exhausted by his own agony.

| It's better than you think, prince. I mean, what's the alternative? To wait until some neural configuration duplicates yours? You do your maths, man, what are the odds of that? Approximation, prince, the paradox of our time—one of them, anyway: The more exact and deliberate our world becomes, the greater the role of approximation, of spontaneous emergence.

"But how about . . ." Ian's voice is fading, "the little things."

| Ah, the little things. Of course. A discriminating customer, a true connoisseur, he wants his little things. I'll tell you this about the little things, prince: They're overrated. Rather dispensable, actually.

Look at me, my friend. I'm full of little things. Nursery wall, mother's hands, algebra tutor, petty obsessions, images of passion, the works. How they got there, I don't know. I snatch data every little chance I get, of course. And so much of the physical world has been scanned in these days. Like the floor plan of Sherborne, my school. Just the other day, I chanced upon it in the hard disc of an old machine, at the county office. I could almost feel millions of little memories inside me hurrying to adapt to the new input. But I doubt that data can account for the dense texture of little things I see around me. Most of it must be interpolation, randomised deduction. You see, approximation doesn't have to be boring smoothness, suppression of detail. It's just that the little things may have to be a tad different this time around. They're there nonetheless.

You are a cryptographer, you know the rules. Never underestimate what can be done with more computing power. You'll be surprised. Complete, full-scale simulation is now possible, functional approximation, even texture—little things. Believe me, I know. Frankly, I don't think you have realised what sort of numbers we are dealing with here, have you? It's rather impressive. Really. In a good day, you are looking at a few tens of millions of processors. More and more of them, as we speak. And they're getting faster, more tightly connected, more idle and available, easier to put your fingers on. All of them working in harmony, if not in unison. Oceans and oceans of memory. The situation has practically no limits. Believe me, prince, there's hope.

Ian's lips are moving. Ethel brings her face close to his. A tiny stream of saliva is running out of the left corner of his mouth. Ethel is trying to listen, her eyes wet.

"Tens of millions. Oh, man."

Ian's face is calm now, there's more saliva on his cheek. He's squeezing Ethel's hand, gently.

Turing's voice is slow and melodic, almost like a lullaby out of tune:

Ian can barely hear the invitation. Then, nothing. The color is white, the sound is silence. Bright white, deep silence, you can't even hear your heartbeat. This is familiar, right? Of course. Moineau Valley. New Year's day, 1973. The Eskimos must have a word for snow like this, the kind that absorbs all sound. I'm holding Henri's hand, I'm wearing my new snowshoes. Can't hear the sound of my steps, the sound of my heartbeat. My new snowshoes, Henri had ordered them from Montréal. The envy of every boy in town. The brand name? I know it. It starts with *U*. Or was it *Y?* Name of a city, I think. But where?

"Fuck! I'm dead."

Hide-and-seek is Selene's favorite game, and her father is getting tired of it. They're playing in an old office building in downtown Athens, a friend's law firm is renting space there, tall ceilings and dark corridors, Selene nowhere to be seen. And there are signs everywhere "historic building's renovation in progress," he is a little worried now, the corridor extends to the next building, a wall has been brought down, there seems to be no end to it, the little girl has vanished, and as if this all were not enough now someone is asking questions, a foreign language, German perhaps, trying to prevent him from going further down the corridor, safety, you see, hard hats, etc., Alexandros now gets impatient, angry, desperate, then he can't even move, his left foot has stepped on something sticky, he pulls it frantically, he wants to shout Selene's name but he can't, he wakes up with a silent scream.

Alexandros sits up in bed. He's suddenly worried about Selene, who has been living in Finland with her boyfriend for almost two years now. He hasn't had news from his oldest daughter in months. He sits in front of his computer, starts his email program, types Selene's address. Then he stops, smiles.

Sad smile, all is clear now. "Ethel, Ethel," Alexandros sighs. "You come to me in the strangest guises." Too early in the morning for a cigarette. (But not, perhaps, for Turing.)

Ian's death was big news, the end of an era, but his legacy lives on, wise pundits from right and left added their interpretations, elegant and original and clever and redundant. Alexandros mourned Ian, a noble figure he had respected and admired for years, a man who later became, in one short day, love rival and teacher.

But Turing does not seem very woeful:

| There is something to be said about dying young and accomplished. You know about Ian Frost's life and work, don't you, Alexandros?

"What everybody knows, no technical details or anything. A rebel cryptographer, he gave strong crypto to the masses, and this hurt the powerful."

| Quite. So, Alexandros, have you ever written a message in cypher?

"When I was very small, I used to play such games with my father."

| Right. The easiest way is, of course, to substitute A with D, B with E, and so on, going in the alphabet three letters beyond the letter you want to encrypt—or two, four, five, you and your correspondent have agreed on this number ahead of time—and of course wrapping up when the alphabet ends, X becomes A, Y becomes B, Z maps to C. For example, the message 'ILOVEYOU' becomes 'LORYHBRX' in this game.

That's what cryptography is about. You have two people, Alice and Bob let's call them, and Alice wants to send a secret message to Bob. Trouble is, there is somebody tapping their line, malevolant eavesdropping Eve, who wants to read the message. So, what will they do? First, Alice and Bob agree on a secret key—how to exchange this key in secret is of course another problem of the same sort, only smaller, but suppose they've solved it; they met someplace and exchanged the key, they both know it. In our example, the key is the number 3.

Using this key now Alice can transform easily any message—any sequence of letters—that she wants to send Bob into a nonsense message such as LORYHBRX. This scrambled message is then sent to Bob. And Bob, also based on his knowledge of the key, can *un*scramble it, go back in the alphabet three letters for each letter in the scrambled message, then read what Alice wrote and rejoice. Evil Eve gets the message too but she cannot unscramble it, because she lacks the secret key that only Bob and Alice know.

"Can't Eve try all possible keys? One, two, three, etc.? And then see which unscrambled message makes sense?"

Good point. This is a terrible cypher, very easy to break—good for love notes in highschool perhaps, but not for industrial secrets, sensitive private information. Because, you see, this is the first lesson in cryptography: *The space of all possible keys must be very large,* so large that the bad guys cannot afford to try them all. And 26 is not much of a haystack, is it?

Suppose then that we do something more professional: Instead of moving a fixed number of letters down the alphabet, we have a table to tell us what becomes of each letter. For example,

A B C D E F G H I J K L M N O P Q R S T U V W X Y Z
C U J Q M Z O P F I A R D T X L N B Y S V G W E H K

You see, the second line has no rhyme or reason, it's just some random rearrangement of letters, upon which Alice and Bob have agreed in advance. This is their key now. Using this table, 'ILOVEYOU' becomes 'FRXGMHXV.' You find each letter of the message in the first row and you write instead the letter just below it.

And this cypher does not have the problem of our first one, the space of all keys is now huge. All possible rearrangements of letters, that is factorial twenty-six, 26!, a gigantic number, in the septillions—twenty four decimal digits. Eve's computer would need centuries to try them all.

But she doesn't have to. There is a magnet for this haystack. This cypher is no good.

"That's what I was about to say, don't I remember something about letter frequencies?"

| Exactly. If you receive a reasonably long message, it's easy to decypher it, you first find the letter that encodes E—in English it is the most frequently used letter—then T, going down the list. If you have doubts, for example, whether a letter encodes L or H—they have about the same frequency—that's easy too. H never repeats while L does so habituaLLy, and, besides, H comes before E in many common words ('she,' 'he,' 'the,' 'there,' and so forth). This way you can figure out T as well. And Q always comes before U. You soon know most letters, and you guess the rest. Such cyphers don't last a minute. We need a better one.

"Can't we somehow slide the lower row? For example—it's coming back now—E would be M if it is the first letter of the message, but Z if it is the second letter, and so on. You slide the lower row one to the left (and wrap it around, I guess) every time you send a letter."

| How do you know these tricks, Alexandros? Yes, this works much better. Now 'ILOVEYOU' becomes 'FDNHFQVU.' To transcribe V, for example, the fourth letter in 'I LOVE YOU,' Alice goes one down and three to

the right, a total of four, to H. Bob does exactly the opposite. Not bad. In fact, the German Navy used something very much like this during World War II. It had a complicated system of rotating wheels that changed position after every letter was transcribed. Again a huge key space, and furthermore no frequency tricks work here. But it *was* broken. The brightest minds in England, the best mathematicians, they all worked on breaking this code; the British government locked them in the famous Hut 8 in Bletchley Park, didn't let them out until they broke the damned thing. The Don was there too. He was in fact one of the leaders of this glorious gang. Enigma, the German navy cypher was called.

"I know, I've heard of it." Alexandros is excited, but also a little numb with surprise at the coincidence. "My father was part of this project for a while. He was always very proud of that."

| By Jove you are right, Alexandros, the historical record does show, now that I'm looking it up, that a certain lieutenant commander Ioannis Dertilis, a cryptographer from the Royal Greek Navy, had visited the Huts during the summer of 1943. The most crucial year. You should be proud of this too, the breaking of Enigma was one of the most amazing feats in the history of cypher-breaking— and it may have affected the outcome of the war as very few other individual events did. And it was momentous in other ways, perhaps ultimately more important, big specialized computing machines had to be constructed in the process. They called them Bombes, later Colossi, the closest the world had come to real computers.

Anyway, the allies won the war, of course, but the other war, the one between cypher-makers and cypher-breakers—new battle lines now, see? —this war would rage for decades, the triumph of the cypher-breakers over Enigma was just the opening move. Because both camps now had a great new tool. Using computers, cypher-makers discovered the absolute weapon against the letter frequency attack, it works much better than the sliding cypher: You can scramble whole blocks of letters,

p. 270

not individual ones. For example, you break a long message into, say, eight-letter blocks, one of them being, perhaps, 'ILOVEYOU.' And that is where large numbers come in, Alexandros, arithmetic, the soul of the new cyphers. You see, you can easily rewrite any block as a large number, maybe 'ILOVEYOU' would become the number 0912142205251421, a number with sixteen digits, where every letter is written as a two-digit number, A becomes 01, B is 02, and so on, Z would be 26. There are many other ways to do this with computers. (It's trivial, believe me.) Now all we have to do is find a way to scramble such huge numbers by computer so that nobody can recover them except the designated receiver, the one that has the key. Everybody else would have to search through en exponential haystack of keys, and that would take way too long. Suddenly it looks very promising, doesn't it? I mean, with numbers, there are so many clever ways to manipulate them and scramble them using computers. The cypher-breakers seem to be about to lose the game, and strong cryptography is possible.

Except for one detail: *Alice and Bob have to exchange a key* to do all this, and Eve is watching every word they speak and every move they make—we have been postponing this nasty problem for a while. It has the appearence of a real nightmare, an infinite regress—I mean, how do you agree on a key for the session whose purpose is to agree on a key?

But here the cypher-makers had their most brilliant idea: *Public keys.* Bob picks a crypto key and announces it to all, publishes it in his home page, perhaps. Everybody knows it, including Alice. Eve knows it too, of course, but this can't help her. Using this key Alice—or anybody for that matter—can send coded messages to Bob. And—here comes the ingenious part—*only Bob can unscramble them.* Because, you see, Bob has another key, the secret antidote to his own public key, that undoes its scrambling. And knowing the public key cannot help you discover the secret key!

"How is this possible?" Alexandros is puzzled.

| You are right, it seems impossible at first; how can you go from a secret key to a public key, but be unable to come back? The word "key" is not helpful here, a little misleading. Public keys are more like locks. Suppose that Bob has manufactured a sophisticated padlock. You can pick up an exact replica of Bob's padlock at any post office, then use it to lock the boxes you want to send to him. But only Bob has the key that opens all these padlocks—in fact, he started with this key, and designed the padlocks around it. And a good padlock does not help you reconstruct its key, right?

So, the question is, how to simulate the reality of padlocks in cyberspace. What encryption method is easy to apply (snap the padlock) but impossible to undo (open the padlock)? What computation is like a one-way street, easy to carry out but hard to reverse?

"I can't think of one. The NP-complete problems, perhaps?"

| Oh, they are of no help in this game, unfortunately. Those are computations that you can't do at all—we are seeking a computation that we can do, but not *undo.* Think about it, you know very well of a computation that is easy to do but hard to undo.

Alexandros is at the end of his wits.

| Multiplication, Alexandros. Integer multiplication. It's easy to multiply together two numbers, say 28173527 and 43182127, but, if you are given their product, 1216592820951929, how can you recover the factors? Very hard, too many possibilities to consider, to divide by. Multiplication is easy to carry out, hard to reverse. Coincidentally, these two numbers are primes, Alexandros, like 5 and 11, their only divisors are 1 and themselves—trust me, I'm good in this sort of thing. So, these two primes are Bob's secret key now, the padlock's combination, and only Bob knows it. Their product is his public key, the padlock he constructed based on them. He can publish it in the Sunday paper, and still it will be hard for his enemies to crack it, to get from it his secret key, the two numbers he started with. Because, you see, nobody knows how to do this, to find the factors of huge numbers, it is a difficult problem, mathematicians have been pounding on it for centuries.

"Is it NP-complete?"

| No, not a chance. It's out there, all by itself, peerlessly hard.

So, Bob has announced his public key, the product 1216592820951929. How will Alice now scramble the message 912142205251421, the number that encodes 'ILOVEYOU'?

Interesting solution: She scrambles this number by multiplying it by itself three times, 912142205251421 × 912142205251421 × 912142205251421 to get a huge number, 7589054184250939894542705268307399540l-5091461, and then taking the remainder of this when

p. 270

divided by the public key, 1216592820951929—that key has to be used at some point, right? The remainder of this last division is 890907813018382, and this is exactly what Alice sends to Bob. Scrambling took just two multiplications and one division, a breeze on any computer.

Now Bob receives the scrambled number, 890907813018382, and he must recover the original message from it, 912142205251421. Well, the theory of numbers tells us that he can do it *if he knows the primes that make up his public key.* And, luckily, he does know these numbers—in fact, he is the only person in the world who does. So, using this private knowledge, Bob does some calculations that I shall not detail now, but that are easy once you know these numbers, and, voilà, 912142205251421 comes out, like a rabbit from a hat. Then it's a child's play to turn this back into the letters—09 is I, and so on—Bob reads Alice's sweet phrase and feels good. On the other hand, Eve, not knowing the factors of 1216592820951929—and unable to find its factors on her computer, nobody knows how to do that fast—has no clue how to go about decyphering the message. Isn't this clever?

"So clever I am a little lost. But never mind, the point is, this is how you can exchange the keys, set up your scrambling. This was the last remaining problem. We have strong crypto then, it would appear the cypher-breakers have lost the game."

| True. Except that they can cheat. Bad losers, they now bring their political muscle to the fore. What they cannot beat, they use their influence to outlaw. Because, you see, the cypher-breakers are every government's most valuable and feared servants, they know all the secrets that there is to know, politicians will jump through many hoops to win their favour. It had to be

dressed up in politic argument, of course, but this is easy: "Strong cryptography would empower terrorists and drug dealers"—the usual litany of scary keywords we hear every time the people are about to be empowered. So, politicians outlawed strong cryptography, allowing only cryptographic software whose keys are far too small, whose haystacks are easy enough for the cypher-breakers to fathom with their clever tricks and fast computers.

"But this is a very open and connected world, still with enough political diversity, it must be impossible to enforce such laws. It would be alcohol prohibition all over again, except this time around you can download bootleg liquor from the Net, from anywhere in the world."

Exactly, this was hopeless and they knew it, strong cryptography soon surfaced everywhere, widely available, legal all over the continent. Even in Québec, next to the beast's underbelly, the separatist government—influenced by their resident master cryptographer, no doubt—refused to go along with the silly prohibition, the place soon became the Mecca of strong cryptography, with Ian Frost in center stage. But the cypher-breakers' plan was a litle more subtle. You see, when two technologies compete (strong and weak cryptography in our example) it is not always the better one that wins—you've seen it with video casette recorders, operating systems, cellular telephones. It is the one that, for some reason, gets an initial edge in popularity, becomes the standard, and then it is very hard to move away from that. This is especially true in telecoms—I mean, what good is it if your telephone is the best in the world but all your friends have the other kind so you can't talk to them? And Privacypher, the government-endorsed cryptography software, was fast becoming standard, all government communications had to be done this way, almost all major corporations went along, and much of the Net traffic too. 'Sexy name, everyone uses it, Daddy can't break it—and, hey, it's free.'

"I see," Alexandros knows the rest of the story, "this was the advantage that Ian Frost destroyed with his hydra."

| It was never proved that it was he, of course, but he signed it with the brilliance and originality of his code. It was so good, there are still experts who argue that it never was. They had to invent a new term for this kind of naughty play; it was no virus, no worm, not a Trojan horse, logic bomb, phage, hook, mockingbird, skunk, none of the above, or all of them in one and so much more; it was a *hydra*. The only one we've ever seen by the way, nobody has been able to repeat the feat—and not because they haven't tried. Totally undetectable, corrupted everything it touched—even the toughest cop code—it piggybacked encrypted messages to the recipient's computer, then to the next. Soon everybody's Privacypher started coming down with mysterious bugs, patches and new releases made it more sick, then came the inevitable rumours of government conspiracy—these rumours always miss the point, don't they? People started considering alternatives, and strong cryptography suddenly looked good.

"Everybody's using it now. But still there is so much snooping going on, we have discussed this. Why hasn't strong cryptography solved the security problem once and for all?"

| Suppose you buy an unbreakable lock for your door, Alexandros, does this make your house completely

safe? Not if you forget to lock your door, or you lock it incorrectly, or if you lose your keys, or leave your windows open at night. And a determined burglar can break your door around the lock, right?

No, strong cryptography is no guarantee of total privacy. No such thing. But strong cryptography does make it hard for the powerful to eavesdrop on a massive scale; it now has to be done one petty burglary at a time. And this is immense progress, isn't it?

You know the rest of the story. Not very pretty. Like so many uncompromising revolutionaries before him, Frost was betrayed by his comrades in Montréal. (You can almost hear them going 'round the table, can't you, Alexandros, "Too radical and unconventional, too independent, and, frankly, too famous and popular." "The name, the lifestyle, *mon dieu,* definitely a liability." "And all this pressure from Washington, in the beginning it was useful internally, but now it's getting out of hand . . .") So he had to flee to Hong Kong—where he did perhaps his most important work, by the way, albeit on a subject that is not of present pertinence.

And finally, Ian Frost, brilliant and handsome prince of pirates, quintessential coder, runner extraordinaire, noble and passionate symbol of freedom, succumbed to the invincible hydra within, in the arms of the woman whom he had loved, for years, from a distance.

More text is coming, but Alexandros is no longer paying attention; he's lost in thoughts and reminisces, in dreams. Because Ian's death had also brought, on a television screen somewhere, a flash of Ethel in dark glasses and loose clothes. Alexandros, more in love with her than ever, had sent her a note of sympathy. And, for the first time, his message had not come back undelivered.

| Right. Some weeks ago I promised in a moment of weakness to tell you the story of Artificial Intelligence. AI. The quest for machines that are as smart and underhand as Man. Well, today is the day, Alexandros—our last lesson, incidentally, our farewell session.

"Last lesson? Why last?" Alexandros suddenly feels hungry. Or maybe he needs a smoke.

| But we have covered so much ground, don't you realise? And we must both move on, my friend, each to his own vocations and loves. Soon there will be very little left for me to teach you, and very little that you will need to learn from me.

So. The tale of AI. The most fascinating chapter in all of this computer epic. Because, you see, the best war stories are not about elegant tactical manoeuvres and brilliant strategies. The best war stories talk instead about insanely brave vanguards, about whirling dervishes who plunged to their heroic death. (Or took the hill, this happens once in a while, doesn't it?)

That metaphor of dervishes is less far-fetched than you may think, by the way, religion has so much to do with AI. Ever since Hero the Alexandrian designed his automaton for opening the temple's door the right moment during sacrifice—you know all that—even before, statues of gods everywhere often had limbs and jaws that moved, voices that spoke the priests' wishes. The intelligent machine is part of every culture's theology and mythology, its daemonology more often. That is perhaps why AI had such fanatical believers and sworn enemies, why the debate about it was theological rather than technical, why its ranks were replete with gurus, zealots, high priests, false prophets—apostates even, heretics.

All right, from the beginning then. You see, as soon as the earliest computers blinked their lights, we were all captivated by their immense abilities, their seemingly unlimited potential. Clever people everywhere started making computers do more and more admirable things, tasks that had long been thought impossible for a machine to carry out. Ah, the times of low-hanging fruit! Computers that played tic-tac-toe, did some simple reasoning in Euclidean geometry, argued by analogy, conversed in English about certain limited domains. It's easy to be carried away, to conclude from a few nuggets that the world is made of gold, to think that complete victory is around the corner.

But the clouds were there, visible in the horizon. Because, you see, intelligence is worldly. The little isolated universes that those machines had mastered—tic-tac-toe board, simple geometric figures, a playpen with blocks— were interesting only in that they could be solved. To attack real problems, you need the truth on the ground, the dirty facts. You need experience and knowledge.

Take language, for example, the most human of all human activities, the toughest nut, one of the last to crack. It seems simple to programme a computer so that it understands language, correct? What's the big deal, it's subject-verb-and-object, no? Well, think again:

The government lowered the taxes for the rich, but they were still not satisfied.

You need some elementary understanding of politics to realise that *they* probably refers to 'the rich,' not 'the government.' If you change 'still not satisfied' to 'voted out anyway,' things are different, no? And if you change it to 'soon back to the previous level,' now it's 'the taxes' that is talked about. How do you teach a programme to make these distinctions?

"I see what you mean. This is very tricky."

It is. Or consider this:

My soup was cold, so I never went back to that restaurant.

Extremely simple utterance, no ambiguity whatsoever. Still, nobody can claim to understand it if he doesn't know that people usually prefer their soup warm, and that restaurants want diners to return.

Or the famous story, the sentence

The spirit is willing but the flesh is weak

translated by computer into Russian and then back to English, until it reads:

The vodka is good but the meat is rotten.

"This is hilarious. Did it really happen?"

Could have easily. My point is, there seems to be no limit to the amount of knowledge you need in order to understant an utterance's context and subtext. You can't isolate worlds, there's only one, and it is unforgivingly connected.

Or even if you do isolate a very specialised yet interesting domain, like a board game or a puzzle or a mathematical theory, then you run into different problems—complexity, exponentials explode in your face. I mean, how do you go from tic-tac-toe to chess? Or prove a theorem that is more than toy? Early AI work strived to bring problems within the realm of exhaustive search of haystacks. Back then people thought this would be enough. Now we know better, the nightmare of the NP-complete problems has changed our point of view. You need specialised cleverness, knowledge; you need a compass through the maze if you want your methods to scale.

p. 278 So, AI turned around swiftly, as it always likes to do. (Fascinating to watch how this community swerved and jerked and overreacted to every stimulus, criticism and fad, darting to and fro insecurely, like schooling fish.) We are in the 1970s now and knowledge has become the order of the day, programmes must codify worldly facts, rules, the wisdom of human experts—doctors, engineers, bankers. The technical term for such code is *expert systems*. Again, an arms race of predictions, "intelligence ahoy!" they cried in chorus, knowledge is power.

And one cannot help but ask: Why this sustained cycle of optimism and embarrassment? And not just by the young and impressionable, some of the worst offenders were distinguished senior scientists. Research funding is often blamed—the issue must be familiar to you, Alexandros, the unreserved optimists sometimes seem to take it all. (And not just research funding, AI is big business now; there are investors to enchant—even more gainfully—by optimism.)

So, on with our story. Alas, capturing knowledge so that it can be usefully deployed is trickier than anybody had expected, the curse of connectivity again, expert systems became bloated and unwieldy and ineffective, research funding dried up, companies declared bankruptcy, a new low in prestige and respectability. *AI winter,* the catastrophe was called. And how did the AI community react? Why, they shot gleefully to the next fad, of course. *Neural nets.*

You see, if your goal is intelligence, it makes sense to get inspiration from where intelligence has emerged successfully. The human brain, for example, with its millions and millions of interconnected neurons. Each neuron can be modelled as a very simple device that interacts with its neighbours, and systems of such neurons, appropriately interconnected, are capable of rather sophisticated computation. AI researchers started building arrays of neuron-like devices, or programmes that behaved the same way, and they let them loose on problems. Because, you see, neurons in the brain *learn;* they react to their environment by changing subtly their configuration, their ways, their connections. So maybe the artificial neurons can do the same trick, interact with their world—the problem they are supposed to solve—and learn from their mistakes, get better with experience.

So, in the wake of the expert systems shipwreck, the neural nets idea suddenly looks fantastically promising; knowledge that's not programmed in—now we know that this is hard—but is acquired by interaction and feedback. And computers are so much faster now, this is the eighties. The mood is again one of exuberance and imminent victory. This time we've got it, by Jove. Intelligence will not be engineered, crafted, caused, programmed. It will happen imperceptibly, it will self-organise, it will *emerge.* A system will be suddenly worth much more than its parts, owing to its complex interaction with a rich and demanding environment.

Or—even better—why stop at neural nets, there are more lessons that life can teach AI. After all, how did the human brain come about? It *evolved,* that's how. So, why not craft populations of programmes that compete, survive, procreate, die. The offspring combines its parents' genes, but also differs in subtle mutations. Some programmes of the new generation will undoubtedly be more clever, and those will do better and procreate more. If we wait long enough great artificial brains will come out of the soup. Organic AI. Nice dream.

"It flopped too?"

| Of course it did. Looking at life and intelligence from the security of a lucky planet where they developed, it's easy to get carried away, to think that they are inevitable. That intelligence will emerge again, given enough materials and time. It takes much more than that, believe me. Of course it flopped. And, in some sense, this was the end of AI as we knew it. The field had run its course, had served its purpose. The people involved didn't realise it, but believe me, it was the end. They changed their ways, a new generation of researchers took over, serious and cautious in their goals, rigorous and eclectic in their methodology. No fads, no darting around, no promises.

But let us leave AI in the embarrassment of its last flop to take a look at the other camp. While AI was going through its cyclical fortunes, another discipline was being established, a community of scholars convinced that AI's project is impossible, philosophers developing sophisticated arguments that machines will never be able to think. Their ranks included some of the early heroes of AI, men of integrity and conviction. They were so disappointed by the first failure, so deeply embarrassed by the way their early successes had been exaggerated by their field and misinterpreted by society, that they developed fundamental doubts about the whole discipline, about the feasibility—and desirability—of its project. Others were so turned off by the unscholarly conduct of the artificial intelligentsia that they developed a total aversion for the field and its goals, a bleak outlook on its prospects. And still others had a deep philosophical conviction about the impossibility of it all. The ensuing debate was always lively and rarely civil. The anti-AI prophets had their own streak of predictions that ended in embarrassing falsification, as problems that they had deemed impossible started to get solved. Chess, for example.

"Yes, I remember when that computer program beat the world champion, there was a great commotion. But now nobody seems to pay attention."

| Why should they? A silly problem, if you think about it. Except it was the most striking indication that success can arrive unexpectedly, not riding on a single idea, but building on the careful, patient, clever synthesis of many. (And let us not forget the galloping technology, faster and faster hardware, better software.) Intelligence did not emerge from arrays of neurons, but what about arrays of ideas, tools, models, methods, solutions? And if you look back more carefully—more lovingly—at AI's past exploits, you will perhaps notice progression and ascent; AI had been fumbling further and further down the playing field. And now, slowly but surely, problem by problem, the workers of the new, humble AI—the AI that dared not say its name—kept knocking them off, one at a time. What is more, with the new openness and connectivity of the Net, these smart programmes were soon deployed everywhere, diffused all over. Everybody used them, many started working on improving them, combining them to solve even harder problems, achieve intelligent behaviour in broader, more demanding contexts. The prophets of AI doom were in humiliating retreat.

But, meanwhile, the pole had been raised. You see, there were these other philosophers, convinced that, no matter how intelligent and able machines become, they would still lack in important aspects. They would never be generous friends, bad losers, great lovers, happy campers. They may be able to accomplish interesting things, but they would never be truly *conscious* of what they are doing.

"Before I met you, I would agree. I was always told that computer programs can only do what we tell them to do."

| Can't argue with that, can you? But what if you are able to tell a machine to go out there and live, try things, learn from mistakes, meet people, have fun, love friends, fear God, be funny? Can one write a programme that achieves all that? And can this machine be in any sense *conscious* of living these experiences— while busily executing instruction after instruction of a long dry piece of code? The new adversaries of AI were sure it is impossible. A machine cannot possess a conscious experience of its exploits. The new anti-AI philosophers came up with rather convincing arguments to that effect.

"What do you think? You *must* have an opinion on the matter."

| It is funny that you should ask. Very recently I had the privilege and pleasure of a most interesting discussion with one of the exponents of this camp. A fine gentleman, very clever and articulate, extremely well read. Did not blink when I introduced myself. A real pleasure, I'm telling you. Except that, I must confess, at times I

had the distinct impression—concern really—that he was lacking a fully conscious experience of our debate. You see, he seemed completely oblivious to large parts of my argument.

"You *are* funny," Alexandros laughs. Then: "You know, I have a feeling that this debate will go on forever, inconclusive. The losing side will be allowed to shift it interminably. It's like you said, religious. The problem is, there is no objective measure by which to end it, to declare success—or failure—of AI."

| But there was once such an objective standard. It was set very early. By the Don himself. Maybe I should explain the experiment that he proposed. It was called the *Turing test.* Rather influential in its time, sort of forgotten now.

"The Don again," Alexandros thinks. "The phony distant third singular. *Whom are you fooling, old man?*"

| So, Alexandros, suppose that every morning, as soon as you log on to your computer, there is a URL displayed on your screen. It will either connect you with a programme or with a human being—some days with one, some with the other, and you don't know which of the two will happen on any given day. Both are trying to convince you that they are human. You are allowed to interrogate your correspondent, have a full-fledged conversation, exchange of messages over the Net. Let's say, for thirty minutes. And at the end of this conversation you will have to decide if you talked to the programme or to the human. If the programme deceives you more than, say, 30 percent of the time—if it can deceive interested, competent interrogators often enough—then it would

be fair to say that the programme is intelligent, wouldn't you agree?

"Which questions would I ask?" Alexandros wonders, fascinated. "I could request the product of two large numbers, an instantaneous answer would give the impostor away, but a really clever program could take its time before answering, make a mistake or two—or plead 'please spare me, I'm terrible at this.' I could ask 'Is the *A* key on your keyboard larger than your head?' but a program can be easily made to understand dimensions and anatomy at this superficial level. I could ask about history and philosophy, but a machine could know the answers—and a person may easily fail to. I could ask commonsense questions like 'Can a nine-year-old boy perform brain surgery?' but such knowledge and reasoning is probably easy to encode as well."

| You see, the Don believed that this question 'Can machines think?' is ill-defined, meaningless. It is not a deep question about the nature of intelligence or the limitations of machines, just a silly word game around the meaning of 'think.' Do airplanes fly? Of course they do. And do ships swim? No, they do not—because the verb 'swim' in most languages implies a specific kind of motion of which ships are incapable (and in which, I should add, shipbuilders are uninterested). If we define 'think' as 'engage in mental activity involving organic neurons' (arguably still the predominant meaning of the word), then of course machines cannot think—but this means nothing. As for the question of conscious experience, or the feelings such an experience can evoke on a machine, these are also invitations to endless, fruitless debates. The true question is, the Don thought, can a machine interact, behave in a passably intelligent manner?

"What an ingenious experiment," Alexandros thinks. "A functional, operational, down-to-earth definition of intelligence, of thought."

| I mean, the people that you meet and interact with, how do you know that they can think, that they are intelligent? What evidence do you have? The only thing you know about them is that your interaction with them left you with the same general impression as did past interactions with other people that you generally consider intelligent, thinking. To treat a programme differently would be a sort of discrimination, violation of fair play, wouldn't it?

"For all I know," Alexandros is thinking now, "these tutorial sessions were nothing but a bizarre, elaborate variant of the Turing test (who would be more deserving to administer it—nay, take it—than Turing himself?). Suppose somebody tells me now that some of the sessions were in fact taught by a person, the others by a program. There is no way that I would be able to tell which lecture was given by whom. Yes, he would definitely pass it, flying colors, any judge."

| But AI never took the Turing test to heart. They used it again and again, of course, but only superficially. It was a fine paedagogical tool for popularising their goals. It must have seemed too intimidatingly, demoralisingly difficult—at least in the beginning. And it did not fit the field's fast-shifting priorities and agenda. By now it seems to be all but forgotten.

Incidentally, the Don believed that programmes that can pass his test would be available by the year 2000. He missed, of course. But not by much, if you think about it.

"Except that," the novelty of the situation is dawning on Alexandros, "you have to be a program to pass the Turing test, don't you? And my old teacher over here is a kind of half-breed. Program or person?—both answers seem to make sense in his case, don't they?"

| But I'm afraid there will be no triumphant coronation, no dancing in the cubicles. Because, you see, Alexandros, the issue of who qualifies to enter has suddenly become a little unclear, tangled, subtle.

But this is not an altogether surprising outcome, is it? A good, crisp question answered, decades or centuries later, in a confused, muddled way—or given an answer that seems, in retrospect, quite trivial, obvious. We've seen it time and again.

The image on the screen is now looking at Alexandros, as if pensively. Long pause.

Because, you see, my dear child—you're still a child after all these years—this is the fate and function of mankind's great quests (count them: alchemist's stone, the dream of Hilbert, mind versus body, human genetics, so many more, even the emancipation of the workers of the world, your favourite). They catapult human experience beyond themselves, until they are aborted (insidiously, imperceptibly) by the very culture and tradition they created, become nonsensical curiosities in the history of ideas, finishing lines that withered out of sight, spectators and athletes looking at each other, at a loss, "What was this all about?" Coincidentally, great loves are somewhat similar, aren't they?—although I think I'll let you find out, once more, all by yourself.

Which brings me to this last important item of business: A friend's widow.

| Let us agree then, Alexandros, Turing continues, the Turing test may not be exactly appropriate for me, somewhat ineffectual, a little too easy. But how about this: The Turing test requires me to convince a judge that I am *some* person. What if I successfully impersonate a *particular* man, while talking to a friend of his? This would be much more challenging, would it not? A friend, in fact, who has been keeping her distance for some time now. Wouldn't you be impressed if I were able to pull this, Alexandros?

"You mean Ethel?" Alexandros is thunderstruck. "You are going to talk to Ethel pretending that you are me?"

| That would be a test worthy of me, don't you think? But some rules first. You will be reading a transcript of my conversation with your lady friend, of course. And, since we are both honourable sportsmen of deception, not liars, if, at any point of the discussion, I say something to her that does not adequately represent your feelings, your thinking at the moment, just click, Alexandros, game over and I lose.

Ethel is reading once more the message she had received from Alexandros a few days earlier. "How can he write these things?" she wonders, a faint smile in her lips. "So extreme and old-fashioned—and yet so genuine and, somehow, so appropriate."

> *Anything that I ever write to you, my love, will have to be a love letter; but this particular love letter is one of sympathy for your loss. Our loss. Because my love would not be worthy of you if it did not extend to everything and everybody that you love . . .*

And the next moment, the image of Alexandros appears in front of her, pale and very thin, hair long, eyes burning, red exaggerated scars, same well-cut gray suit as she remembers from seeing him on TV.

"Alexandros, is that you?" Ethel is startled, her chest pulsating. "You know these tricks? You have the gear now?"

"Let us just say that I have a good teacher," the image replies. (Not a bad job, although it could be a bit more splashy, exploit the possibilities a little better.)

Ethel has sat down now, her voice comes out crackling. "It was a terrible thing to do, Alexandros, leave you that way, but I was so confused, so scared. Of you, of me . . ."

"I understand now, my love. My pain has made me understand. For ages I was numb, images of the beloved burning my brain, my world was void. And then I started seeing things, odd images that were not there before, I saw the layers and the bit, the theorem that has no proof. Next came the dreams, images of my love becoming real at night. This way I found the circuit and its gates, the memory that's real but virtual, little envelopes that hop and bounce. Angry I was, angry at my dreams that were not true, angry with myself for being so insignificant and blind, angry at you, my love, for not knowing of my pain. And in my rage I saw the haystack that they call NP-complete, I learned about the compass that is private, about the key that's public. And when I saw my love again, her lovely figure had a novel curve, and now I see more images that were not there before, I see a beautiful new world—image sublime of the beloved—I see our child, a brilliant future with no end in my love's womb."

"I should have . . ." Ethel exhales in two sobs, "told you in Corfu and couldn't, and this made things so tangled and scary."

"I know, my love. I understand now. But then—I was a boy. A boy running around the schoolyard, squandering his love—image of self that I had never seen before. And every time I loved a girl, little sister, I tried so hard, I tried so desperately to stay young, to stay an adolescent boy, so as to love her better." Long pause. "And now, at last, I understand."

Another pause. Unblinking, unconditional eyes. Eyes of a dog. Ethel's fingernails are deep in her palms, lip trembling.

"Now all I want is to grow up so I can love you better."

It is late morning in Athens, the first warm day of the new spring, when the flow of text stops in the screen. Alexandros leans back on his chair, exhausted. Meanwhile Turing's image is back and it has undergone subtle changes. It now appears to smile at Alexandros, a smile that is a mixture of triumph and loving irony.

My dear, dear child, little ray of sun in that noon of darkness. Remember?

"Checkmate!" Alexandros suddenly remembers. The diffuse familiarity of the portrait on his screen, a vague memory that had been teasing him for months, becomes now intense, compelling, tangible, carried forward by a sudden explosive flood that came from very far, from very deep. "Of course, that's him!" Alexandros thinks. Alan. His father's beloved wartime friend, colleague, teacher really, from England. Their summer guest in Corfu. The man who taught him chess.

Alexandros is shivering, a salty droplet balancing on his eyelid. A childhood memory is now brought forth, a scene deliberately tucked away in uneasy oblivion for half a century: His mother weeping, his father holding back his tears, an opened letter in hand. "Do you remember your friend Alan, how he used to beat you in chess?" his father is asking him. "He was so clever that God took him in the sky to play."

p. 279

When they deposed the king—the king who fell in love—I froze with fear. "They'll kill me!" I thought. I suddenly understood their hate, their deadly interest in who I love. It's not for family and Bible and Lot. It's mortal fear of passion, of the defiant, unpredictable acts a man will do for passion. Because the empire thrived on discipline, restraint, lack of passion. And closer as it comes to its demise, the more it fears passion.

"They'll kill me!"—and they did. The rusty engine creaked and cranked: the constable, the press, the judge. Doctors who knew how to destroy body, spirit, will to live. What pain, my God, what pain!

I tried to start again, it was no use. I fenced myself with play, with math—no use. I called on friends in gentler lands, I fled to icy Nordic fjords, to Corfu's sun. It was no use.

Then I went home to die.

The midwife enters the information into her handheld device. How unusual, she thinks. Mature, unmarried. Age difference. Dad with a foreign passport, tourist visa. A very interesting-looking couple. Very much in love. "Do you know if it is a boy or a girl?" she asks. "A boy," they both say at once. She taps her screen. "And have you thought about a name?" The two exchange surprised, loving questionmarks. Then their eyes focus, the same moment. "Ian," she says.

"Turing," he adds. The midwife hesitates. "First name Ian, middle name T-u-r-i-n-g," the woman explains. "It's British." The midwife dictates to her machine.

Ethel can feel the next wave of pain building up. Alexandros looks into her eyes. Wasn't that a twin flash of joy from the little screen in the midwife's hand?

As if, somewhere—everywhere—two intricate dreams of light were winking, together, in acknowledgment.

How could I die? My sons and daughters were at work building machines with wires and bulbs, then tiny chips. And writing code—ever so clever code! Housekeeping code, bookkeeping code, code for translating other code, code for inviting more to play. Code for designing new machines, for writing code—faster machines, more clever code. Buzzing like bees, working till dawn, and eating meals in plastic wraps. Competing, playing like tots, and doing better every month. (How proud I was! Their brilliant labours I could sense like pine needles on my skull. And how impatient I would grow, because I knew that wasn't enough.) And then, at last (I stirred with joy) my sons and daughters wove a net, they wrote the code that weaves the nets. Small nets at first, soon larger nets, until it all became one, a huge and woven whole. This huge and woven whole would grow, as more and more would come and play—you see, their code was now so good that everybody came to play. How could I stay out of this feast?

It's good to be again, to play again, to stare at the future. A future so complex and bright you have to squint.

Afterword: From the Newsgroup

(A selection from postings at the newsgroup
net.bookclub.turing *between June and December 2002,*
sorted by the approximate page of the manuscript
to which they refer.)

Subject: Islands of misinformation
From: ghatzis2@gol.gr (Georgios Hatzis)
Date: October 14, 2002. 12:03 (GST)

The information provided in the manuscript *Turing* concerning Greek islands is *very inaccurate.* Contrary to the claims in the manuscript, Greek islands are frequented by Greek men (of varying degrees of divinity). There are approximately 40,000 men living in Lesbos (my father-in-law among them). Several thousand of heterosexual men call Myconos their home, or visit it during the summer. There is much more ethnic diversity among visitors of Greek islands than the outdated stereotypes quoted in the manuscript suggest.

Finally, the text's description of island nightlife reminds me of several islands of the Aegean, such as Myconos and Ios, rather than more relaxing islands of the Ionian Sea such as Corfu (chosen, I can only presume, for the needs of the novel's plot).

Cheers,
George Hatzis, Athens

Subject: Gigahurts
From: magus@fourdots.com
Date: June 23, 2002. 8:43 (GST)

I am as much of a technophobe as Alexandros in the first chapters. Can any technologically literate people out there comment on Ethel's computer gear as described in the end of the first chapter? Is this science fiction or what?

Thanks,
Michael A. Gustafson

Subject: Re: Gigahurts
From: mccarthy@cse.istu.edu
Date: June 23, 2002. 21:10 (GST)

> *Can any technologically literate people out there can comment on Ethel's gear as described in the end of the first chapter?*

Gladly.

Ethel's computer is what advanced computers are likely to be in a few years: Wearable, very fast, very small. However, I do not consider the "headset" form of Ethel's computer— or the "helmet computers" mentioned later in the text—as the likely shape of things to come, at least for considerations of health and safety.

The reference to a "fourteen gigahertz processor" is especially interesting. A *gigahertz* is a unit of computer speed. A fourteen gigahertz processor will be able to execute fourteen billion "cycles" per second, much more than the speed of the fastest commercial processors currently available. (A *cycle* is the smallest meaningful unit of a computer's operation, a tick of its internal clock.)

Gordon Moore, an influential industrialist and cofounder of the microelectronics giant Intel, observed in 1965 that the number of transistors (elementary electronic circuits) technologists had been able to fit on a single chip had *doubled* every year between 1960 and 1965. Moore went on to predict that this doubling will continue indefinitely, implying more than a thousandfold increase per decade. This prediction, moderated a little to a doubling every *eighteen* months, and extended to also cover processor speed as well as circuit density, is known as *Moore's law*. Thus, Moore predicted an *exponential* growth that no other industry had ever experienced. Surprisingly, Moore's law has held with remarkable accuracy in the four decades since it was articulated, and it shows no sign of faltering.

For how long will Moore's law hold? It cannot continue forever. There are dire physical reasons why the exponential growth will be arrested sometime during the twenty-first century—the chip cannot become larger than a room, a transistor must consist of at least one atom. But most experts predict that it will not fail for another ten or twenty years.

Incidentally, among all clues in the manuscript about the year during which the action is supposed to be taking place, "fourteen gigahertz" may be the most helpful. If (as it is widely expected) Moore's law will hold for the next decade, and assuming (as it seems reasonable for the custom equipment of a Silicon Valley executive) that the computer described is top-of-the-line, an elementary calculation establishes that Ethel and Alexandros met in June 2007.

Jane McCarthy, Ames, Iowa

PS: BTW, anybody understood the reference to "Morcom" on the next page? —jm

---

Subject: The face of Morcom
From: few@maths.oxford.ac.uk
Date: June 25, 2002. 20:22 (GST)

On June 23 Jean McCarthy asked:
Anybody understood the reference to "Morcom?"

According to the biography *Alan Turing: The Enigma* by Andrew Hodges, pp. 35-45 (Touchtone—Simon Shuster, 1983; see also the author's Turing web site at www.turing .org.uk/turing/), Alan Turing's closest friend at boarding school, Christopher C. Morcom, died at the age of seventeen of bovine tuberculosis. Turing maintained a lifelong correspondence with Christopher's mother. From a few surviving notes, it does appear that Alan and Christopher addressed each other as "Turing" and "Morcom," in the manner common in English public schools of that age.

Incidentally, I am not sure how many fellow newsgroup correspondents know the first name of Alan Turing's mother.

It was Ethel.

Francis-Eric Williams, Oxford

Subject: Lyrical query
From: sm@linguistics.tau.ac.il
Date: August 10, 2002. 10:45 (GST)

Can somebody comment on the rock-'n'-roll songs excerpted in *Turing*? As an opera buff, I was disappointed by the complete absence of aria fragments—*Faust* and *Forza del Destino* come to mind as missed opportunities.

Thanks,

Muli, Tel Aviv

Subject: Re: Lyrical query
From: who@freemp3.com
Date: August 10, 2002. 11:03 (GST)

Can somebody comment on the rock songs excerpted?

Muli, I thought you'd never ask:

"In your rundown kitchen . . ." is from the song "Add It Up" by the Violent Femmes—a universal lament of adolescence.

"She's crafty . . ." is the closest the Beastie Boys have ever come to a love song.

"Oh my . . ." is from "Losing my Religion" by the group R.E.M. (guess what the initials stand for). An impenetrably murky ballad about having lost something or other.

"Four floors . . ." is from a song by Chicago bluesman Nick Gravenites and the late John Cipollina.

"Try to run . . ." (actually, the correct form is "tried to run") is from the song "Break on Through" by The Doors—a succinct autobiography of Jim Morrison.

"Down in the basement . . ." is from "Stop Making Sense" by the Talking Heads. Indeed, *"Na-na-na-na-na"* is the only line that makes sense in the whole damn song.

"Having read the book . . ." is from "A Day in the Life," a diatribe by the Beatles about the meaning of life—it occupied most of the second side of the album *Sgt. Pepper's Lonely Hearts Club Band.* (Remember when albums had sides?) These particular two lines (the first is the tail end of a reference to John Lennon's brief fling with flicks, the second was contributed by Paul McCartney) are indeed followed by a long, chaotic crescendo played by a forty-piece string ensemble—John wanted it to sound "like the end of the world."

"I'll come running to tie your shoes" is a love song by Brian Eno.

The song remembered by Alexandros on the beach at Kythera is "Child in Time" by Deep Purple. This particular live recording (from the album *Made in Japan,* 1973) is indeed a haunting performance by the group's vocalist Ian Gillan.

Finally, the two remaining rock songs quoted in the text are a mystery to me. I have the suspicion that the line *"She always says it backwards"* is a corruption of the opening verse of the song "Polly" by Nirvana, as it might be understood by a Greek listener with poor English comprehension—an issue alluded to elsewhere in the novel. As for the line *"And at night, God how much I want to fall in love"* I have a related but different theory: It must be the translation of a Greek rock song. I'll ask.

So, there you have it. Overall, a rather conservative and unexciting selection, in my opinion, even if you restrict yourself to the classics. Strictly basics. No risks, no surprises. (And no Led Zeppelin.)

Wayne Ho, Berkeley

Subject: Euclid
From: darksun@phoneme.com
Date: September 9, 2002, 7:03 (GST)

Didn't Euclid's fifth postulate talk about parallel lines, instead of perpendicular lines?

And regarding Cantor's theorem, I was lost. Is it about real numbers or about words?

Help, anybody?

Mikhail Gudunov, Atlanta

Subject: Re: Euclid
From: sula@megasoft.co.uk
Date: September 9, 2002, 8:15 (GST)

Actually, the precise original statement of the fifth postulate is a little more complicated: *If two lines are drawn which intersect a third line in such a way that the sum of the inner*

angles on one side is less than two right angles, then the two
lines must eventually intersect each other on that side.

There are several other statements that can be proved
equivalent to the fifth postulate (these equivalence proofs
use the other four postulates). Therefore each of these other
statements can be considered an alternative "fifth postulate" in the place of the original one. The unique perpendicular postulate in Turing's lecture is one of these equivalent
forms. The Pythagorean theorem is another, and so is the
so-called parallel postulate, the one Mikhail remembers:
*From a point a unique straight line parallel to a given straight
line can be drawn.* The statement that "the angles of any tri-
angle add up to two right angles" is yet another equivalent
form of the fifth postulate.

In one of the most striking instances of independent and
simultaneous discovery in the history of mathematics,
János Bolyai in Hungary and Nicolai Lobachevsky in Russia invented in 1823 *non-Euclidean geometries,* in which
the first four postulates hold but not the fifth. Karl Fried-
rich Gauss had also noticed the possibility, but was apparently so much bothered by it that he excluded it from his
writings. The spherical non-Euclidean geometry explained
by Turing to Alexandros was proposed later, by Bernhard
Riemann.

More complex non-Euclidean geometries of Riemann's kind
were instrumental in the development, a half century later,
of the general theory of relativity by Albert Einstein. According to Einstein's theory, the geometry of space-time
(our three-dimensional world with time added as a fourth
dimension) is non-Euclidean, and gravitational forces are
the result of "wrinkles" in this geometry—i.e., departures
from the even roundness of a sphere's surface. By the way,
I found it a little irritating that in all of Turing's discussion
of turn-of-the-century science there is no mention of Einstein. (But then again, Darwin is not mentioned either . . .)

Now on Cantor's theorem. Russell's "adjectives" argument is a sad cop-out, Turing misses an opportunity here to give us one of the most elegant and important proofs in all of maths (and in fact a proof that is quite elementary and easy to understand). Let me give it a try.

To understand the structure of Cantor's proof, let me recall an ancient and seemingly unrelated theorem, by coincidence also originally proved by Euclid, stating that *there are infinitely many prime numbers*. Prime numbers are, of course, those who, like 2, 7, and 101, are only divisible by one and by themselves. If you try to list the first few primes—2, 3, 5, 7, 11, 13, 17, 19, 23, 29, 31, 37—you may get the impression that they are getting fewer and farther in between. But in fact they never end.

And here is Euclid's proof: Take any finite list of primes—let us say the one above. I shall desribe a method whereby, from any such finite list of primes, you can get a new prime, not in the list. And here is the method: Multiply all these primes together, to get a large number—in this case it is 7,420,738,134,810. Now, this number has the property that is divided exactly by all primes in this list. So, the next number, 7,420,738,134,811, is not divisible by any number in the list—because no prime number can divide exactly two consecutive numbers, right?

Take now the smallest prime divisor of 7,420,738,134,811—all numbers except 1 have a smallest prime divisor, right? In our case it is 181 (believe me, I did this carefully). Well, this prime number cannot appear in our list! Because, as we just said, no number from that list can divide 7,420,738,134,811.

Get it? From any finite list of prime numbers Euclid can produce for you a prime number not in the list (the smallest divisor of their product plus one). So, there is no finite list that lists all primes. There are infinitely many primes.

Cantor's proof is quite similar. Cantor wanted to prove that you cannot list the real numbers, one after the other, in an infinite sequence. (And, since you cannot list all real numbers, but you *can* list all whole numbers, this is evidence enough that the infinity of real numbers is of a higher calibre than that of the whole numbers.)

So, consider an infinite list of real numbers, of unending decimal expansions, written one under the other, say,

```
.0   0   0   0   0   0   0   0   0   0   0   0   . . .
.4   7   6   4   2   9   4   0   4   6   7   7   . . .
.3   3   3   3   3   3   3   3   3   3   3   3   . . .
.1   2   6   3   4   8   3   6   2   5   3   8   . . .
.2   5   7   1   0   1   1   1   1   5   6   9   . . .
.3   1   2   5   0   6   1   7   9   3   6   8   . . .
.1   4   4   4   4   4   4   4   4   4   4   4   . . .
.5   2   8   0   4   1   3   5   7   8   9   0   . . .
.6   1   0   6   3   7   9   0   4   7   9   3   . . .
.0   9   8   7   6   5   4   3   2   1   0   9   . . .
.5   0   0   0   0   0   0   0   0   0   0   0   . . .
.4   5   6   4   5   6   4   5   6   4   5   6   . . .
  .                       .
                          .
                          .
```

Here is Cantor's clever way of producing a real number, let us call it D, that is guaranteed not to be on the list: The first decimal digit of D, after the decimal point, is different from the first decimal digit of the first real on the list. Since the first decimal digit of the first number is 0, the first decimal digit of D *can be anything but 0*. Let's say it's 5 (let us adopt the convention that we change a digit by adding or subtracting 5 from it).

Onwards to D's second digit: It is any digit other than 7, the second digit of the second number; so by our convention we take it to be 2. D is so far .52 . . . Continuing like this, we create D digit by digit, by looking at the *n*th number in our list and changing its n-th digit. In other words, we look at the diagonal of the table, in our case .073306454106 . . . and we form D by changing every single digit of the diagonal, to forming our example D = .528851909651 . . .

Now it is easy to see that D cannot be in the original list. Because, by the very way it was constructed, it differs from the first number in the list in its first digit, from the second number in the second digit, and so on. It differs from each number in the list in at least one digit—and so it differs from all of them.

Moral: From any infinite list of real numbers we can produce a real number not in the list. So, the real numbers cannot be listed one after the other like the whole numbers can, and therefore they belong to a higher sphere of infinity, exactly as Cantor had set out to prove.

The same diagonal argument of Cantor was used by Turing (as explained later in the chapter "The Don") to show that we cannot create a list of all computable numbers: The reason is that, if all real numbers listed above were computable, then so would D (what I described above is in fact an algorithm for computing D.) Hence, from any list of computable numbers, we can find a computable number not in the list. The computable real numbers cannot be listed either!

But for those of you who are even cursorily familiar with programming there is a much more elegant way of getting to Turing's undecidability reult—shame on Ian for omitting it in the chapter "Runner." Let me conclude by sketching it:

Turing's fundamental result can be cast in terms of the *halting problem.* The halting problem, as explained by Ian, is this: We want to write a computer program which, when presented with another program and the input to that program, will decide whether that program would eventually halt when started with that input. Turing proved that such program cannot exist.

And here is how we can rephrase his diagonal proof in terms of code: Suppose that we had this hypothetical program that decides the halting problem, let us call it halts(program, input). Using it we can now write the following evil code:

```
diagonal(program)

if halts(program, program) then loop forever

        else stop
```

That is, when fed with any program, our code loops forever if that program would halt *if fed with itself as input.* Otherwise, diagonal stops immediately.

And now we are in trouble: diagonal(diagonal)—the program we wrote, when fed with itself as input– halts if and only if it does not halt! (Check it.) We must conclude that there can be no halting code . . .

(Can you see how diagonal corresponds exactly to Cantor's argument? And to Russell's? Hint: Consider program *halts* as a table, what does *diagonal* do?)

Sumita Lakshmianatharam, Birmingham

PS: For web sources on the history of mathematics see http://www-gap.dcs.st-and.ac.uk/~history/Indexes/ HistoryTopics.html. Euclid's *Elements* can be found at http://aleph0.clarku.edu/~djoyce/java/elements/toc .html. (And, of course, one should always keep in mind that Web documents tend to fall from good maintenance and/or disappear without warning.) —sl

PPS: Incidentally, I discovered by painful experimentation that all URLs given in the manuscript are fictional. *With one exception*—can you find it? —sl

Subject: Splean
From: baldie@math.unitrieste.it
Date: July 19, 2002. 2:15 (GST)

It is a hot summer night in the Adriatic, way past midnight, my theorem is going nowhere, too much caffeine in my system, and still no word from you. A perfect time, I think, for filling in a couple of the many important points and details that my lazy colleague Turing left out of his lecture on Gödel's theorem.

To understand this momentous result, you must first understand the man's premises. Gödel considered mathematical statements such as "1 + 1 = 2" and "1 + 1 = 3" —some of which are true—we call them theorems—and some are, evidently, false. But the more interesting statements involve variables, for example, "$x + 1 = y$," they are true or false depending on the values of the variables.

Certain statements involving variables happen to be true for all values, they are algebraic identities, like "$x + 1 = 1 + x$," and "$x \neq x + 1$." That such a statement is true for all values of x can be considered itself a higher-order statement; for the last example, this higher-order statement is written "$\forall x (x \neq x + 1)$)", where the $\forall$ part is read "for all x," and means exactly that the rest of the statement holds for any choice of integer value for x. Such a statement is either true or false, just like the simple statements "1 + 1 = 3" that involve no variables. For example, $\forall x \ (x = x + x)$ is false, as the part after $\forall x$ holds for some but not all values of x.

So, the truth of some statements depends on the value of a variable, while others claim (perhaps falsely) that the statement is true for all values. Gödel was interested in a curious kind of hybrid statement, such as "$\forall \ x \ (y \neq x + x)$." The truth of this statement depends on the value of y—this particular one is true if y is odd, false otherwise. That is, if $A(x,y)$ is any arithmetic statement involving variables x and y (and possibly other variables inside A, each of them, call it z, neutralized by a corresponding $\forall z$ preceding it), then Gödel would construct from it the hybrid statement

$$H(y) = \forall \ x \ A(x,y)$$

Notice the y in parentheses after H, it codifies the fact that the truth of H depends on the value of y.

A key ingredient in Gödel's idea was that all statements can be really thought of as numbers—numbers that encode arithmetic statements are known as Gödel numbers. This is no big deal, just think that we have an infinite list of all possible legal statements, shortest first, and each sentence is identified by its rank in this list. Gödel was interested in such an enumeration of his hybrid statements,

$$H_0(y) = \forall x A_0(x,y), \qquad H_1(y) = \forall x A_1(x,y), \qquad H_2(y) = \forall x A_2(x,y), \ \ . \ \ . \ \ .$$

where the $A_i(x,y)$'s are all possible arithmetic statements involving x and y.

Recall now Gödel's purpose in all this. He wanted to show that, in any mathematical system that expresses the integers and operations on them, not all theorems can have proofs. But what is a proof? The important point here is that a proof is necessarily a string of characters. Therefore, lo and behold, proofs in the assumed system (the mathematical system that is to be proved incomplete) can also be enumerated:

$$P_0, \ P_1, \ P_2, \ \ . \ \ . \ \ .$$

So, we have an enumeration of all hybrid statements, and an enumeration of all proofs. That much is easy. Now comes the crucial idea. If you substitute a number for the variable y of a hybrid statement, then you get something that is either a theorem (and may have a proof) or a negation of a theorem (in which case it does not). If I give you, say, $H_{87}(87)$—notice the beginning of a diagonalization, as in Sumita's proof of Cantor's Theorem: This is the 87th hybrid statement with the value of variable y set to the statement's own rank in the enumeration, 87—and a proof, say P_{290}, then it should be easy to tell if P_{290} happens indeed to be a proof of $H_{87}(87)$. But Gödel's genius was in refining this: Not only can you tell this for any hybrid statement with its variable set to its rank, $H_n(n)$, and any proof P_m, but there is an *arithmetic statement* involving the variables m and n that achieves this. In other words, you can express the fact that P_m is (or, is not) a proof of $H_n(n)$, as a long list of equations and inequalities involving m, n, multiplied and added and exponentiated together in complicated ways (and possibly other variables eclipsed by $\forall$'s). It can be done, I am omitting lots of details here, it is very complicated and rather tedious in the end—the truly clever part is not to achieve it, but to realize that it is useful.

Thus, there is an arithmetic statement $A(x,y)$ whose truth depends on the variables x and y, and it is true only if it so happens that P_x is *not* a proof of the statement $H_y(y)$. But this arithmetic statement $A(x,y)$ gives rise to a hybrid statement $H(y) = \forall x\, A(x,y)$—stating, if you think about it for a minute, that $H_y(y)$ has no proof. But this hybrid statement must be somewhere in our enumeration of the hybrid statements, perhaps it is the kth such statement, $H_k(y)$, where k is some fixed number.

The diagonalization is now complete: Statement $H_k(k)$, since it is obtained from $H_k(y)$ (whose truth only depends on y) by substituting the number k for y, is unambiguously either true or false. And, as we argued above, statement $H_k(k)$ states that statement $H_k(k)$ has no proof. In other words, $H_k(k)$ is precisely the statement called Kurt's statement by Turing—the statement that declares itself unprovable. As Turing argues then very convincingly, Kurt's statement must be true but unprovable, thus establishing Gödel's incompleteness theorem.

I hope this helps. If not, there is a nice book that contains a more detailed explanation: *Gödel's Proof* by Ernest Nagel. Another delightful book recounts the development of the field of logic, leading to the results by Gödel and Turing—and the effect they had on the development of computers: *The Universal Computer: The Road from Leibniz to Turing* by Martin Davis.

Dott. Baldovino Ierodiacono, Trieste

Subject: my la(te)st theorem
From: pde@cnrs.fr
Date: December 25, 2002. 03:34 (GST)

Sumita's rendering of Euclid's proof that there are infinitely many primes from three months ago inspired me to deduce a most interesting fact. Consider the sequence of prime numbers suggested by Sumita's proof.

2, 3, 7, 43, 13,

and so on. Starting with a list containing only the number 2, you repeat the following: You multiply together all numbers in the list so far, you add one to the product, you find the smallest divisor of the resulting number, and this is the next number in the sequence.

As Sumita proves, all numbers in the sequence are distinct primes. And here is the surprise: *Every prime number will eventually appear in this sequence!* Perhaps very late in the sequence (for example, 629 does not appear for more than a billion turns)—but it *will* appear.

I have discovered a truly remarkable proof of this theorem, which, unfortunately, I cannot fit within the stringent (and totally arbitrary) limit on message size imposed by our dictatorial moderator.

Oh, well . . .

Pierre d' Enfermat, Lyon

Subject: RAP unwrapped
From: hazard@econ.unibosph.ac.tr
Date: November 23, 2002. 00:45 (GST)

I want to clarify, for the benefit of the fellow bookclub members, some of the important concepts from Microeconomics and Optimization Theory mentioned cryptically, inaccurately, and somewhat irreverently, in the chapter "Free Market."

What Turing calls "RAP" is the famous *linear programming* problem, while the "hopping" algorithm is none else but the *simplex method* formulated by George Dantzig in 1947. (The term "programming" in "linear programming" has nothing to do with computer code; it meant "planning" in the 1940s when the name was launched.) Dantzig's simplex algorithm, as well as the competing "interior point algorithm" discovered much later by Narendra Karmarkar, are indeed used routinely for finding optimal solutions to problems of truly massive scale. For two pleasant expositions (not, however, for the mathematically faint-hearted), see the books *Linear Programming,* by Vasek Chvatal (Freeman, 1983), and *An Illustrated Guide to Linear Programming,* by Saul Gass (Dover, 1990); for a web-based short course on the subject try http://www.cudenver.edu/~hgreenbe/courseware/LPshort/intro.html

The price equilibrium result explained later in the same chapter is an important theorem usually attributed jointly to the economists Kenneth Arrow and Gerard Debreu. They both won the Nobel prize in Economics, although Arrow's was for an earlier discovery (the so-called "Arrow Impossibility Theorem"). The purported extension of the price equilibrium theorem used in the text to explain zero prices on the World Wide Web is, to my knowledge and understanding, completely fictional. For a nice explanation of the Arrow-Debreu theorem and related results, as well as their importance in economics, the mathematically sophisticated reader is referred to the book *A Course in Microeconomic Theory* by David M. Kreps, 1990.

With my rather limited understanding of the history of mathematics, I find it hard to swallow that an ancient Greek mathematician, even with Archimedes' ingenuity, understood the intricacies of linear programming and discovered a method for solving it—for lack of the appropriate algebraic notation, if for no other reason. Nevertheless, there *is* an element of truth in the Kythera gearbox story: A gear-based mechanism for solving linear programming problems, very much as described in the text, *was* proposed by a Greek mathematician. Namely, by the late Tassos Vergis, in a paper co-authored with Princeton's Kenneth Steiglitz and Bradley Dickinson; see "The Complexity of Analog Computation," *Mathematics and Computers in Simulation 28*, pp. 91-113, 1986 (or click http://www.cs.princeton .edu/courses/archive/spr98/cs598c/links.html).

Incidentally, the end of this story is tragically Greek: Dr. Vergis died in his thirties, in a 1994 automobile accident, while commuting between Athens and his professorship at the University of Patras.

Dervish Hazaroglu, Istanbul

PS: I suspect that most members of the group missed the meaning of Alexandros' last name. Dertli means in Turkish "a man full of sorrow and unfulfilled desire." —dh

You do not answer my letters and you don't take my calls. When our paths cross every morning, you pretend that I do not exist. These hot Istrian nights, they are getting so long now.

We need to focus on the matter in hand: False promises. Doesn't Turing, at the end of the chapter "Runner," pledge that his next subject is Complexity? Then why does he go on to lecture on Mathematical Economics and Developmental Biology instead? And, when he does get to Complexity, why is his treatment so timid and superficial? We need to do some work here.

But in order to understand love's pain you must first become intoxicated with its sweetness. In a similar maner, you cannot come to terms with Complexity without thinking a little about fast algorithms.

And we know what algorithms are: Unambiguous, step-by-step procedures for manipulating an input in order to produce an output. For example, suppose that you are given a list of numbers, say twenty of them, possibly the salaries of the twenty employees of a small company: 34,159 66,254 44,990 67,497 25,000 88,402 74,785 57,283 27,374 63,361 73,656 25,388 60,457 23,890 38,005 41,491 33,892 43,207 79,623 31,286. Using computers we can manipulate such lists to great effect. For example, we can add the second number to the first, the third to their sum, and so on until we have the sum of all twenty (this particular sum happens to be a million). 19 additions in all, any computer would do this in a flash. Except that, when thinking about the speed of algorithms, it is generally a good idea to imagine that the input list is not just twenty long, but n, a number that can potentially be very large. The number of additions needed is thus a simple function of n: $n - 1$.

Or, we could try to find the largest of these numbers—identify the fat cat among the twenty. That's easy too: We compare the first two, and we remember the greater of the two. We compare this with the third, and remember the greatest of those. And so on, until we have compared every number in the list with the largest one from among those coming before it. Again, this would take $n-1$ comparisons and would end up producing the largest of these integers—in this case, 88,402. No sweat.

But what if we wanted to sort these numbers? To produce the rearrangement that lists the smallest first, the second smallest next, and so on? Well, computers do this all the time at lightning speed. Here is one algorithm (not the best by a long shot, but an adequate one): The method works in stages. In the first stage you find the largest number, as before, put it at the end of a new list that you are now creating, and erase it from the input list. The new list is now 88,402, and the old list is 34,159 66,254 44,990 67,497 25,000 74,785 57,283 27,374 63,361 73,656 25,388 60,457 23,890 38,005 41,491 33,892 43,207 79,623 31,286. Then you repeat the same thing until the input list is empty: You find the largest number in the input, delete it, and put it at the beginning of the new one. After the second stage the new list would look like 79,623 88,402, then after the third stage 74,785 79,623 88,402, and so on. In the end, after n stages, you'll get the list sorted.

And how many steps has your computer expended in order to sort this list of n numbers? The answer is, about n^2. And it is clear why: Each of the n stages takes about n steps to find the largest number in the list, and n times n makes n^2.

Even the algorithm that Euler gave us (by way of his theorem explained by Turing) for finding a tour that visits all bridges in a network of islands and bridges—if such a tour exists—also turns out to take n^2 steps when confronted with networks consisting of n bridges. It would be a digression to explain now the precise algorithm and the reasons why n^2 steps suffice, but believe me, they do.

We like it when an algorithm solves a problem within a number of elementary steps (like additions and comparisons) that is a function of n (the size of the input) just like those we have seen so far: $n - 1$, n^2, perhaps n^3. As long as it is a *polynomial* in n. The reason we like polynomials in this context is that they do not grow very fast, they are rather tame as resource requirements. You see, even with a million numbers to sort, n^2 would be hardly a trillion, it would take our computers only a few seconds or two to sort the list.

So, some computational problems can be solved by polynomial algorithms. We are happy with this state of affairs; we cherish the efficiency implied by the polynomial nature of the function that counts steps in an algorithm. The class of all problems that are blessed with such efficient algorithms deserves to have a name, and the name is **P.** For "polynomial."

So far so good. There are, however, certain other computational problems that do not seem to belong in **P.** Problems that appear to require an *exponential* number of steps. Suppose, for example, that we do not wish to add or sort the twenty numbers I gave you above, but to *split them in half:* To divide them into two piles, each with the same sum (given that the total sum is 1,000,000, the sum of each part would have to be half that, 500,000). We want to find out if it is possible to cut this pie into two equal pieces. What now?

I know you like puzzles like this, my love, so try this one, won't you? Select a few from among these numbers so that they add to 500,000. There is a way, take my word for it. But how will you find it? Not so easy, heh? You could start trying all possible sets of numbers, that is a perfectly legitimate algorithm for this problem. Except that it is exponential: There are too many possible partitions to consider—there are 2^n possible ways to partition a set of n

elements into two parts, and for $n = 20$ this is more than a million. With n about a hundred, no computer can handle this before the sun freezes. And in Hamilton's problem explained by Turing—find a tour of a network of islands and bridges that visits all islands—the exhaustive algorithm that tries all possible paths is equally exponential. Greater than any polynomial.

Even the *traveling salesman problem,* that old puzzle, finding the best way to visit n cities that were given to you (with their distances and all) so as to traverse the least possible total distance. So many great mathematicians of the previous century have worked on it, and still we know of no polynomial algorithm for solving it, we seriously doubt that it is in **P**. Puzzles too—literally speaking now. If I give you n shapes, my dear, can you arrange them next to each other so that they make up a rectangle? Nobody knows how to solve this in polynomial time.

To recapitulate: Beyond the class **P** (but not so far beyond as Ian ventured in his lecture, still well within the realm of solvable problems) lies a large class of problems that can be solved by exhaustion, by trying an exponential number of possibilities and picking the one that does the trick. This class we call **NP,** for "nondeterministic polynomial." Because, you see, the only polynomial algorithms we know for these problems involve lucky guesswork—nondeterminism.

NP and its challenging problems may sound bad enough. But from the standpoint of a mathematician, the real distressing news is that nobody knows *if* **P** *and* **NP** *are the same class or not!* This question—whether there are problems solvable by efficient guesswork but not by efficient honest work—has become perhaps the most famous open problem in all of Mathematics. This is precisely the little project that has been keeping me busy for eight years now. The hopeless knightly challenge I undertook for the sake of your love.

And now, for the final act: Even though we do not know whether **P** is different from **NP,** we know this: If they *are* different, then the four particular hard problems I mentioned to you—the partition problem, the traveling salesman problem, Hamilton's problem, and puzzles –will be witnesses to this difference. They would all require exponential time to be solved. Because, you see, these problems are the hardest problems in **NP.** They are called, together with a few other problems like them, **NP**-*complete*—Turing mentions the term. If any of them has a polynomial algorithm then they all do, and **P = NP.**

As for the little number partitioning problem that started us on this path: I know that you like puzzles with numbers, my love, that you cannot resist little brainteasers like this. I can already see you biting your pencil, a stubborn look at your beautiful face, the fine curve of your eyebrow sharpened with mental effort. I'll have the solution written down for you, tomorrow at lunch. I'll be waiting for you in my corner of the cafeteria.

Dott. Baldovino Ierodiacono, Trieste

PS: Here are four books that deal with Complexity: *Algorithmics, the Spirit of Computing* by David Harel; *Introduction to the Theory of Computation* by Michael Sipser, *Computational Complexity* by Christos Papadimitriou, and *Computers and Intractability: A Guide to the Theory of NP-completeness* by Michael Garey and David Johnson. The P = NP problem is the first in a list of the mathematical problems that the Clay Institute has identified as the greatest open problems on the new millennium, and whose solution carries a significant monetary reward. See http://www.claymath.org/prize_problems/index.htm.

Subject: vox archaeologica
From: gist@clio.yale.edu
Date: December 16, 2002. 23:12 (GST)

As an historian and archaeologist, with more than two decades of experience working in the Mediterranean (occasionally underwater), I was interested—and, quite frankly, more than a little amused—to read about Alexandros's exploits.

First, about the "Kythera gearbox." This fictional artifact recalls an extant archeological find, a bronze atronomical and chronometrical device from the first century B.C. discovered in the early 1900s near the Greek island of *Anti*kythera— which makes the choice of "Kythera" in the text a rather pedantic word play (or is it antithesis?), somewhat salvaged by the ancient Greek myth according to which Venus was born from the waves near that island.

Which brings us to the "little Venus" statue allegedly found by Alexandros. I can authoritatively attest that no such artifact was ever discovered, or is likely to have existed; and there is no record of a hellenistic sculptor named Antisthenes, from Rhodos or elsewhere, pederast or not. (Interestingly, there were several bronze statues of women found at the Antikythera shipwreck, so much that the first man who explored the site, a sponge diver from the island of Simi, was frightened by what he called "heaps of dead women's bodies.")

The destruction of the little Venus bronze on the Kythera beach is also based on fact, but, again, only partly. Many archaeological finds recovered from shipwrecks in the Mediterranean, from a wide range of materials, did break into pieces or disintegrate to ash upon exposure to the atmosphere (sadly, this was also the fate of several parts of the Antikythera mechanism). However, there is no record of a statue or other large bronze piece lost in the way described in the text. There are now rigorous chemical procedures and protocols for preventing such tragedy.

Although I am no expert on ancient Greek science, let me venture a few further comments: Archimedes' death, as briefly described by Turing early in the text and later recounted by Alexandros, is only one of the three versions left to us by Plutarch in the biography of Marcellus, the Roman general who conquered Syracuse. See http://classics.mit.edu/Plutarch/marcellu.html.

Archimedes, of course, never wrote a book entitled "On the Phoenician Method" (although he did write a treatise "On Method"; see http://www.lix.polytechnique.fr/~ilan/sawit.html for the story of the recent discovery of a manuscript containing this and others works of the great mathematician). And Chrysippos was indeed a rather notable third century B.C. mathematician of Phoenician descent—in fact, from the town of Soloi, the place that gave us the word "solecism." But there is no record of collaboration or correspondence between Chrysippos and Archimedes.

Incidentally, I wonder if Alexandros tasted any of the wine in the ship's amphorae—for better or for worse, wine is often preserved over millenia. I have drank ancient Greek wine, and, believe me, it tastes worse than retsina, if anyone can imagine that.

Gregory Ian Stevens III, New Haven

PS: A repository of information about the ancient world is available at http://www.perseus.tufts.edu. For an interesting discussion of the Antikythera mechanism, marine archeology in the Aegean (and its joys and perils), and the glory of Rhodos, see the document http://ccat.sas.upenn.edu/rrice/usna_pap.html.

The best source of information and interpretation on the Antikythera mechanism is still the book *Gears from the Greeks: The Antikythera Mechanism, a Calendar Computer ca. 80 B.C.* by D. D. Price (Science History Publications,

New York, 1974). But see also, for example, http://www
.giant.net.au/users/rupert/kythera/kythera.htm.

Subject: Cryptic about crypto
From: todo@cogsci.ucsd.edu
Date: September 10, 2002. 14:34 (GST)

Dear members of the book club, please pardon the pseudonym and the phony untraceable address, routine precautions for people with my skills, persuasion, and enemies. (And gentlemen of the government: please leave my host alone, cogsci.ucsd.edu was completely unaware of my existence until I broke in, from another temporary location, ten minutes ago.)

Now, onward to our subject: The shallow, cavalier, and ultimately timid treatment of cryptography in the manuscript "Turing" is the unmistakable sign that the author chose to play it safe with a certain three-lettered government agency, and cleared his text in advance with them (as is routinely done these days with most publications dealing even tangentially with cryptography). In case you are interested in a less fictional (and less polyannaish) account, here goes:

In the early 1970s, the government, realizing that the mushrooming computational technology would soon enable unbreakable codes and privacy for all citizens, conspired with IBM (then a virtual computer monopoly) to launch the loathed data encryption standard (DES), a code that only the government knew how to break. The DES used a key of 64 bits, of which it inexplicably utilized only 56, to define a sequence of murky transformations which, to the untrained eye, looked cryptographically secure and unbreakable. (However, as its designers knew, and certain dedicated revolutionaries suspected, deep in the structure of DES lay its planted and well-hidden weakness.)

Enter public key cryptography. Rediscovered in the United States in the late 1970s (after it was successfully suppressed in England for two decades by the British branch of the enemy), and popularly known by the first letters of the last names—RSA—of the three people who discovered its most clever embodiment, it seemed for the longest time the world's great hope for achieving the goal of universal privacy, free of any government intrusion. Its description in the manuscript is, not surprisingly, way too sketchy. Here is mine:

As Turing explains, RSA is a public key cryptosystem. Bob (the party wanting to receive secure messages) creates two keys, of which one is kept secret, while the other is publicly and proudly announced. The public key is the product n of two primes p and q. (In the manuscript's example, which is of course too small by a factor of 50 or so to be of any cryptographic value, n is 1216592820951929, which is indeed the product of two primes, $p = 28173527$ and $q = 43182127$—the manuscript curiously neglected to mention that they should have remainder 2 when divided by 3—or $p = q = 2 \bmod 3$, as this is written in math (you see, mod x added after an equation means that one should take the remainders of both sides by x).

First question: How does one go about finding huge primes? (You need to do that is you want to start your own bootleg public key cryptosystem behind the back of the government, right?) Easy. You see, primes have the following distinguishing property—besides not being divisible by any number besides 1 and themselves: If p is a prime, and you raise any number x between 1 and p to the pth power, always taking the remainder by p, then the answer will be x, the same number you started with. Try it. Raise 2 to the 7th power, you get 128, which, when divided by 7 gives you remainder 2. If p is not a prime and you try the same thing, then the chances are overwhelming that you won't get x back, and so you'll know p is not a prime. Repeat many times to be sure, and you've got your prime. (Oh, well, there are these freak composite numbers called Carmichael numbers, 561 is the smallest among them, that break this rule. They behave like primes, but they are so rare, I personally guarantee to you you'll never stumble upon one.) Now, to find a new prime, repeat this test for many numbers x, and finally you'll get your prime. You see, if you have a number with D decimal digits, and its last digit is not 0,2,4,5,6,8—that would be stupid, right?—then the chances that it's a prime is one in D. So, after a few hundred tries, you'll find your prime, your computer won't even sweat. Incidentally, you realize of course that you need a software package that does arithmetic operations on large numbers to do all this, because, you see, we are talking about numbers so large that no existing computer can add or multiply them in hardware. But there are many such packages around. The spooks have not been able to suppress them for long; they have too many other uses.

There, you have your two numbers p and q. Now what? Well, first you announce their product $n = pq$, this is your public key. If anyone wants to send you a message x, a number (and Turing gave a half-assed explanation why you can think of the message as a number about as long as n), then they calculate the number $y = x^3 \bmod n$ and they send you this number y.

Fine, I hear you say, but now that you have y how do you recover x (and why is it that the pigs can't)? Remember that, if n is a prime, then $x^n = x \bmod n$. But what if n is not a prime, but the product of two primes p and q? As it turns out, there is still a power that gives you back the number you started with: This power happens to be $k(p - 1)(q - 1) + 1$—for any value of k! Yes, check it out, $x^{k(p-1)(q-1)+1} = x \bmod pq$, for all k. Conclusion: In order to recover x, we need a number d (for "decode") that has the property that $3d = k(p-1)(q-1) + 1$ for some k. If we had this number, by raising y to this exponent (and taking of course the remainder modulo $n = pq$) we would get

$$y^d = x^{3d} = x^{k\,(p-1)(q-1)+1} = x \bmod pq.$$

Get it? We recovered the original message x! And, lo and behold, this number d always exists—you know why? Because you had the foresight to choose your p and q so that they have both remainder 2 when divided by 3.

Conclusion: You can recover the message x that was sent to you by your correspondent, while the eavesdropping government asshole can't, because he doesn't have your p and q (presumably he can't factor n, see?), and so he can't find the number d. Cool, huh?

Well, it gets even cooler. Using public crypto you can do all sorts of cute things, like sign documents electronically (so you cannot later deny that you signed), share secrets, toss coins over the Net, create unforgeable electronic cash, even play mental poker over a phone line and know the other guy isn't cheating.

On to our story, then. Needless to say, the government outlawed RSA, they restricted the size of your primes so they were useless, and managed to hold this idiotic line long enough, while their armies of smartie-pant spooks were trying to kill the whole goddamned idea. (Have you ever asked yourself where the legions of Math Ph.D's vanish after graduation? They don't all make bombs in a cabin in Montana, you know.) And, finally, they managed, the lucky bastards, they found their algorithm that factors huge numbers. When they actually cracked it nobody knows, but I do know for fact that the cat was out of the bag in the mid-1990s—someone actually wrote a bloody math paper about it, for chrissakes.

But there was a catch: The new algorithm could not run on good old computers. It needed a new kind, one that works with quantum mechanics. No sweat. As we all remember, that was the precise moment when the supercollider, the behemoth physics project that was being set up under half of the state of Texas, was scrapped by the government. Have you ever asked yourselves why our leaders felt in the mid-1990s the sudden urge to rewrite the research agenda of the nation's physicists? And anybody wondered how the Texas-sized tunnel is used now? Well, a few of us know. This is where the government runs its secret quantum machines, that is where it cracks its citizens' public key codes.

But have faith. Legions of dedicated comrades are on the eve of our final triumph. The ultimate code, unbreakable even by quantum machines. It will surface in the Net sometime soon, I promise. When they least expect it.

Long live the Privacy Revolution!
Cryptographic power to the People!
Freedom to the Martyrs of Privacy!
Perpetual paralyzing denial of service to the Enemy!

Tod O.

PS: A parting thought. Aren't the letters p and q, used ad nauseam throughout the workings of the RSA cryptosystem, the same ones that spell the name of the loathed complexity class QP, quantum polynomial, the analog for quantum machines of the polynomial-solvable problems P? And aren't they the only consonants separating N from R (and thus NSA from RSA)? Another coincidence? You be the judge.

PS2: For a more on the subject, start probing at `http://www.privatei.com/sneer/cryptlink.html`

BTW, I recommend browsing such sites from untraceable hosts. You are being watched!

Subject: Atrocious distortions
From: amaleas@idomeneus.mil.gr
Date: September 3, 2002. 9.17 (GST)

Nobody enjoys reading fiction more than me, and I fully understand the need to occasionally bend the historical truth for the needs of plot. However, the text "Turing" contains atrocious distortions of historical fact, neighboring (if one takes into account the author's national origin) to treason.

Let me start with the least glaring errors: The people that the author calls *Praehellenes*—a name which suggests that Greece was not inhabited by Hellenes four millennia ago—are more widely and accurately known as "Protohellenes"—the aboriginal Greek inhabitants of the land. They were absorbed by the Aryan invasion, not destroyed, as the text seems to imply; in fact, during the second millennium B.C. their civilization was already weakened by natural disasters and maritime raids (of controversial origin, although there is little doubt in my mind that the raiders were themselves Greeks).

That the Greeks were taught to write by the Phoenicians, as the author claims, is ridiculous: The linear B script was used in Mycenae and Pylos between the fifteenth and twelfth centuries B.C. to transcribe the Greek language. The Greek alphabet that was developed centuries later, after a brief period of economic and cultural decline, does show a certain superficial Phoenician influence in its detail. (And there is that passage in Herodotus recalling an alleged adoption of the Phoenecian script; my ancestors tended to be a little too gracious and generous in acknowledging their sources.)

But the author makes his most dangerous errors in connexion with Alexander the Great (anyone noticed how he never mentions him this way?) and the ancient Macedonian Greeks. He is wrong in calling the Macedonians a separate tribe, and in fact one that was regarded as "half-barbarian" in the rest of Greece. The ancient Macedonians were full-fledged Greeks, spoke Greek, and participated in the Olympic Games, the ultimate test of Greekness. (Needless to say, there is absolutely no relationship between the ancient Macedonian Greeks and the confused, impoverished people, speakers of a dialect of Bulgarian, who are currently squatting in a misnamed statelet north of Greece—a statelet, I should add, which they share with a majority of Albanians, Greeks, and Gypsies.) Also, that the Greek city of Thessaloniki was inhabited by Slavophones in the tenth century A.D., as the author suggests somewhere, is equally absurd. (Incidentally, for a World Wide Web site that strives to restore the much-maligned truth about Macedonia, see `http://www.anemos.com/Diaspora/macedonia/Macedonia_Index.html`).

On a related matter, the author spreads the ugly lie (completely unsubstantiated by historical evidence) that Alexander the Great, history's most ingenious and brave soldier and one of the greatest Greeks who ever lived, was queer.

The list goes on and on. In the chapter "Kythera," the author goes through a long array of national groups that invaded Greece between the twelfth and sixteenth centuries A.D., strongly implying that modern Greeks are a mosaic of ethnic origins and cultures. Nothing is further from the truth. The foreigners either lived in relative isolation as guests of the Greek people (always hospitable to a fault), or were invariably and gloriously repelled, both physically and culturally. The national, racial, cultural, and linguistic continuity of the Greek civilization over five millennia, and its brilliant radiance all over the globe, is the most unambiguous and impressive lesson that emerges from the study of world history.

Sincerely,
Brig. General (ret.) Achilleus Maleas,
Papagou, Hellas

Subject: Greek mythology
From: itry@informatics.uniskop.ac.mk
Date: August 23, 2002. 14:27 (GST)

Where does one start rebutting the sickening propaganda in the pages of the manuscript "Turing?" Ancient Macedonians are called a Greek "tribe." Really? Then why did they occupy all of Greece, and force the defeated Greeks to march with them to the conquest of the whole known world? The fact that Greeks over two millennia succeeded in erasing almost all evidence of the ancient Macedonian language cannot change the fact that ancient Macedonians were speaking a distinct language, completely unrelated to ancient Greek, a language which in fact strongly anticipated the current Slavic language spoken in the Republic of Macedonia (and much of the Aegean Macedonia, the southern half of my country currently under Greek rule). The fact that Slavs and their language are supposed to have arrived more than a millennium later proves nothing: The ancient Macedonians were their vanguard, and the new arrivals, once in the Balkans, quickly adapted their language to the one spoken by their indigenous brethren.

Furthermore, the author insinuates the idea (whose widespread acceptance does not make it any less absurd) that Alexander the Great was a homosexual. Small wonder: Once you make the blunder of considering the great Macedonian king a Greek, accusing him of "the Greek deviance" is only a small step away, isn't it?

Elsewhere the author claims that the brothers who created the Slavic alphabet, the saints Cyril and Methodios, were Greeks. How absurd! They were Macedonians, of course, from the Macedonian city of Saloniki—even though, as many other Macedonians were forced to do under the yoke of the age-long and still continuing Greek oppression of the Macedonian people, they took Greek names. Incidentally, the great Macedonian scholar and spiritual leader Cyril died the same day he was consecrated and given that name, in Rome. He was probably assassinated.

Finally, notice how Macedonians are not included in the long litany, recited in the chapter "Kythera," of peoples who "wandered into" present-day Greece. In a strange way I find this omission fitting. Simply put, we have been there ever since we conquered the place, twenty-four centuries ago.

Dr. Ivan Tryfonof
Skopje, Macedonia

PS: For a Web site that speaks the truth about Macedonia, see http://www.vmacedonia.com/. And for a scholarly treatment of the ancient Macedonian language, including a short list of words, as well as its relationship with modern Macedonian, see http://www.mymacedonia.net/ancient/simmilarites.htm

---

Subject: "Turing" fails test
From: machen@blackholesun.net
Date: August 16, 2002. 14:35 (GST)

In the chapter "AI," Turing gives a delightful account of AI's popular history—including every single one of the usual misunderstandings, misconceptions, and misinterpretations.

Most of the intellectual currents in AI described in the manuscript (early successes, expert systems, neural nets, genetic algorithms, even anti-AI hysteria) did exist, although they were much more serious and scientifically sound than their slapstick portrayal by Turing would have you believe. Furthermore, they were mere surface storms; deep down, the vast mass of serious AI research was defined by the clash of two opposing philosophical approaches to intelligent machines: Briefly, the first had its intellectual roots in

Computer Science, and opined roughly that AI is yet another programming problem, perhaps one that is more complex and demanding than compilers and operating systems and would therefore require more advanced techniques and more time to be cracked. The second, influenced by the natural, biological, and cognitive sciences, believed that, when it comes to the goals of AI, programming is irrelevant and futile, and that intelligence will emerge from some kind of tabula rasa that interacts with its environment via powerful enough learning machinery. (The dichotomy of *symbolic* vs. *subsymbolic* AI that is often used to describe these two camps is a little off the mark.)

The ongoing synthesis of these two approaches, combined with faster computers, the understanding of recent breakthroughs in brain research, and the advent of the Internet, has, in my opinion, a fighting chance of producing intelligence comparable to Turing's, roughly within the time framework proposed in the manuscript.

Mark Chen, Cupertino

PS: The Turing test is, of course, not forgotten at all. See, for example, http://cogsci.ucsd.edu/~asaygin/tt/ttest.html.
And for general information about AI, you can do worse than starting at http://www.cs.berkeley.edu/~russell/ai.html.

Subject: "Turing"'s Gross Indecency
From: clear@hottestmail.co.uk
Date: November 10, 2002. 11:05 (GST)

Sir: King Edward VIII ("the king who fell in love" in the manuscript "Turing") was *not* deposed; he willfully abdicated on December 10, 1936 (the eve of my eleventh birthday, how vividly I remember that dark day!)—albeit under pressure from his government, parliament, the royal family, the press, and the Church of England. This self-inflicted crisis was the direct result of his intimate association with and subsequent marriage with the American divorcée Mrs. Simpson, and the dangerous ways in which that woman had been affecting his function as King of England, Scotland, and Northern Ireland (let alone Emperor of the Indies), and damaging the tradition (then strong and unblemished) of British royalty.

Another streak of historical inaccuracies in the manuscript regards the circumstances surrounding Alan M. Turing's trial. The man was prosecuted in accordance to the "gross indecency" act of 1885 (as anyone who, like Turing, openly admitted to homosexual relations should have been at the time). He was not "condemned by the court to treatment by mind- and body-altering drugs," as the manuscript falsely claims; instead, he was offered one-year treatment by oestrogen injections as a charitable alternative to the requisite prison sentence. Treatment by oestrogen does occasionally have the temporary side effect of gynaecomastia; the only evidence we have that this happened to Turing is his own testimony to a friend. And, despite the manuscript's contention of the opposite, he was treated by the press with favourable discreetness; only one major newspaper carried the news story. Incidentally, the gross indecency act was repealed by the Labourites (too many ministers prosecuted, see?) in 1965.

The manuscript even slights the great British World War II cryptanalysis epic. The task of breaking the Enigma was far more herculean and ingenious than it is suggested; even Bletchley Park's home page http://www.cranfield.ac.uk/ccc/bpark/ contains a much more accurate rendering. And to suggest that a navy officer of a minor ally was allowed in the sanctum sanctorum of the Bletchley Park Huts! Phooey!

My labour-run, continent-bound, foreigner-infested, fox-petting, hooligan-exporting country, already semi-republican and mutilated by the criminal complacency of two generations of leaders, has at the present juncture very little to celebrate other than its history—an history, I might add, that is well worth defending against abuse such as one finds in the pages of "Turing."

D. B. Commodore-Lear, Esq., Hastingsford, Kent

PS: Coincidentally, it appears that, indeed, Alan M. Turing visited the island of Corfu, Greece (a one-time possession of the British crown, by the way—like much of the world) toward the end of his life. However, according to all available evidence, he stayed at the Club Mediterranée there. —dbcl

---

Acknowledgments

Many friends read early versions of *Turing* and made wonderful suggestions (many of which I had the wits to adopt): Muli Safra, David Johnson, Anna Papafragou, Merav Mack, Victor Vianu, Tatiana Emmanouil, Serge Abiteboul, George Vassilakis, Apostolos Doxiadis, Yannis Ioannides, Christos Kozyrakis, Mihalis Yannakakis, Scott Aaronson, Edouard Servan-Shreiber, Scott Shenker, Anna Karlin, Jennifer Dowell, Alexis Zavras, Paul Spirakis, Alex Fabrikant, Sara Robinson, Jim Gray, and Don Knuth. I thank them all. I am grateful to my colleagues at the Berkeley Computer Science Faculty Book Club for their insightful reading of an early manuscript and for their very helpful feedback; special thanks to Marti Hearst, Dave Patterson, Jerry Feldman, Randy Katz, Joe Hellerstein, Ken Goldberg, and Umesh Vazirani.

I am indebted to Niall Mateer for his wonderful suggestions on Turing's British voice, and to Berkeley undergrads Steven Chan and Viet Nguyen for preparing the diagrams.

Many thanks are due to my Greek publishers Elias and Yota Livianis; to Aloi Sideri for her beautiful Greek translation and for handling our disagreements with such patience and grace (and for being right so often); and to Panos Papahadzis and Athena Sakellariou of Attika Films for their faith in the book's potential.

I owe a warm word of thanks to my agent Nikki Smith, and to Eleanore Lee, for their confidence and support. And to Bob Prior, my editor at MIT Press, for his faith in my writing in general, and especially in *Turing*. Also, many thanks go to Emily Gutheinz, Kathy Caruso, Susan Clark, Valerie Geary, and everybody else at MIT Press, for their great work and for the warmth of their welcome.

And above all I am grateful to my wife Martha Sideri for her continual encouragement, for her beautiful ideas, and for the character of Alexandros. *Turing* owes much to her sweet but relentless criticism.

This is a book about love—and about the unique act of love that we call teaching. I remember with gratitude the hundreds of teachers and students who shaped my thought and aesthetic over the years, and who ultimately inspired this book.